Vampire's Promise

IMMORTAL PROTECTOR

BOOK THREE

STEPHANIE FLYNN

Small Fish Publishing

USA

First edition
Cover design by Stephanie Flynn
ISBN eBook: 9781952372612
ISBN Paperback: 9781952372605
ISBN Hardcover: 9781952372667
ISBN Large print paperback: 9781952372674

Library of Congress Control Number: 2022912272

Also By Stephanie Flynn

Find my catalog at StephanieFlynn.com

Immortal Protector series

0.5 Vampire's Distraction

1 Vampire's Deception

2 Vampire's Secret

3 Vampire's Promise

3.5 Elf Bound

4 Vampire's Demand

Immortal Protector Side Tales

Deer Holiday

Love Claws

Depths of the Heart

Matchmaker in Time series

STEPHANIE FLYNN

0.5 Minutes to Live

1 Seconds to Act

2 Hours to Arrive

3 Days to Hide

4 Years to Savor

Pirates in Time series

1 Pirate's Prize

2 Pirate's Treasure

3 Pirate's Plunder

Time Travel Romance Shorts

Fateful Time

One Crazy Time

If you like your urban fantasy without the romance, too, check out Stephanie Flynn's other name, Marie Flynn!

I

The Guilt Rages On

Daisy

I CLIMBED UPSTAIRS TO my bedroom with my cell phone in hand, typing a frantic text to my sister, but I stopped before sending it. How was I supposed to explain our dad had died over a text? Or that I was the one who gave him a 'heart attack'? *On purpose.* I deleted the text and tossed my phone onto the bed. I was a terrible witch and an even more terrible sister.

In my closet, I pushed aside all my everyday clothing, looking for something with enough pizzazz for tonight. I could wear my repaired little black dress, but I wanted something extra special. I had nearly half a dozen bridesmaid's dresses, but none of them were remotely appropriate, except one—a shimmery navy-blue knee-length number, so fancy I hadn't worn it since. It didn't coordinate with the necklace Oliver had gifted me, but I wouldn't take it off for anything. The locket had been his mother's, and now it hid a vial of Oliver's blood—an insurance policy.

I was never going to use it, but it set Oliver at ease, and that was enough for me. Plus, the vintage style was growing on me, and bonus points for my not having an allergic reaction to the unknown metals. It was classy, just how I imagined his mother had been.

While I prepared for a fancy dinner with my vampire boyfriend—who didn't eat but insisted on the specifics of the date—guilt gnawed at me. I needed to tell my little sister what I'd done at Borealis Medical Center, if she hadn't already seen the highlights on the news. I sighed and returned to my phone. If I didn't rip the bandage off, my date was going to be spoiled. Texting wouldn't suffice. Not for this. I tapped Lily Barrett's number and waited through the rings.

"Daisy?" she answered. Huh. She answered.

"Hey," I said lamely. How was I supposed to tell her such life-changing news?

"What's going on?" she asked. I heard shuffling in the background. Lily was busy, and I didn't want to interrupt her day or...destroy her week, but I had to. As the older sister, sometimes I had to do the heavy lifting.

"Look, there's no easy way to say this, but Dad's gone, Lily. I don't know if you've heard, but he had a heart attack." I squeezed my eyes shut, waiting for the denial and anger, expecting to be yelled at for telling her such grave news so flippantly. In my defense, I didn't know where Daddy's little girl had been hiding out, so I did what I'd thought was best.

"The explosion at the hospital," Lily said calmly.

"Yeah."

"It wasn't a heart attack, was it?" Her voice was smooth, as if she'd already known the story had been a lie and only wanted to confirm her suspicion.

"It was, but it wasn't." Technically, it had been a heart attack, but did it count if it were deliberately caused by magic? I figured my sister was already working that out in the silence that followed.

The knife of guilt twisted harder.

I didn't know how much longer I would have my sister's attention before she went radio-silent on me again, so I said quickly, "Since Mom's gone too, we have to deal with their house—settle the estate, and stuff. I'm on paid leave from work because of the explosion, so if it's a good time for you, we could start packing up the house this week."

"When is death ever a good time?" she asked flatly.

"It's not. I'm sorry." I pressed a fist to my forehead. My sister deserved more compassion from me, but since I'd killed the man in a cold, hard rage, I was struggling to show I cared. Because I didn't. Lily had missed a lot during her absence. She'd probably be on my side if she knew everything.

Silence stretched.

"Are you okay? Lily, talk to me." She was the only family I had left, and as the older sister, I felt a duty to keep her safe—to do what our dad had failed to do.

"Yeah, yeah. I'll be there in a couple of days." Lily ended the call.

I dropped onto my bed. Lily needed time to process. Maybe I should've led with good news, like she didn't have to stay in hiding because of the cure in her veins. Since I'd activated my dormant witch DNA, my blood had changed, and the vampire weapon would no longer exist without starting from scratch. Since the mastermind and his pet scientist were both gone, Lily and I were both safe. After so many losses, I supposed I was a bit numb to it all. I wished Mom were here. She'd been a saleswoman focused on making people happy. She could've broken the news and consoled Lily better than I did.

With that dreadful task complete, I headed back to my closet. I slipped into the navy dress and coordinating heels. It was amazing was a simple change of clothes could do for the psyche. Feeling a spring in my step, I went to the bathroom to freshen up and style my hair. Pretty soon I'd be joining my boyfriend for another one of his indulgences. We'd just had an amazing weekend at a resort near Green Bay—*his* resort—and I was consciously aware of how I walked. I'd rather people thought I was a klutz on heels than know the truth—so much sex.

Good thing too much sex didn't exist—unless it interfered with work, although that never stopped my first partner, Megan. She and emergency department nurse Kevin Fontaine had spent copious amounts of time in the utility closets at Borealis Medical Center. I'd envied them. For a short while, I had Oliver as a partner, but he'd quit before we had the chance to sneak into the naughty places.

Frankly, it was for the best. A vampire with no medical training had no business working as a paramedic. A vampire at all had no place working as a paramedic—a serious conflict of interest. I had to admit there were a few benefits, but not enough to justify the risk. Besides, I didn't want to mix love and work—the distraction being genuinely dangerous to patients. So now I couldn't be happier, and with an exciting evening planned, I didn't want to think about work at all.

I found my mascara and made the requisite stretched face to apply it without poking my eye out. A knock on my bathroom doorframe turned my head. I narrowly avoided stabbing my eye.

My roommate, a leggy brunette with sun-kissed highlights, leaned against the opening, assessing my appearance approvingly. She was a witch, in the best way, helping me control my newfound powers so Oliver and I could have a normal life. And by normal I meant spending my entire human life with an immortal vampire, which already encroached on the definition of normal, until I'd become a witch myself, a vampire's mortal enemy. Yep, totally normal life.

"How was your weekend?" Allison Kincaid asked.

"Dreamy. Oliver wined and dined me. The grounds at the Courtyard Inn are beautiful...not that I saw much of them." I sent Allison a devious smile.

"I bet," she said dismissively. I wouldn't want to hear about her sex life, either. "How are you feeling lately? Did the throttling spell help offset those urges?"

Allison always helped me when I needed it, including nurturing my baby witch abilities. When I'd first activated, I'd been so far out of control, I couldn't function without murdering every vampire I encountered. The last thing I needed was to land in prison for murder and expose vampires to the public. Or risk a repeat of history. Oliver had explained what had happened last time—the Peshtigo fire of 1871—and I was not interested in joining witches on a vampire hunt-turned-mass-accidental murder. So Allison cast a spell on me.

"Honestly, the spell almost felt like I was worse, but I was a complete mess over it, so undoubtedly my emotions fueled the chaos and made everything harder. I didn't think I could handle this at all, but it's okay now." I held out my hand to show off another of my gems. "Oliver gifted me this ring, and the urge to kill vampires stopped. I feel like myself again, and it's great! But I really appreciate your help. I really, really do."

Allison inspected the jewel with a frown. "And this ring works?"

"Like night and day, it flipped a switch." Now we had all the time in the world to enjoy ourselves—or at least the next few decades—but I wasn't going to think about our expiration date tonight. I faced the mirror and popped open my mouth again while swiping at my lashes.

"Great." Her enthusiasm was seriously lacking, and that worried me.

"Everything okay?" I asked her.

"Just a spell not working as expected. I've got a shift at the bar tonight, so have fun. Don't break any furniture."

I chuckled. "I don't plan to. Hey," I said as Allison turned to leave. She stopped. "Is there a spell to fix furniture, or...you know, the plumbing...like how you mend clothing?"

"I'm sure someone thought of it at some point, but I've never seen one. You'd have to dig." Allison headed down the stairs and added as an afterthought, "I need a roof over my head, so practice on small stuff in your room."

The plumbing wasn't that big of a deal. I'd mastered the art of putty. And when I spent my time searching ancient texts, it was for a spell to cure vampires entirely. I'd been told its existence was a rumor, and so far, it had been like hunting for a needle in a sand bed at the bottom of the ocean. I was certain there was one, but I had no proof, and all efforts had been in vain. Even though Oliver had promised I'd never spend a day in a nursing home, I couldn't give up hope. Someday we could still have kids and grow old together.

That was a dream worth deciphering ancient grimoire spells.

I brushed out my hair and pinned back the sides. A swipe of lip gloss finished my look.

A ring of the doorbell downstairs told me I was just on time.

2
Explosive Dinner

Daisy

THE RUMBLING OF THE V8 beneath me while Oliver worked the pedals and shoved around the shifter was...so...damn...sexy. I didn't want the ride to end, but he parked his candy-apple red 1967 Ford Mustang Shelby with white racing stripes in the gated parking lot of Schooner Landing. This high-end, nautical-themed restaurant across the river in Menominee was reserved for special occasions and people with deep pockets, which excluded me. Naturally, I had never been here before, and I repeatedly smoothed my short dress and fussed with my pinned locks, hoping I didn't embarrass him.

"Everything is going to be perfect," Oliver said, patting my bare leg. My boyfriend wore a custom-made suit, as always. His tailor had to be a magician, but my firm and energetic vampire would make my heart flutter in torn sweatpants, unkempt beard, and mussed hair.

I think I preferred his mussed hair, actually.

Oliver climbed out of the car and—with normal human speed—assisted me out of the black leather bucket seat. A breeze off the bay shook the tree branches dotting the sidewalk and kicked up my hair, making a nest out of it. Most days, I wondered why I bothered.

"Have I told you how absolutely stunning you are?" he asked, pale eyes gazing into mine while he brushed a deviant lock away.

I blushed. "Twice. You look fine yourself, but you know that."

"Indeed. But I'm concerned you're trembling," Oliver said, leading us across the parking lot and holding the restaurant's door open for me.

"I'm fine, really." I'd studied ahead of time. Salad fork. Soup fork. Ahh, soup *spoon*. Dinner fork? Dinner knife. Since he didn't eat, he'd be watching me, which was...weird, but he'd insisted he liked watching. Maybe he'd steer me in the right utensil direction.

Oliver eyed me warily as if not believing me. "If at any moment you're not feeling well, just let me know."

"I'm fine," I insisted. "Really." But that was a fib. I didn't want to ruin the celebratory mood. After this last magical meal from Oliver's fantasy weekend getaway, I had to return to reality. And my current reality was dealing with the fallout from my magical explosion at work and joining my sister in cleaning out our parents' house.

Adulting sucked sometimes.

The friendly hostess led us to our reserved seats. Recessed lights cast a soft glow over the front of the house. Muted sky-blue accents offset the pale brick walls. Floor to ceiling picture windows overlooked the bay, where a red lighthouse glinted offshore, and seagulls coasted in the breeze. It was serene, and the gentle murmurs of diners were easy to ignore.

Oliver pulled my chair back, a crisscross design of metal reminding me of nautical nets, and he pushed me under the table. I picked up a menu while Oliver seated himself across from me. He seemed nervous himself, which was wholly unlike him.

"Everything okay?" I asked him.

Oliver's sly smile reappeared, the one that made my heart skip. His fingers knitted together and rested on the closed menu. "Always. Pick whatever you want. Nothing is off limits."

In case the menu here differed from the online version, I skimmed the offerings and I smiled in relief. It was the same. The server appeared and asked for our orders. Oliver requested a tequila, as usual, and nothing else.

Was it getting hot in here? I asked for water, cold water.

"Just water. Are you sure?" Oliver asked, suspicious. He could read me like an open book—or listen to my heartbeat becoming quicker.

"To drink," I said, trying to ease his concern, but I worried more by the minute, which was dumb. Oliver loved me. He wouldn't judge my fine-dining skills—or lack thereof. I'd tried very hard to ignore what came next—the misery of adulting—but I was still...I don't know. A nervous wreck? A warmth nestled under my skin, heating me like an idling engine. I smiled at Oliver's style of metaphor. He was rubbing off on me. And ice water was exactly what I needed before I started sweating in my navy blue bridesmaid's dress.

And then I asked for what I really wanted and could never consider ordering. What could I say? I was a hungry woman.

"Then I'll have..." I pointed at the menu and read my choice. "New York strip and Caesar salad would hit the spot, if that's okay." I primarily subsisted on spaghetti and other pasta dishes. My roommate, Jamie Harris, was a master at whipping up boxed waffles, and when the occasion tickled his fancy, he upped the skills a notch or two, but not this high.

"It's my pleasure to offer you anything you want," Oliver said.

The server made notes and collected our menus. "Drinks will be up soon."

Not soon enough. I unfolded my napkin, trembling, and took in the order of utensils. A couple of each. I glanced around and realized no one was seated close enough to judge which I used. As a complete fish out of water here, I risked embarrassing myself only to the server. "This place is very fancy."

Oliver reached across the table and held my hand, and immediately his gaze settled on our hands. He had to feel the anxious heat rumbling beneath my surface. So embarrassing.

"Things have been hectic lately, and I hoped a change of scenery would help make the most of our time." The sadness in his voice was confusing.

Typically, things of that nature—like, for instance, our expiration date—hardly popped into his head because time itself didn't affect him, so his recent fixation on time was unusual. I leaned forward and whispered, "You're immortal. Why does time suddenly concern you so much?"

Oliver smiled softly. "Because you're not."

As he'd reassured me, we had decades before I became a geriatric, but I secretly hoped someday we could become geriatrics together, nursing-home free. So, time was for me to worry about. Not him. "But there's nothing we can do about it." I touched the elegant pendant hanging around my neck. The insurance policy that I'd never use—but that didn't stop my curiosity. "What was it like when you...? Did it hurt?" I pictured him writhing in pain in that filthy, dark cave filling with smoke, fangs forming and descending in a fit of agony, morphing from human into an apex predator. My stomach knotted, and heat once more flushed through me.

I was a little too young for perimenopause...

The server returned, and we released our hands and leaned back. She settled a glass in front of each of us and reassured my food would be up soon. Although she didn't really look at me too much. When she left, Oliver finally answered.

"Your head feels like it's tearing in two. Your teeth, of course, hurt as the fangs rapidly form in preparation for the first feed. The light sensitivity stings your eyes. You chill as your body begins to use its own blood supply as an energy source. That's why if you don't take that first feed, you'll die. The good news is you only have to deal with the transition once, and the benefits are...well, you've seen them." Oliver waggled his eyebrows suggestively at me.

Oh, yeah. I knew the benefits.

"Besides the sun, the hunger is the only downside. It never goes away. You learn to manage it, some better than others."

I shuddered.

"Every human smells like the best food you could imagine after starving for weeks. A baby vampire can't control it, but even those who can may succumb during moments of weakness."

I remembered Evangeline—torn hospital gown, disheveled hair, bloodied and dirty—snarling and attacking Newt's throat for the cure. Positively horrifying. "I'm sorry you had to go through that."

"If I hadn't, I never would've met you."

I flushed hot with his sweet compliment, and I really needed to fan myself. I swigged down some ice water, but it wasn't cold enough.

The server returned once more and lowered a plate in front of me. She turned to Oliver and said, "Are you sure there's nothing I can tempt you with?"

Oliver's lips quirked, he and I thinking the same thing: just her vein. "A refill, please."

The server took his glass and rushed off with a smile.

Medium-rare and singed with grill lines, the steak begged to be devoured. I sawed off a bite of juicy red tenderness and popped it into my mouth with a soft groan. Oliver watched closely, almost as if he were jealous. Before I could ask if he was reminiscing, the server returned with his refill, and she set it in front of him.

"How are things?" Her question was directed at Oliver, but I didn't blame her. The man stood out in a crowd. As Oliver responded positively, she glowed, and my chest puffed with pride. This stunningly handsome man only had eyes for me. Besides, if the server saw his bite face, she'd run screaming. My lips lifted in a private smile, and I cut another slice off my steak.

"Well, if there's anything I can do, let me know." She moved to the next table, clearly less enthusiastic about her elderly customers at table seven.

"Is that how it always goes? I mean the flustered flirting." Heat continued building, but this time it had to be the hot food sliding down my throat. I swallowed another gulp of ice water. "She would've sat in your lap if you'd offered."

"It's the predatory nature of our species. I have no proof, but I think it's pheromones. We lure the prey in and then feed."

I snorted. "Pheromones? I think it's more your face and clothing."

Oliver grinned. "I *am* dashing in a sleek suit."

"You're also dashing without it." I scooped up another bite, slowly sliding it into my open mouth and groaning as I teasingly slid the fork out.

"Is that so?" His eyes flashed with desire.

My body heated a few more degrees. I was going to start sweating buckets soon. The water wasn't good enough, and I wasn't helping by flirty with the sexy vampire across from me. As much as I didn't want to, I needed a subject less...distracting—the proverbial version of a cold shower. "Does your brother get the same attention?"

Oliver's soft rumbling engine shut off. "We haven't spent much time together, but Soren's never complained to me. He's more interested in feeding and partying, usually at the same time. I tried to steer some direction into him, but no one has caught his eye. Someday maybe he'll find a woman to tame his ass. Just like mine."

I laughed. "Your ass is far from tame."

"I'm a regular stallion at your service, but my bed prowess is not why I brought you here."

I swiped up the last of my delicious plate while Oliver watched me intently. Even that gaze burned heat through me. Would I draw attention if I made a fan out of my napkin? I cocked an eyebrow at him. "So this wasn't just another of your spontaneous luxury dates?"

Oliver was calm, serious, and I set my fork down. He reached for my hand. My initial reaction was to refuse, and I didn't know why, but I placed my hand in his. Heat surged through my fingers, like a hot blanket dragging across my body. The nerves returned, and sweat trickled down my back.

"When I was a much younger man, I'd tended the farm with my father from before dawn until long after dusk. My future was nothing but backbreaking work—pure survival—without time for pleasure. I'd promised myself I would do whatever it took to escape that mold and have the life I'd always dreamed."

The vampire squeezed my hand in an unspoken message. Heat grew rapidly. With my other hand, picked up my napkin and waved it at myself. Screw it. I was miserably hot.

"After decades of careful strategy, I accomplished that goal, and I thought I would be content, but a gnawing feeling haunted me, as if something was missing. When I'd bumped into you—twice—at the breathtaking wedding of Abby Barrett, you stole my heart, and I realized it wasn't a *something* at all, but a *someone*."

Heat surged again, and now I recognized what was happening. This wasn't anxiety or nerves or perimenopause—thank God. This was magic, and it was angry. "Oliver," I said in a worried tone.

Oliver's thumb rubbed along my knuckles. "Daisy, I don't believe in coincidence. I planned on sweeping you off your feet as soon as it was safe for me to do so, but something bigger than me brought me to your car accident. Now, with you by my side as my partner, my best friend, life has meaning. And I want to live every moment with you. Daisy Lynn Barrett, I promise—" Oliver started, with his heart on his sleeve. In his other hand, Oliver revealed a palm-sized tiny jewelry box. He opened the lid, and a gem the size of my thumbnail glinted under the recessed lights.

A proposal. He wanted to marry me. A *vampire*. The magic whispered in my ear: an *evil* vampire who attacked and *killed* humans for food and *pleasure*. Something was very wrong. I pulled my hand free and stared at the onyx ring on my finger. It wasn't black anymore. It was as clear as a diamond. Allison had reduced my magic, and the ring put a cap on it completely. Had my magic destroyed it? Drained it? But how? Regardless of wanting to know what had happened, the important thing was my safety net was gone.

"Oliver, you...you have to get out of here," I said shakily.

Oliver snapped the box shut and slipped it into his suit jacket. His grim features were processing my warning instead of assuming I'd rejected him. "What is it? What's wrong? Daisy, talk to me."

I flashed him the onyx ring, and his eyes widened. The urge to kill the enemy, no matter my choice, surged. All the emotion in my body funneled to my hands against my will. The rainbow colors of power were blindingly bright.

Oliver could use his vampire speed to get out of here faster than I could run away. I climbed to my feet. "Go! Go now!"

The clatter of silverware and murmurs of the customers' conversations stopped abruptly. They stared at us, not knowing their lives were in danger.

Oliver rose and dropped bills on the table. "Let's get out of here."

He scooped me by the arm and we headed toward the door, but we moved slower than normal human speed. I was in heels. My knees were failing to function, and I trembled with the urge to release. I probably looked like I was having a stroke, and it felt like the clock was ticking on diarrhea, because I squeezed my muscles—every single one I could focus on—to hold it together. But rather than one orifice to worry about, the magic was going to exit every pore on my body all at once. I whispered in my panic, "There's no time. I can't hold it. You must go, and then I'll be okay. Everyone around us will be okay." As long as they didn't see I was the source of what came next.

Oliver's face twisted. "Daisy, I love you, and I'm going to marry you. We'll get through this—"

"No, we won't," I interrupted, my voice cold and foreign. As if I no longer controlled myself, I dropped the fight. Now I only trembled from exhaustion. Magic rushed to my hands, and an invisible spear of power shot straight into Oliver's chest. The impact blew him back and slammed him against the pale brick wall. He fell in a heap.

The release felt good. Amazing. Pain-free. I grinned with satisfaction.

Shouts of panic filled the air. While the elderly at table seven remained seated, eyes wide in confusion, younger customers ran for the exit. Chairs fell. Tables scraped the floor. Silverware clattered and wineglasses tipped. Staff ducked behind the bar. My magic was supposed to protect humans, but now they were terrified. Neutralizing the threat was a bigger concern—a small sacrifice for the greater good—something Jamie had told me about the Peshtigo fire of 1871. I supposed I couldn't be so disgusted with his comments anymore.

I was one of them.

Paying the staff no attention, I marched through the dining room of abandoned round tables and approached the limp body of Oliver Rockwell, a vampire who needed to die.

3

Too Good, Too Soon

Oliver

I LOATHED BRICK WALLS. The pain they inflicted was entirely unnecessary, and with vampire hearing, they didn't give humans the privacy they expected, so truthfully, brick, as well as concrete, were pointless building materials. Tomorrow I'd drown my headache in tequila. Today, I rubbed the back of my head and tried not to let a baby witch kill me.

People screeching for the police and emergency services filled the front of the house, but Daisy's approaching footsteps were the only warning I needed.

"I told you to go, but as always, you never listen." Daisy's voice was foreign to my ears.

Daisy's mother, Stacey Barrett, assured me the onyx ring would last two weeks. In truth, I wanted a lifetime, but two weeks was a better outlook than I expected with her heritage, but all we had were days. The magic had taken her from me. With a groan, I climbed to my feet. "Daisy, this isn't you."

"I don't know what's wrong with me," she said in her normal voice. "Please go. I don't want to hurt you. I don't want any of these people getting hurt."

I rested my hands on her shoulders, and just a taste of the power surging through her shocked me like roasting-hot static electricity. I'd never felt something so strong before—not that I'd touched a variety of witches in my day. But still, the power coursing through her was alarming. "I promise I'm never giving up on you. Know that."

Daisy's eyes watered. She fought this for me, but I didn't want to burden her any more than I already had. I would go, after I reassured her I would always be there. "When you're ready, I'll be waiting. You are my forever."

The light and love in her eyes blanked, and the woman I knew melted away again. This was no longer my Daisy, but the witch losing the battle with her instinct to kill vampires. The creepy voice returned. "Vampires are the scourge of this planet. Created by magic, they will be destroyed by magic. Goodbye, Oliver. It's been nice knowing you." Her arms reached out to her sides, palms up to the ceiling.

I underestimated her speed. Before I could vampire-blur out the door and scoop her up on the way, the deep rumbling explosions from her hands shook my hypersensitive eardrums. I clapped my hands over my ears and folded to protect myself as debris rained down. Ceiling tiles fell and broke on the tables and chairs. Wood beams collapsed, shattering plates and glasses. Water lines were broken and pouring along the dining room. Insulation tufts lazed on their way down. People screamed. Electricity crackled. This was multiple times worse than her explosion at Borealis. A lot of people were witnesses and at direct risk. "Daisy, stop!"

Her face fell with regret, and her hands trembled. "What's happening to me?"

"We need to get you out of here before the building comes down."

She craned her neck around and gasped at the destruction. "Stop me. Please stop me. I don't want to do this."

I pulled Daisy into my arms and led her across the dining room, or what was left of it. The ceiling groaned, and the few remaining beams moaned under the strain.

Her excessive heat warmed my body—the build to her next explosion. "We need to move faster." I scooped Daisy into my arms and speed-rushed her outside. Setting her on her feet, I said, "Stay here."

She wrapped her arms around herself, the guilt evident on her face. If I didn't act quickly, that guilt would be worse—crushing, tormenting—and she wouldn't survive it.

I raced back inside and found the elderly couple on the floor near their table. I lifted the woman first and brought her out a side door. She stood on wobbly legs and pressed a hand to her head. Before she could regain her bearings, I returned for the man, and against his protestations, I picked him up and rushed him out to the woman.

"Harvey!" The woman fell on the man in relief.

Harvey cradled his wife as if it were their first time. "Are you okay, Lenore?"

"Thanks to this incredibly strong young man, I'm fine." Lenore flashed me a grin, and they coddled each other in gratitude.

Meeting their eye contact, I said, "A gas leak destroyed the restaurant. You're going to be fine." After they nodded, that was my cue to finish the job.

Returning inside, I found the bartender huddled with the phone. She was speaking to emergency dispatch. I lifted the young blond to her feet and captured her gaze. I repeated the cover story.

The ceiling groaned again, and we both looked up. "We have to get out of here now," I said.

The bartender silently agreed and took the cordless phone with her. We walked painfully slowly, and as we neared the front door, the ceiling collapsed. With a second to spare, I pushed the bartender outside, but I was knocked to the floor by falling ceiling joists. A two-by-six impaled my back and pushed me to the floor. I cringed at the spike of blinding pain but realized it wasn't a fatal blow.

Just inconvenient.

I sucked in a breath of dust and, on all fours, I lifted myself up, sending the beam further through me. On my feet but hunched, I had enough leverage to twist until the beam fell sideways, taking me with it, and I pushed myself free of the enormous stake. I fell to my knees, gasping at the pain and coughing as the cloud of dust settled around me. That was going to leave a mark. I healed quickly and stretched to my aching feet and brushed off the mess. I'd worn a dark suit, which would camouflage the blood, but I wasn't going to have a fun time explaining the massive hole in the back of my coat. With an eye roll of frustration, I listened for more victims, but there weren't any. Everyone else had escaped, and I joined them, not wanting to inconvenience my tailor any more than I already had.

Darkness had fallen, and the survivors huddled together for safety under the lights. From one survivor to the next, I altered their memories. No one needed to know about a rogue new witch with uncontrolled abilities killing vampires without regard to innocent bystanders. A gas leak was far easier to swallow for all humans.

Emergency services pulled into the parking lot just as I'd finished. Climbing out of the driver's seat was someone completely unexpected, not because I knew the young man with buzzed brown hair and the face of a youngster who hadn't quite sprouted facial hair, but because of what he was.

A vampire.

A vampire paramedic.

Speaking from personal experience, who was this guy trying to protect...or impress? Because it better not be my Daisy.

And on that note, I needed to find Daisy. Pushing through the bewildered customers, one with a napkin still tucked at his throat, I looked for the face I needed, but Daisy was nowhere in sight. Her roommate Allison was here. I ducked away from her and headed for the illuminated parking lot, but my Shelby sat empty. I turned in place. Where did she go so fast?

Until Daisy got her power under control, she was a danger in the presence of any vampire, myself included. I ducked into my car and slipped my cell phone out of my pocket. The screen had remained intact. Daisy would be pleased to hear she didn't destroy this one. On my lock screen notifications, I had one message: *I'm safe. Stay away from me until I can figure this out. I'm sorry. I love you.'*

I hated those words. They impaled my chest like the beam in the restaurant had, but I didn't have a choice right now. I slipped a hand into my suit jacket and popped open the ring box. It was still like new. With a sigh of relief—at the custom-designed jewel remaining intact, not the replacement cost—I tossed it into the glove box. What a failure of a proposal. I should've known better than to pledge my life to her when she was in a temporary state of control. Next time, I wouldn't screw it up. Next time, she would be herself.

To get there, I needed answers, and that started with Stacey Barrett.

I spun out, knuckles blanching on the steering wheel, and I dialed her mother.

4

More Bad News

Daisy

WHEN MY EX HAD proposed to me that night in the park, I'd been pissed at Oliver and Pierce over the series of compulsions they'd done to me and the wild truth of what Oliver was. I'd carried my stupid high heels and walked home barefoot, alone, fuming. That must've been very hard for Oliver to watch, since he would sacrifice himself for only a few extra minutes with me—like when I'd nearly destroyed his sun ring in broad daylight.

And now, for those few extra minutes with me, an expensive luxury restaurant was unstable...to say the least. Countless people were hurt. I couldn't stomach the death toll. The guilt must've gotten to Oliver, since he was now zipping back into the building to rescue people I'd hurt. I should be over there, helping, apologizing, calling the damned cops and explaining my story before accepting the cuffs and the free ride downtown. But the farther I was from Oliver, the quieter my magic became, and the more myself I could be. I didn't want to cause any more trouble, and being locked up wouldn't help me with this cursed magic.

Since I *needed* to kill Oliver when we were close, I couldn't get into his car, and I doubted he'd let me walk home this time, barefoot, alone, not entirely fuming—more like a frustrated calm. Plus, the walking distance was far greater, so instead of doing what I should've been doing, I'd texted Allison for a ride.

'Hurry. It's a matter of literal life and death.' I sent.

'Be there in five.'

While making my way toward the road—away from the growing crowd—a creaking sound, like wood splintering, caught my ear. Then a growing rumbling and the dull thrumming of a building collapsing in a massive cloud of dust. My stomach knotted. People screamed. More ran in my direction, pushing past me. I didn't see Oliver. More accurately, I didn't feel Oliver. I should've been devastated by what I'd done. In reality, I was more afraid of what I could still do if this didn't get under control. After holding the immense magic back as long as I had, holding back tears was easier than it used to be.

Among the terrified, filthy people, I found my curly-haired brunette, scouring the crowd. I grabbed her arm immediately. "Get me out of here."

Allison took the lead, bringing me to where she'd double parked on the street. Not wasting a second, I dropped into her passenger seat and buckled in. The buckle was physically nothing, but it felt safe, as if the car agreed to hold me away from those innocent people. The car wouldn't let me hurt them anymore. I held the belt like a lifeline.

Allison started the car and glanced out the rearview mirror at the destruction I'd caused. We slipped away from the commotion as the ambulance arrived and meandered its way into the parking lot. "What happened?"

"Alli, I can't live like this. The magic—it controls me, and I'm a danger to everyone." I looked at the guilty palms resting on my lap.

Allison sent me a friendly smile. "You'll figure it out. It's normal for a new witch to struggle with vampires around."

"I can't even go on a date without killing people. According to Pierce, there are many more vampires around than I cared to know. How am I going to function—go to work, buy groceries, or get freaking gas without blowing up the station?"

"Did Oliver survive?" Allison asked softly as we crossed the noisy grate of the Ogden Street bridge into Marinette.

"I couldn't feel him." I slipped out my cell phone, surprised it had survived the blast, and texted him, pretending for the moment he was fine. What were the odds the building actually managed to penetrate his heart with wood or fully remove his head from his body? God, that was gruesome to consider. I texted him the only thing I could: *I'm safe. Stay away from me until I can figure this out. I'm sorry. I love you.'*

The message sat unread. He was still helping people—had to be. Maybe even finding a drink for himself to heal up after I'd thrown him against a brick wall. Yep, he was busy.

Allison turned the wheel, bringing us home. I definitely didn't want to think about magic right now, regardless of my futile plan to find a spell to cure vampires. I had something else I could work on, but it was equally depressing. "Can you take me to my dad's?"

"Sure thing." Allison circled around the block and headed back to Ogden, which connected to Bay Shore Street.

I texted my sister to meet me, but the odds of her answering were slim and even less that she'd want to help so late in the day. "Alli, do you want to help me clean out my dad's house?"

Allison snorted. "Uh, no."

I stared at the phone in my hand, waiting for Lily's reply.

"Hey, it's not because I don't want to. I'm working tonight, and I still have to get ready. Maybe Jamie will pitch in? Try him."

I texted my other roommate, Allison's half-brother, but he declined too. He didn't give an excuse, and I didn't push. Helping me clean wasn't exactly a fun way to help someone deal with the horror they'd just caused.

Sidling up to the curb, Allison said, "For this kind of work, I recommend different clothes, but if you ruin that dress, I can teach you how to fix it."

I gave her a half-assed lift of my lips and climbed out. My sister's car was already in the parking lot, shockingly, and I stepped inside the old family home. A weight settled on my chest. Greg was dead, by my own hand, and Mom was dead by his own hand, sort of. Pictures were dusty. The fridge I'd stocked daily with meals for Greg was now empty. The sooner we cleaned out this place, the sooner it could sell, and I'd never have to step foot inside this casket of nightmares again.

Lily appeared around the corner and stopped short. She tugged an earbud out of her ear canal and tilted her head. "Where have you been all day? And that's what you're wearing to clean a house?"

I looked down at my navy-blue cocktail dress. "Why not? I paid good money for this bridesmaid dress. I'd like to get my mileage out of it."

Lily shrugged. "I'm tackling the primary bedroom next. What's on your agenda?"

"Bathroom."

Lily's face pinched in disgust. "Good luck." She disappeared back into the bedroom, a little more enthusiastic than I'd expected.

Shrugging it off, I dropped my purse and went to the bathroom. Greg spent most of his time at the lab, so the bathroom wasn't too bad. I donned elbow-length cleaning gloves and kneeled by the bathtub, first dumping the partially used soaps and shampoos into a wastebasket. Then I scrubbed the tub with more vigor than needed, even coaxing a little magic into it, because finding ways to drain it helped me function.

To fill the void in the house of death, Lily turned on the TV, but I insisted she turn it off. Twice I'd destroyed buildings and deliberately harmed others. I was a danger to vampires and, by collateral damage—to humans. At this rate, I needed to lock myself up in a basement far away from everyone. I snorted to myself. That torture dungeon in the suburban house with the rowboat decoration would work just fine. An image of Oliver nearly dead from stab wounds from his ex and the vampire serum courtesy of Greg made me snap the scrubby brush handle. I stared at the broken pieces and hurled them into the tub in frustration. They clattered around and slid.

"I need more garbage bags," Lily announced, rounding into the bathroom with papers in her hand. "So many more bags. I didn't know Dad kept *everything*, and this house is full of old memories I don't want."

"Ditto," I mumbled. A part of me harbored anger at Lily. She'd encouraged me to accept the witchcraft and free her from being hunted by elves for the cure in her blood. I didn't want it, but when Evangeline had staked Oliver, it happened. Now my life was a nightmare, and her cheerfulness only made it worse.

"What happened here?" she asked, leaning toward the tub.

"It broke." I sighed in frustration and sat back on my heels.

"I got into the safe, and I found a copy of Mom and Dad's will." Her tone was dry, discouraging, and she shook the papers in her hand.

The Good News Fairy shit on us again. "What does it say?"

Lily flipped pages and read, "I, Dad, blah, blah, blah, bequeath to Pharmaceutical Development Inc. of Green Bay, Wisconsin, blah, blah." Lily skimmed. "I think this means all his cash assets have been bequeathed to PDI." She paused. "Since Mom's previous death meant all her cash assets belonged to Dad..."

I snorted again. "I can't believe this."

"Does this mean we have to sell the house, settle the estate, and give every penny to that lab?"

I rose and gestured for the papers, not wanting to believe the audacity. Lily handed them to me, and I read them. "I think this means the house and contents and vehicles are left for us to deal with—you know, things that take effort and cost money. But yeah, all his investments, savings accounts—all the liquid cash—belongs to the lab. None left for us to handle this mess, and they'd both signed. The lab that stole our childhoods, killed our mother, and destroyed our father is the benefactor. We've been spanked over and over, and now, just when we thought there was a chance we'd get a lollipop, we get spanked again. What a legacy."

"What's the date on the document?" Lily asked, perhaps thinking what I should've—they'd been coerced.

I shuffled the pages back to the signature sheet and crinkled them in my fist. "The will's dated before I met Pierce."

"Like a few months?" Lily pressed on, still hopeful.

"A few years." As the implications sank in, I dropped onto the toilet lid. "Pierce wasn't compelling Dad to recreate the weapon and steal me for the purpose. They were truly friends with aligned interests. Maybe Newt set this in motion, but I don't know how far back their business went, only that the true purpose of the serum caused Dad to rebel—briefly—and Mom was killed for it. Who knows? Maybe Dad explained to Mom that the lab was creating the greatest gift to mankind, and they didn't need convincing, compelling, or a spell to sign their life away to his life's work."

"That lab is a curse," Lily said.

"No kidding. Well, I'll place an order online for a pile of cleaning supplies. I just need to check my accounts, so I don't end up with another overdraft fee. I'm going to have to charge Jamie and Allison more rent." Which I felt terrible about. They weren't exactly rolling in it either.

Lily looked at me grimly. She didn't offer, but I suspected her situation wasn't much better than mine.

I peeled the gloves off and freed my phone from the confines of my tight jeans pocket. I logged into my bank account app, and I frowned. Something was wrong.

"What is it?" Lily asked.

"I'm not sure." I had a little too much money, and my debt payments hadn't cleared. Well, shit. Just what I needed—another mess to clean up. If I got late fees...

My heart pounded in my chest. Why couldn't one thing go right?

I logged into my mortgage account to see if the payment was pending on their end, but the balance was way off. The app was probably doing a maintenance update. I never tracked those notices. Of all days for the app to be wonky...

I logged into my student loans and...same thing. The companies weren't related. What were the odds both were performing updates at the same time? So weird. I frantically checked the balance on my car note, and it was wrong too. Way wrong. What the hell? Was someone playing a sick joke on me?

I rose and paced the bathroom while the customer service line rang at the bank holding my car note. The last thing I needed was a repo when I had to get to work. After fighting my way through the menu bot, a representative finally answered, and I gave her my account information.

"There are no pending payments, Ms. Barrett."

Now I was even more puzzled. It wasn't possible several different financial institutions were doing updates or maintenance at the same time, all showing the wrong balances. My hands trembled. There had to be a mistake, and I didn't want to get in trouble. I said, "The balance isn't right, though. I didn't pay off my car."

"Hmmm. Let me see here. Your account was paid in full. A caller requested the payoff balance," the friendly voice said into my ear. "Congratulations."

"Thanks." I hung up and blinked, dumbfounded.

"Paid off?" Lily repeated.

I darted her a look of confusion and worry. My stomach swirled, and I dialed my mortgage and student loans one after the other and received the same responses—*Paid in full. Congratulations. Confirmation is in the mail.*

The mortgage, my student loans, and my car payment were all paid off, and now I had an unusually flush bank account. My knees gave out, and I fell onto the toilet lid with a loud *thunk*.

Lily rushed up to me and rested her hands on my shoulders. "What happened? What did you find out?"

"I have no debts left—all paid in full with one stroke of the pen." How the hell? I stared completely shocked at the foreign feeling.

"Must be nice to have a rich boyfriend," Lily said flippantly.

"What?" I asked, confused by how she'd made that leap.

"Who else has pockets as deep as Oliver's? What was that—six figures?"

"Well into the six-figure range." I guess I'd never thought of it before, but I supposed she was right, and I didn't know anyone else that generous who had the means. I trembled, trying to process the implications. The freedom. The lack of worry. No longer chasing my tail from one payment to the next and buying the cheapest bread from the day-old rack just to make sandwiches for lunch and stocking up on spaghetti sauce when there was a sale. No longer worrying about filling my gas tank to the top. I pressed a hand against my forehead, trying to slow the spin of my brain. "And I tried to kill him earlier."

"Clearly, he didn't take it personally."

I laughed for the first time in a while. "What a great way to thank him after he tried proposing."

"He did what?" Lily folded down next to my lap.

"That was the explosion at the restaurant." I gave her a twirl of my fingers. "Witchcraft is back, and it's pissed. I couldn't stop it."

"The news said it was a gas leak. I figured that was a lie. Is he okay?"

I paused, swallowing back emotion before answering. "I thought we had forever, but the onyx ring he gave me only lasted a few days. After the explosion, I sent him a message telling him to stay away until I can recap this magic. He hasn't read it."

"Daisy," Lily said hesitantly. "Your situation is awful. I get it. I do."

"What?" There was a 'but' in her tone, and somehow, I didn't think I was going to like what she said next.

"But since you don't need the money now, I want to keep the house. Live in it, you know? And I'll need help with the taxes and things...for a little while." Lily looked at the floor, unwilling to meet my confused gaze.

"What about those 'old memories' you just mentioned?"

"I'll redecorate and purge all the sadness, but it's a house I could never afford on my own in a convenient location on the beautiful bay. I can't give that up." Lily gripped my hands, pleading for understanding. "I've been living like a nomad, hiding from the elves, ever since Dad told me what he did with my blood. I want a home that stays in one place, and I don't want to burden my friends with my baggage on their couches anymore."

It was all bad memories to me. "I may not have debts anymore, but I'm not exactly flush. I'll help you with what I can. If you really want it, keep it, but you're going to need a job."

"Thank you," Lily said, beaming, and gave me a quick squeeze. "Make sure you get the bathroom extra sparkling."

I frowned.

"I'm kidding...kinda," Lily said, spirits higher than they should be.

"You should thank Oliver. He is someone special—so damned special—and I don't deserve him." I went back to looking at my palms.

"We both have things to celebrate. You're not broke, and I have a home, so I'll make you a deal."

I was listening.

"It's partially my fault you're stuck with the magic keeping you two apart. Finish helping me clean the house, I'll help you find a spell to fix you—no matter how long it takes. " Lily offered me a hand. "Assuming...you know..." He was alive? I silently finished for her.

My sister in my life? My sister pouring over boring grimoires for me? My sister helping me get back into Oliver's arms? How could I say no to that? I took it, and she tugged me to my feet. "You bring drinks and snacks. I'll bring coffee and cleaning supplies. And after—paint. So much paint." I waved my hands around. "This house needs to say, 'I'm Lily, and I'm an independent young woman'. No offense to Mom's taste."

"Deal." Lily bit her lower lip in restrained excitement. "So what did the ring look like?"

Pretending Oliver was alive turned out to be easy. I smiled, remembering the sparkles. "Stupidly big, like I'd need a life preserver to go swimming or risk drowning. Stunningly beautiful and expensive as hell, as you'd expect. Frankly, I'd be afraid to wear it at all, not wanting to lose it or have it stolen. It's that fancy."

"I wish I could've seen it."

I wish I could've been wearing it.

5

The Deal

Oliver

I'D USED MY PHONE to browse local properties for sale, and since we were in the middle of a housing slump, there weren't too many. Then I narrowed down the results to the most expensive listings and narrowed further by homes clearly empty in their photographs. Results: two.

The first had been a bust. I pulled to the curb of the second—the suburban home in Menominee with the rowboat decoration in the landscaping. There were no lights on or any signs of life, but I could sense a vampire's presence. I sighed. Why this house? Why was this suburban home so attractive to female vampires?

While grumbling to myself about returning to the site of my most recent torture, I climbed the steps and checked the knob. Unlocked. I pushed the front door open, waited a beat for a surprise attack that didn't come, and lifted a palm. Using a hand was a wiser move than face-planting, but as expected, no invisible barrier existed.

I entered the abandoned property. The only wonderful memory I had was my hallucination of Daisy while I'd slowly died. But Daisy had found me and, despite being terrified of the act, she'd offered her wrist and saved my life. That was the woman I'd fight to the ends of the earth for.

So here I was.

"Stacey!" I called as I passed through the living room and into the kitchen. I repeated my call, and with a whoosh of air, Daisy's mother stood before me, decked in a respectable skirt suit set. It wasn't designer, but the cut fit her well. She grinned like an old friend.

"I don't suppose you're in the market for another property?" Stacey opened her arms for a hug. My business associate always loved a healthy paycheck, and I appreciated her quality service. Her being my girlfriend's mother and our favorable relations was a perk.

"We need to talk," I said, pulling away. "Starting with how did you get into my house?"

"Nicole knows me. She invited me inside." She folded her arms across her chest as if offended.

I hated finding out my home protection had...loopholes. "She didn't know you'd had a change of lifestyle."

"I imagine not. Now, it's my turn. Why aren't you with Daisy?"

Human Stacey and I had a business relationship for many years, and she'd complimented me on various attributes she admired, but despite her high opinion of me, she hadn't wanted me anywhere near Daisy. But once my old friend shifted to my side of the hidden world, she pushed me to be with her daughter. "And I would be, but the onyx ring you gave me wore off."

Stacey flinched. "It was supposed to last two weeks. Are you sure?"

"Schooner Landing," I said simply. The news had been covering it extensively.

"I see you made it out alive." Stacey turned on her heel and went deeper into the kitchen. The green-eyed beauty with silver tinsel in her hair like highlights fished out a wineglass from an overhead cabinet and ducked under the island, retrieving a bottle of Merlot.

"All I did was sit next to her." And propose, but her mother didn't need to know that yet.

"Then you'll need one of these, too." She collected a second glass and poured for both of us. "When Daisy was a teenager, I worked most of the time. You know how agent's hours are all over the place. And with her father's first love being the lab, we left Daisy and Lily to spend time with my brother-in-law Marc and his wife Lisa. Daisy's cousin Abby was like a sister to her. My in-laws spent more time with my girls than I did. For years, I didn't know Lisa held the contents of the Barrett family legacy." She passed a glass of wine to me.

Never one to turn down a free drink, I swirled and sipped. The fruity notes and hint of vanilla were top-notch. "Witchcraft."

"I also didn't believe in it. The stories of her ancestors were too far-fetched to be believed. Henrietta Barrett burned at the stake for being a witch?"

Clearly, she wasn't a history major. "You show such disdain for the past. Why did you name your daughter after her, then?"

"That was entirely Greg's idea. He hoped that passing along the name would encourage Daisy to follow in her ancestors' footsteps. I didn't mind the name Daisy, so I didn't object. Little did I know that vampires were real and becoming a witch was protection. It almost makes up for his being a shit father." Stacey paused and sipped. "Nah."

I stifled a chuckle.

"Marc Barrett had a close relationship with Daisy's paternal grandmother. He'd fought throughout his childhood to activate his witch DNA, but never had any luck. He'd tried teaching Abby, but as a non-believer, she didn't have any interest, so he tried pushing the family legacy through my girls. I refused to have that rubbish in my household, and whenever Marc brought it up to Greg, he'd deferred to me. Hindsight is twenty-twenty, as they say. Now I wish I could've been there, guiding the girls, helping them. Could you imagine how powerful Daisy and Lily could've been by now if I had chosen to believe?"

I didn't want to imagine.

"Since the girls could've protected themselves, Greg wouldn't have made their blood the weapon and the cure. They never would've been at risk." Stacey's gaze met mine.

I understood what she meant, and I finished the thought. "Of meeting someone like me."

Stacey shrugged. "I've since changed my mind, obviously, but those haunting thoughts have kept me searching for an answer."

I didn't have an answer either, but I had an idea. "Without the ring, Daisy is completely out of control. She's a danger to herself and everyone around her—myself included. Magic is grounded in emotion. Tell Daisy you're alive. Explain all this to her. She's been through a lot lately. Having her mother back could only help stabilize her."

"Why do you think I gave you that ring? If I waltzed up to her, she'd level me in a second. Your age gives you an advantage. You can give her the news more easily than I can."

"She loves you," I pressed.

"And you're telling me she doesn't love you?" Stacey sipped her red wine.

"It's different."

"Daisy thought I was gone and buried, and she mourned me. I'm sure she mourned Marc, Lisa, and Abby more, as much as it hurts to admit. And now I drink human blood. Tell me how a new witch would take that news without a working onyx ring."

"She understands our world now, and we can take precautions to protect you, but by withholding the truth from her, she'll only hurt worse once she finds out. Daisy needs to know sooner than later."

Stacey leaned forward with a playful smile on her lips. "I agree, and you need to tell her."

"And if she explodes in another fit of magic?" Because that was a guarantee in her current state.

"You're a vampire. I think you can figure out a way to stop her." The leveled gaze from Daisy's mother told me all I needed to know. If Daisy couldn't control herself, Stacey wanted me to turn her.

I finished my glass in a single swallow.

"We have a mutual interest in Daisy's well-being, and as my long-time business associate, and might I add, friend, can I count on you?"

I'd given Daisy a vial of my blood only for an emergency. Using it was a last-resort and her choice only. "We both agreed she won't ever take the change, and I'm not going against her wishes."

"Then you'll need to be creative." Stacey set down her wineglass.

I didn't appreciate what she was implying.

"Pardon me, Mr. Rockwell, I need a different kind of drink. Unless you care to join me once more?" Stacey asked with a sweet lilt.

I needed to avoid lactose as much as possible, and the hygiene of many humans left me wanting. "I have a stocked refrigerator."

"Your loss." Stacey disappeared out the door in a *whoosh* of vampire speed.

Daisy becoming a vampire would solve the problem separating us, but I couldn't do that to her. I wasn't that selfish. I was going to do whatever I could to find another solution for Daisy to be reunited with me.

6

The Partner Is...

Daisy

MY BOSS SET UP a temporary emergency service department on a different wing of Borealis Medical Center. Luckily, when I'd exploded on Greg—literally—I hadn't damaged the ambulance garage. Our temporary breakroom was shared with the outpatient nursing staff. I didn't mind the extra traffic and new faces. Besides, they had a bigger television, a cappuccino machine, and more couches, which might've been leather—I couldn't tell, but Oliver could've. I smiled to myself. He could've determined the brand just by looking at them, and likely the year crafted. A man of style, luxury, and expensive taste.

And I wanted his hands all over me. I wanted to walk down the aisle with him. I wanted to be his forever.

Instead, guilt weighed heavily on my shoulders, and everywhere I looked, I watched for faces of disapproval for what I'd done, even though Oliver wiped all their memories when I destroyed a wing of this hospital.

My new partner was a transfer from another department, so I presumed she didn't need a tour. While waiting, I sat on the leather couch with a grimoire. I paged through the ancient text, hunting for a spell to help me cure vampires, but worried thoughts continued to intrude. I couldn't think of any nurses who showed an interest in EMS, and its pay cut. Should I introduce them to the hidden world around me? I didn't know how long I could keep up the animal bite ruse if such an occurrence happened again. Or what if we were attacked? Could my magic save us both? What if I exploded near my new partner? I couldn't erase memories.

I exhaled slowly and turned the page, trying to focus on the faded lettering.

Now that Oliver had paid off all my debts, maybe I should switch careers to one where the public wasn't at risk. But then, who would I be? I helped people. I saved people. Without that purpose, I was...lost. And I couldn't even think of anything else appealing to me.

The breakroom door opened as nurses filed in, grabbing quick bites to eat between call lights. I looked up, eager to make eye contact with my new partner, whoever she was. An inkling too small to worry about tingled deep within my psyche. I recognized that feeling, but it didn't make sense. There were no vampires here, and if Oliver was remotely near the building, I would know.

While I returned to my book, more people funneled in and out, and finally, a pair of shoes stopped by my feet. I looked up and smiled. "Hey, Kevin. What's up?" I closed my book, set it on the table, and rose.

"I'm your new partner." He held out a hand to shake formally.

I grinned at the unnecessary gesture but accepted his grip. Heat rushed to my hand. In surprise, I pulled free and widened my eyes in surprise. This uncontrolled magic was alerting me to humans now. On top of everything else, I couldn't handle my magic getting worse. I needed Allison and Jamie now.

"Is something wrong?" he asked.

I gave him a fake smile. "Not at all. Actually, I'm thrilled to have a partner with experience for a change. You know how that's been lately. But I need to make a call quickly. Excuse me." I ducked out of the breakroom and pulled up Allison's contact in my phone. "Come on, come on," I urged as the line rang.

"Daisy? What's going on?"

I exhaled in relief and whispered frantically, "I'm at work and my magic is like a furry, four-legged pointer ready to pounce on a quail."

"You have a vampire in the building?"

"That's what I'm trying to tell you. There aren't any—only humans. I can't be attacking my patients or my partner! I don't know what to do. Help me, please, Alli. God, just take this away."

"Whoa, slow down. You're feeling an urge to kill *humans*?"

"It's a light tingle, but it's there, and that's how it began with vampires—slow at first and then...*boom*. How do I stop it? My new partner is probably confused as hell right now."

"Daisy, listen to me."

I was.

"Magic feeds on emotions. The stronger your feelings, the stronger the magic."

"I know, but he's a friend. I can't just shut him off like a stranger."

"He's not much of a friend if you didn't know he's a vampire."

I snorted dismissively. "Kevin isn't a vam—" I cut myself off before innocent ears heard my crazy talk. "He's not. I've known him a long time as an ER nurse, and he'd dated Megan. There's no way he's—"

"Daisy, you need to accept that if you're feeling the urge to kill, the target isn't human. The magic only wants to destroy vampires. In all the years I've practiced, in all the texts I've scoured, there's never been a case of magic going after humans. Never." Allison hung up.

That was it. I had to spend the rest of my life cowering away from society or killing vampires. I wasn't a hermit, but I wasn't a murderer either. How was I going to live like this?

"Hey, Daisy, you look good." The familiar voice both drained the blood from my body in disgust and coursed relief through me because he'd lived. I slipped my phone back into my pocket and turned.

With a smile dancing on his lips, Pierce Evansson's deep brown eyes crinkled. Large white glamoured wings folded behind his muscular frame. His navy polo stretched precariously across his broad chest, and his baggy cargo pants likely held a stake, because the elf never left home without a vampire weapon at hand. And that was my proof. Pierce was best friends with Kevin. He'd never accept a vampire in his life.

Kevin was human; my magic was broken. Allison had no idea how to fix it.

From our rocky history, I went on the defensive immediately and said dryly, "I'm thrilled *you* survived the blast."

"Are you?" Pierce leaned in.

As always, he missed the sarcasm. Ultimately, I was relieved he survived only because I didn't want the entire elf clan hunting me down. "Yeah."

Pierce's gentle smile was genuine. "I'm proud you can hold your own now." He leaned in closer and whispered, "Kick some vamp ass for me."

I frowned.

"There you are," Kevin said, approaching from behind Pierce.

As nurses wheeled patients down the hallway, the tingle of heat returned. Maybe there was a vampire nearby, not that I'd be able to identify them. Unlike the wings on the elves, vampires didn't walk around with fangs descended or anything. But that just confirmed my need to find the spell to cure vampires. It was my only hope of controlling this ridiculousness.

"Hey, Kev, what's going on?" Pierce asked and gave his friend a custom handshake.

"Just looking for my new partner."

Pierce's gaze bounced between us, confused. "Her? You're Daisy's new partner?"

Kevin folded his arms across his chest as if offended. The two of them were similar except Kevin was younger and shorter, but they both had trimmed hair, shaven faces, and the bulky muscles common among gym fiends. "Is there a problem with that?"

"You know a medic's pay is dirt compared to nursing. Why would you choose a pay cut?"

Kevin relaxed his posture. "The same old regulars looking for medication refills or pain meds are...getting tiresome. I find assisting with accidents and injuries far more energizing than sickness, and being on scene, like the explosion at Schooner Landing, was more compelling than these four walls."

He'd already accepted the job before being assigned to me. The department knew I was there. I shrunk away from my new partner and swallowed back a nervous chuckle. "What did you see?"

Kevin's gaze met mine, but I couldn't read his blank expression. The overhead alarm called for us, breaking the tension. I listened for the address and nature of the call.

"I'm out of here, guys. Have fun." Pierce waved and left.

"Are you ready?" I asked Kevin.

"Absolutely." My new partner followed me while I rushed toward the ambulance. As if operating on the same wavelength, Kevin climbed into the passenger seat while I sat behind the steering wheel. I rolled the heavy rig out of the garage and down the county road, lights and sirens wailing for space.

"So, another animal attack?" Kevin asked, having listened to the call details with me.

"Yep." I steered onto the main thoroughfare through town and used my shoulder radio to alert the online physician we were en route.

"We get a lot of these around here, don't we? I mean, I only saw a few in the emergency department, but I heard about it."

"Seems that way." I didn't know how to handle this. Exposing the hidden world wasn't without risk. But not telling him also meant he could be the next Megan or Kayla. Lying sucked.

Instead of stopping, I hesitated through the red lights, as safety allowed, and tailgated a few distracted drivers. While we rolled right by Fully Loaded. If only I could get a drink and some pointers from Allison. I sighed.

I lumbered along the interstate bridge and swung the hefty rig down 38th Avenue, on the north end of town, and as I visualized the remaining directions, my blood turned cold. My stomach churned at the fancy newer-build home with a wooden rowboat and lamp in the front yard. I flipped off the siren.

"Something wrong?" Kevin asked.

"I've been here before." Evangeline's torture house. Now what scourge up and moved in? We were walking into a vampire's scene, but this time I could protect myself—and Kevin—if an uncontrolled vampire decided dinner wasn't over. Perhaps my not-broken magic was still useful after all. But that wasn't the introduction to the hidden world I'd imagined for poor Kevin. How would he handle it?

Panic and quit?

Try to fight and freak the hell out?

Get bitten and die?

Swallowing back a lump, I unbuckled and rushed up the concrete porch steps and knocked. The lights were off, and no one answered. Kevin moved around the yard, searching for something.

"Over here, Barrett!" Kevin stood next to the rowboat in the landscaping, lightly illuminated by the lamp.

My magic was a pointer. His nose was a bloodhound. He hadn't fought me for the driver's seat. I had high hopes for Kevin.

"Need the stretcher?" I called.

"Just come here."

I stopped short at his side, and my mouth dropped open. I'd never seen anything like this. "Well, I don't think they need us."

"We're way past CPR with these people," Kevin agreed.

Four bloody bodies lay heaped inside the decorative rowboat. Lifeless eyes gazed at the sky. Kevin leaned over the bodies and tilted their heads. "Bites all right. Who called this in and left them?"

A disgusted passerby? A horrified neighbor? The guilty party? "That's the million-dollar question."

"I'll get the police over here. There's nothing we can do." Kevin tilted his face into his shoulder radio.

Movement caught the corner of my eye—a woman in a skirt suit, walking swiftly away down the sidewalk in heels with long brown locks flowing down her back. "Hey, wait!" I rushed in her direction, but she ignored me. "EMS, I need to ask you a few questions. Please?"

She still ignored me.

Kevin touched my shoulder, and heat surged through me. "LEOs are on the way. Let's stay by the bodies until they secure the crime scene."

While watching the woman walk away, something familiar about her rang a few tiny bells—like a cat's toy, not a church bell. There was something about that woman, but I couldn't connect the familiarity to anyone I knew. "Yeah, okay," I said absently and turned away, heading toward the victims.

I inspected the bodies myself, getting a closer look at the wounds. These pairs of punctures were all identical. Arguably, they could be described as canine. I preferred vampire.

Kevin appeared clueless, but I wasn't prepared or comfortable telling him the truth. Staring at the victims with pity, my body heated with tingles like a flame springing to life under my skin. My emotions were getting the best of me, affecting my magic even when no vampires were around. Maybe my magic was becoming more sensitive—like a wider range of perception.

I bet that woman in heels was a vampire. I couldn't see her on the sidewalk anymore, but maybe she'd circled around in the dark, and now she was getting too close. As much as I hated my magic, there was relief in knowing I could logic my way through what I was feeling. And I had a built-in alarm system.

"I've seen a lot in my day in the emergency department, but this...this is awful. No one deserves to be treated like this. Are you okay?" Kevin asked, concern soft in his tone. Kevin's famous bedside manner was coming out. Young, attractive, and sweet—clearly, he was one of the good guys.

"Yeah, I'm fine." The tingles grew, and I glanced around the darkened yard, seeking any movement from the perpetrator.

Kevin gazed at the victims. "These marks look like Megan's. Do you figure this is the same dog?"

Not a chance. Evangeline was dead-dead for real. And what dog would lift bodies and stack them into a boat? "Probably. It's the same M.O. I bet that lady walking down the sidewalk found them and stacked them neatly."

"Why?" Kevin asked.

"I don't know. Maybe so kids didn't stumble on them in the morning on their way to school?"

The worrisome thought-train continued to heat my body, preparing for a magical defense—or offense. I pinched my polo's collar and fanned it to cool my chest.

"The police never caught it?" Kevin asked, surprised. "There's been no mention of dogs in the news lately. Where's he been all this time?"

I glanced at the bodies, regretting where this was heading. "I wish I knew."

Sirens wailed in the distance. At least this conversation was over soon.

"It's too big to be a snake, but what else has two fangs?" Kevin asked.

A flashback of my first time trying to solve a Cujo case came to mind—my basketball player. *A snake in his pants.* Oliver's pants. I smiled to myself, but it slid away when I remembered it hadn't ended well. I bent over the bodies to get a better look, in case of movement, and I pointed. "See here? There's no arterial spray. There are no puddles of blood." After a pause, I added, "Someone stabbed them or injected them with something, and this is the dump site." I gazed at the house with the torture room in the basement. Whoever did this didn't need to torture their food. A quick compulsion was easier, cleaner, and less risky. So why this public display? It didn't add up, but thankfully, in a few minutes I could walk away. "But that's for the detectives to figure out."

"So, not a dog?"

Kevin was too innocent for this job, and I didn't want to corrupt him. "I doubt it."

Police cars pulled to the curb, and several men in uniform filtered out of the vehicles, shining blinding flashlights into our eyes. I relayed my knowledge to the officers and gathered Kevin into the ambulance. Thankfully, my new partner didn't ask any more questions, because I didn't have it in me to keep lying.

I drove us back to Borealis, drumming the steering wheel, hoping some kinetic energy would drain some of my triggered magic. I'd already said too much to Kevin, and I had no way to explain an accidental explosion of an ambulance. So I kept drumming and distracting myself with reminders of scrubbing Greg's toilet.

That helped a lot.

7

Locking Down

Daisy

In my living room, with Allison as referee, the tingling heat—the urge to kill—waited to be unleashed on a stuffed burlap dummy the size of a shoe. I wasn't superstitious, exactly, but enough weird stuff had happened in my life lately, so I paused at the target before me. "Nothing bad's going to happen?"

"It shouldn't," Allison said. That wasn't reassuring at all. "The outcome is entirely up to you."

That was even less reassuring. My target resembled a gingerbread man by any other name, except one. "But that's a voodoo doll."

"It's not voodoo," Allison said.

I still didn't believe her. "It has four limbs and a rounded head. And there's a smirk on its face. That's definitely a smirk."

Allison pressed her lips together. "Whether you need to injure for self-defense or kill offensively, you have to be able to function without exploding. So, gather the emotion, focus the energy. The objective is to hit one target, and don't blow it to bits."

So many words of a serious nature. "My insurance probably doesn't cover accidental self-inflicted explosions. Maybe we should do this outside."

Allison chuckled. "The pressure to succeed will help you be more careful. You can do this. When Jamie was learning to harness his power, he blew a car to smithereens."

"Really?" I asked, surprised. All this time, I thought I was the only witch in history who struggled so much to figure this out, leaving me feeling like a complete failure. And now, hope flickered in the shadows of my heart. "What happened?"

"Our mom always encouraged us to find the magic within because it was our only protection, but we had to keep it a secret from everyone, including his dad. Right after getting his license, Jamie asked to borrow his dad's car for the first time. Jamie's dad handed over the keys, proud his son had earned his practice driving hours without a single accident. My brother planned to go straight to a girl's house to impress her with his wheels and his magic. He never made it." Allison smiled warmly.

Since Allison wasn't distraught over it, I could infer the end of the story without offending her. "Car went boom?"

Allison nodded and laughed. "He got behind the wheel, and he was so damned excited, the whole thing blew from his magic. When we rushed to the window, Jamie stood there at the curb, holding the steering wheel. Metal pieces of the car rained down around him. Nearby car alarms honked in protest."

I laughed.

"*They* said someone tampered with the municipal gas line, but we knew the truth. At the time it was hilarious, and even now I look back on it as a funny memory, but it wasn't all good. Jamie's dad left and never returned."

My laughter died. "That's harsh."

"Partially, the man loved his car, but he figured out fast my brother and I were dabbling in the arts, and he didn't approve. Child support ended there, and he's still in arrears."

The hidden world tore apart their family, too. "I'm sorry. That's terrible."

Allison shrugged. "That's one of the reasons why you must master the magic. Now get to work."

I saluted her authority and refocused on the pent-up energy I'd been itching to release since the onyx ring had failed. Although I'd seen horrors similar to the bodies in the rowboat before, apparently the stress of everything lately set my emotions into overdrive. But I wasn't a walking heap of sad potato salad, because my magic used my emotions as fuel, draining them. Directing them into a weapon. Was I becoming like Pierce—an emotionless being incapable of proper human interaction?

My responsibility was ensuring proper handling and safety procedures. Sounded more like a simple corporate policy than a complex, powerful system of power. Visualizing my emotions coalescing from a brilliant ball of color to an organized rainbow. I guided it toward my palms and focused on the creepy little face. The burlap humanoid doll exploded into tufts of polyester.

Allison frowned. "Less power. You have to focus on *how much* power you send. It's like drizzling syrup on your waffles. You don't unscrew the whole cap and dump the bottle over. You must see, in a manner of speaking, what you're doing and choose just the right amount—the right amount of pressure."

"Yes, because pouring pancake syrup and controlling fatal magic are on the same wavelength."

"You know what I mean."

I did. It meant that, exploding car story or not, I wasn't cut out for witchcraft. Apparently, what Allison thought was on par with pancake syrup for her was like juggling half a dozen fiery swords to me. "How long did it take you to master your control after you...you know...?" Killed your dad with the wooden block of knives, I declined to say.

"A few weeks until I was certain I wouldn't burn the fur off the neighbor's cat."

She'd been reassuring me for far longer than that, and so far, it wasn't getting better. If anything, the magic's strength was outpacing my control by a long shot, and with that trajectory, I couldn't see how I'd ever be in Oliver's arms again. The only thing I had been feeling lately was...worry. My shoulders slumped.

Allison rested a hand on my arm. "It's okay. You'll get there."

"And if I don't?"

Allison pulled her hand away. She didn't answer.

"If I don't?" I pressed. I hadn't considered the ramifications of failing to control my urges.

"Back in the day, you'd earn a fearsome reputation and people would stay away from you. Others would target you for the next witch burning. Nowadays, I think they have special asylums," she said slowly. "They're not exactly advertised to the public."

Great. Just great. I sighed. "There's no other option?"

Allison grimly shook her head.

Padded walls and drug-induced nightmares were my future if I couldn't figure this out. "Okay. From the top." I reached my arms out while Allison replaced the doll with another equally horrifying hand-stitched burlap thing that resembled a voodoo doll. Reluctantly, I took aim.

"Remember, less power. Homeowner's insurance..."

"Yeah, yeah," I said dismissively. I already knew the consequences of failure, but yeah, I didn't want to lose my home. Especially now that I owned it free and clear. I still couldn't believe Oliver. Never in a million years did I expect such an over-the-top gift. I'd be grateful until my last breath.

I leveled my hands at the doll, and between a lighter's flame and a fireball was a little green army guy. That was how much I conjured and released, drilling a smoking hole in the region commonly associated with a heart. Not bad, but not the solution I was looking for. "I'm confident I can handle offensive maneuvers. How does this help me with control when I'm out in public?"

"The next time you prepare to burn a hole in my doll's chest, I want you to reel it back, take that pain and anger, and swallow it. That was the reason for one of your first lessons, and that's how you'll handle the public."

"Your solution is to accept a constant barrage of pain from my psyche, roaring fire toward my palms, and dragging the sandpaper rainbows of overloaded emotions back into myself? That's exhausting." And not at all the answer I'd hoped for.

"Keeping others safe around your magic is exhausting."

"Even for you?" I asked her softly, needing reassurance I wasn't alone in the struggle, that I wasn't still a failure.

"Only around vampires—at the club, the bar, the drive-in theater, and the park. Anywhere the public congregates at night, vampires are there, and yeah, it's a struggle."

Allison had said our magic only reacted to vampires, but that couldn't be true. That meant I was a freak, destined never to be in public again until I found the fabled spell to cure vampires. I sighed.

"Once more from the top," Allison said.

A knock at my front door was a welcome reprieve. "Hold that thought." I dashed to the door, grateful for the break, and my sister stood before me, holding a six-pack of soda and a grocery bag. "Drinks and snacks, as promised."

I grinned, happy to see Lily all bright-eyed and bushy-tailed.

Lily held out the bag. "All right, deal's a deal. I'm hyped on coffee and ready to read boring stuff."

"Come on in." I took the burden from her and brought it to the kitchen island, Lily following on my heels. I unpacked a variety of chips, a jar of salsa, a brick of cheese melt, a bunch of bananas, and a pack of chocolate chip cookies—an eclectic mix that matched my sister perfectly. This carb load reminded me that I needed to get back into running. Too many days had passed since I'd last pounded the pavement, but like those nights, tonight it would be brushed aside again.

"Where are the books?" Lily asked, rubbing her hands together and fidgeting. She craned her neck around as if she'd never been in here before. Too much caffeine indeed. No reason to waste a useful buzz.

"Alli!" I leaned around the entryway. "We're taking a break to dig for spells. I need your books." I cracked a can of soda and brought it back over to my practice space in the living room.

Allison shuffled through her chest of supplies. "In here is everything I have. I doubt you'll find anything useful, but you don't know until you try."

"I'll get the rest." I went upstairs and dragged out the box of hand-me-downs from Aunt Lisa. The box Oliver's ring had been in tipped over, and the lid tilted open. Setting down the grimoires, I picked up the symbol-engraved box, and the bottom was ajar. With a frown, I poked a finger inside, and the false bottom moved. "Strange." I lifted it, and three shiny ruby rings similar to Oliver's rested at the bottom, and next to them, a dehydrated sprig of tiny purple flowers. "Even more strange."

Taking the flowers, I replaced the false bottom and tucked the box away. With an armful of books, I returned to the mini-party and spread them out for grabs. "Here's the rest, and Lily, I want you to have this." I offered the sprig to my sister.

She frowned at it. "What is it?"

"Vervain," Allison said, lifting her brows with appreciation. "A lot of it. Where did you get that?"

"Aunt Lisa."

"She's full of surprises," Allison said.

The more Allison told me about witchcraft running in my family, the more I wished to have Lisa by my side to explain all this. Like walking through life during a thick fog, I was lost without her, missing a piece of my own history. I hated the empty feeling where family used to be. At least I still had Lily, but she was just as clueless as me.

"What do you want me to do with it?" Lily asked.

"Oliver gave it to me crushed up inside a locket. He told me to always wear it," I said. "It'll protect you from vampire compulsion and bites."

"But there aren't any here besides Oliver and Soren. You trust them, don't you?" Lily asked.

My mind flashed back to the bodies in the decorative rowboat and the well-dressed woman sauntering away. "I do, but I don't think they're the only ones now." Allison looked at me with concern, so I explained, "Last night, Kevin and I took a call. Four bodies, all with clear fang marks. So, please, keep that vervain on you."

"I can do that." Lily tucked it into her pocket.

"Speaking of vervain," Allison said. "Witches don't need herbal protection. What's with the new necklace?"

My fingers went protectively to the antique locket hiding a vial of Oliver's blood around my neck. "A gift from Oliver." In case of grievous injury, he'd said, I could heal myself. It was the only backup plan until I could have Oliver at my side again. A pang of emptiness tore through me.

"Huh," Allison said and returned to the pages.

"So, what exactly are we looking for?" Lily asked.

"A unicorn hair at the top of Mount Everest, after years and years of snowstorms," Allison said, focusing on the pages turning. "Have you ever been to Everest? You're not finding much there but dehydrated, frozen solid human bodies and so much trash. Humans are disgusting."

Ignoring my roommate's useless answer and unnecessary visual, I said, "Anything that mentions a reduction or elimination in the desire to hunt or kill vampires."

Allison snorted.

"Reduce the desire? But you just said there's another rogue vampire in town. Shouldn't we be making you stronger?" Lily asked.

"Ding, ding, ding, new girl gets it," Allison said.

"I can't control it," I said. "I'm starting to feel the magic when I'm around humans, so I need to put a lid on this before people get hurt, and while you're searching, 'vampire cure' is also a key phrase of interest."

"Now you're asking to find a rainbow unicorn hair flying across the sky with a big flag saying, 'I'm right here, sillies!' before crash landing in twenty feet of fresh snowpack on the mountaintop. It's not happening. This is a waste of time when you should be practicing control." Allison looked to Lily for support.

My sister shrugged and turned the page. "I made a deal."

I stared at my sister. Lily never took my side, and the warm-and-fuzzies flooded me knowing we were on the same wavelength for a change.

"Alternatively," Allison said to Lily. "If another swell of vampires already rolled into town, we need all the help we can get. You could activate your witch side and learn right along with your sister."

Lily looked at me for my biased opinion, and I was happy to oblige. "I wasn't given a choice, but knowing everything I do now, I would never have chosen it. Not a chance in hell. I think it's the most miserable thing ever, and I cannot, in good conscience, recommend you volunteer for it."

Lily considered and spoke softly. "With the weapon gone, vampires don't need the cure anymore, and the elves won't be hunting me to stop them." Her tone suggested she hadn't finished her thought.

"And?" I prompted.

"Instead of having value to a people of strength, I'm just another helpless human about to be caught in the crosshairs."

I didn't like where she was headed with this. I struggled so hard. I didn't want this for her. "Lily—"

"I saw how you were hurt over and over again by vampires and elves even with help. Daisy, I don't have to live in fear anymore, but that's not good enough. I want to be able to defend myself and others while I'm at it."

I couldn't let my sister make a terrible decision, even with her eyes wide open. "You have to get a job to pay for that big-ass house."

"I know," she said angrily, cutting me off.

"But I can't even go to work without this boiling fury within me trying to kill people, and yes, I mean *people*. I'm still a danger to everyone around me. How are you so certain you can help others when I've been at this for weeks?"

Lily stiffened, clearly offended. "You think I can't do this just because you can't?"

"That's not what I said."

Allison watched us both, quietly staying out of it.

Lily didn't respond, only glared at my unacceptable advice. She wanted me to welcome her decision with open arms and praise her noble intentions. If she wanted to struggle with this amount of pain, all for the hope of wielding magic like a badass, I couldn't stop her. She was a grown adult. All my life I'd been told Lily was superior to me, having always succeeded while I struggled, so there was no reason to doubt her success.

Didn't mean I had to like it. I glanced at the carpet and exhaled. "Out of a sample size of three, I guess I'm a special case since no one else struggles with control like I do."

Lily looked at me as if disbelieving her own ears.

I added, "Just because I suck doesn't mean you will."

Lily sat up straighter, a bright smile tugging at her lips. "I want this. I do."

Allison smiled like a proud parent. Another victim for the club. My roommate took her cell phone out of her pocket. "We need Jamie. While he drags his ass out of bed, we can get ready. Daisy, move anything fragile or valuable out of the way."

I sighed and got up. I scoured the area, tucking away photographs and other keepsakes, but I left the broken framed photograph of me and Pierce. It might make good target practice. If not, no harm done.

Lily frowned, watching me with worry on her brow. "Wait, how does this work exactly?"

Allison packed up the books. "Your witchcraft DNA is a dormant defense mechanism. You need a strong emotional trigger to set it off."

"That sounds...ominous. What triggered yours, Daisy?" Lily asked.

As the images hammered my chest and a fresh wave of pain returned, I answered softly, "Evangeline staked Oliver through the chest, and I thought he died right in front of me. It was the worst night of my life, watching him die, when all I wanted was to be strong, to fight with him. All I could do was watch and cry. That broke me."

Lily slumped. "Oh."

"Yeah, *oh*," I snapped. "This isn't something to take lightly. I know you're going to do it anyway, but this magic is the only thing keeping me away from Oliver, and it sucks."

Now I was the danger to my love. Nausea twisted my stomach like a spike-covered mace, swinging and hitting home, knocking the wind from my lungs. I struggled to inhale, and when the breath returned, I swallowed back tears and reminded myself Lily wanted to walk right into my misery. She was an idiot.

"Well, I don't have those attachments," Lily grumbled.

"If you really want it, we can do it," Jamie said, shirtless, wiping his face dry with a fluffy white towel.

"How?" Lily stood to meet him, a mixture of curiosity, fear, and excitement palpable from her. "I mean, is it going to hurt?"

Jamie dropped the towel on the floor. "How badly do you want this?"

"I really want it." Lily squared her shoulders as if she were prepared for what came next.

"Enough to fight through the pain?"

"Pain?" Lily repeated, face twisting with uncertainty.

I couldn't help a lift of my lips. She didn't know pain, but if she went down this route, it was going to be her best friend.

"If an emotional trigger won't work, a physical one will. Can you handle this?" Jamie stretched his arms forward, palms out, toward my sister.

Lily considered, looking for words of advice from Allison.

"You can do this, Lily," Allison said. "Activating the DNA is temporary. Having it is forever."

Forever. I blinked back tears. No way. Somewhere, someone had to have a spell to free me from this overcharge of anger directed at others. I had to find the solution because I couldn't stay away from Oliver Rockwell *forever*. I needed his arms around me, his warm gaze upon me, his car metaphors turning me on. Without him, an emptiness pervaded, slowly draining my life, and leaving behind a husk of who I was meant to be.

Lily turned to me for one final platitude of encouragement, which surprised me. I shook my head. "Living with regrets comes with a steep learning curve. It's not worth it."

Lily stared at the carpet. Her posture changed the moment she made her final choice. "I'm ready."

Jamie's invisible force knocked her off her feet.

My stomach swirled. I couldn't stand seeing my little sister hurt. On the other hand, maybe she'd give up when she'd had enough—long before getting what she thought she wanted. "If this is how you're going to do it, I can't watch. I'm going for a run."

The likely nonexistent spell to ease my innate desire to kill Oliver would have to wait once again. Time to bust out the sneakers and hope my sister was still Lily when I returned.

8
Wingman

Oliver

I GESTURED FOR YET another refill while swiping my finger on my cell phone screen, focusing on a word puzzle. One benefit of vampirism—inebriation took longer. One disadvantage? Inebriation took longer. Tonight, I was firmly in Camp Disadvantage with sensitive ears ringing from the music pumping around us and not enough booze to dull the ache. While my brother wore jeans and a T-shirt, fitting squarely in the youthful crowd, I stuck out with my suit, which unfortunately brought me plenty of unwanted attention, but I would not sacrifice my comfort for a minor frustration.

"What's got you in a mood?" Soren asked, pulling out the stool next to me and lowering himself onto it. He gestured to the bartender for his own refill.

"I'm missing a five-letter word." My finger shifted, choosing scrambled letters that were absolutely real words, but the game wouldn't accept them.

"If I can help you finish that game, so you'll join me on the dance floor, so be it. Let me see."

I tilted my screen toward my brother, and his brows knitted in deep thought. "Bump on a log." Soren chuckled.

This was going to be pointless. I shifted to stand. "I might as well pack up and head home now."

"No, you hold on there." Soren pressed my shoulders down. "*Dreary*."

"That's six letters."

"*Dryer*." Soren pointed to my screen. "It has to be dryer."

The bartender set a pair of drinks in front of us. Soren swallowed half of his in a gulp.

I selected the letters, and the game shimmied with rejection. "Nope."

"*Ready*?"

I looked at him sideways. "I already figured out the elementary words. Impress me, brother, and then I can assist you with whatever conundrum brought you back to my side."

Soren focused hard. Apparently, my success was paramount to his enjoyment of the gyrating ladies.

"Derry."

I glared at him. "That's a proper noun. We snacked our way through a frat party several decades back in Derry, New Hampshire. Remember that?"

"I'd never forget. Try it anyway." Soren finished off his glass.

I slid the letters in the proper order, and the game accepted it. "It's a proper noun," I repeated, irritation lacing my words.

"These aren't your grandmother's games. The puzzle is solved, so you can't use that as an excuse. Now, what's got you in a twist tonight?"

I pocketed my phone. Until I explained, he wouldn't stop bothering me . My little brother was nothing if not tenacious. "Other people had always been keeping us apart, so I could focus on fixing the problem."

Soren made a cooing noise. "Brother, I didn't know you missed me so. But no worries, I'm here now."

Unfortunately.

While I grumbled about his ego, Soren continued, "And if you find trouble again, I'll be there to entertain myself, but I promise to bring a human spectator. You know, for me to snack on, but I'll share if you get hungry after."

I squinted.

"What? I'm generous."

"Always so supportive. Go back to your sweaty ladies." I turned away from him and sipped my glass, wondering what had convinced me to join him tonight in the first place.

"Ah, brother. I'm messing with you. Lighten up. Now, tell me what's got you swimming in the dumps."

If only I could be as carefree as Soren. Instead, I stewed about the dead heart tearing inside my chest. Pride kept my cards held close, but desperation had me laying them down. "As I said, I could target people getting between us, but now it's Daisy herself getting in the way of us being together, and I don't know what to do."

"You miss her terribly, don't you? She's got you wrapped around her little finger." Soren chuckled.

I drank down the entire glass in a couple of swallows, really hating Camp Disadvantage for my lack of buzz. "If you had a woman like her, you'd understand."

"I beg to differ, but if you start finding some fun around here, maybe novel ideas will spring into that depressing mind of yours. Couldn't hurt to try."

A woman smelling of sweat and hops approached, rubbing her arm against mine. She sent a look at Soren and addressed me. "Is this seat taken?"

I gestured for her to sit and returned to my game. Unlike my brother, it was useful in distracting me from my awful conundrum.

She smiled, eyes sparkling with interest, and she held out a palm. "I'm Teri with an 'i'."

I swiped letters to make a word on my game. "I'm taken," I said, leaving her hand dangling. My brother's hand squeezed my shoulder. I added, "But my brother here is completely available."

Soren leaned into my ear. "You're a terrible wingman."

"I'm out of practice."

Terri with an 'i' gave my brother a once-over, and approval lit up her eyes. "Can I offer you a drink?"

Soren beamed. "How wonderful of you to ask. Oli, want to share?"

Looking up from my game, I asked her, "Have you eaten any dairy lately?"

Terri with an 'i' cringed. "You know what? Never mind." She got up and left, swallowed by the noisy crowd.

Soren dropped onto her vacant seat. "She could've been fun. I think you're the only vampire in history with allergies."

"Lactose intolerance." There was a difference.

Soren scooted closer and leaned over my shoulder at my screen. "Pest."

"Some people come upon self-awareness a little late, but at least there's hope for you." I sent my brother a joking twitch of my lips. His face twisted with my insult, but before he attempted a witty remark, I said, "Already did that one."

"Step," he added.

"Nope."

"Then forget it. Why don't you come dance with me and those ladies over there?" Soren pointed out a group of smiling drunk women in skimpy clothes.

"I'm not in the mood."

"Then you haven't had enough to drink." Soren ordered me another tequila, neat. "You can't do anything about Daisy right now, and you were never going to find an answer at a bar with me, so what's still bothering you?"

"Stacey's in town." I swallowed the next refill, and the esophageal burn had long since been dulled by the liquor coursing through my veins. I wished I could feel the buzz just beneath the surface.

"That doesn't surprise me. Wouldn't you go home after getting freed from imprisonment?"

"Daisy doesn't know her mother's alive, and Stacey wants me to turn Daisy into a vampire."

"Huh." Soren drank down the next glass that was supposed to be mine. "When she finds out, she's going to explode again."

"Correct."

"And the only way to stop her is to turn her," Soren added.

"You got it. Mommy dearest gets what she wants, but Daisy suffers a future she doesn't want."

"Damn. Have another drink. Loosen up. The only thing certain tonight is fun." Soren patted me on the shoulder and returned to the women.

I swiped another word, completing the level, and waited impatiently for the graphical fireworks to congratulate me on my wordly prowess.

"Hey there, handsome." And the next one appeared. A redhead, who preferred an unnatural shade, sidled up next to me, pressing her tightly wrapped breasts against my arm.

Ignoring her, I swallowed down my next tequila and squeezed the lime slice between my lips, relishing the tart juice.

Having not received the hint, she leaned in closer, and stale breath blew against my ear. "What's your favorite drink?"

I swiped letters together and made another word. "Blood."

"What?" she asked over the din of the bar.

"Rum," I said, the clear disinterest on my tongue not reaching her temporal lobe.

She slid onto the stool next to me and leaned in, trying to make eye contact, so I appeased her.

"You're gorgeous." Hungry eyes skimmed my fingers, seeking a wedding ring. "Wanna get out of here?"

"Seems like you do."

She beamed with anticipation and took my arm. At once, the shift in her balance had her swaying. "Let's go to your place."

I slipped free of her arm, and her spirits dropped, but she didn't give up. She pleaded, "I can't go alone. Haven't you heard the news?" Her sultry tone had dropped away, revealing...fear.

Now she had my attention. "Hear what?"

"Four bodies were piled on a front lawn in Menominee. Animal attack is what the news says, but I heard from someone who knows a witness, and he said a woman bit them. Police haven't found her yet." The temptress frowned at me. "What's wrong with your eyes?"

I leaned forward, capturing her gaze. "You're going to find your friends, stay by their side, and go home together. You've had too much to drink, and you won't do it again."

She stared blankly into my eyes, and when my compulsion ended, she nodded and stumbled away.

I finished off three more glasses of tequila in rapid succession and threw a wad of twenties on the bar. I'd had enough of this place, and now I had something to focus on. When I rose quickly, a warm buzz finally tickled my brain. I sauntered over to Soren and leaned into his ear. "We have bodies."

"Alive or not quite?"

"Not at all," I answered, resting a hand on his shoulder in urgency.

"Again?" Soren's face fell with a silent whine.

"Let's go."

9

Grasping Control

Daisy

THE *THUNK* OF THE toaster popping made my stomach growl. Jamie lifted the last of the hot waffles, and with a finger-stinging toss, piled them onto plates. He grabbed the syrup bottle and carried the food to the table before sitting opposite me. Allison and Lily sat on the remaining sides.

"Dinner is served." Jamie lifted his fork and knife. It wasn't gourmet tonight, but it was cheap, fast, and tasty. Plus, it was his specialty with an erratic college class schedule. In a couple more weeks he'd be an official college graduate, but I didn't see our random waffle meals ending.

"Lily, you've done remarkably well for a new witch," Allison said, squeezing syrup over her pile.

"Not if you count the police banging on the door." Lily pinched a pair of waffles for herself and stuck her burning fingers into her mouth.

"Why were the police here?" I asked. After I'd stepped out for a run, I didn't return until long after Lily and Jamie sat on my living room carpet, calmly talking. I couldn't face her or her terrible decision, so I had gone straight up to bed.

"She screamed a little too loud for the neighbors, but her witchcraft is alive, and she's doing amazing so far," Allison said, beaming with pride. She passed the syrup to Jamie.

"I convinced the police we were watching a slasher horror movie, and they bought it. Helps that I danced for an officer's bachelorette party recently." Jamie winked.

I rolled my eyes.

"And we spent the rest of the evening practicing," Jamie added.

I glanced around my living room and kitchen. Nothing was amiss or broken. I lifted a brow at my sister. "You did?"

Lily shared a proud smile with Jamie. "Yep."

I accepted the syrup from Jamie and stared at the cap. Small drizzle or pull the whole top off and drown them? I drowned my waffles. When I set it on the table, Lily concentrated on it. I asked her, "You want it?"

"Leave it there." Lily gestured, and the bottle lifted in the air, floated to her, and landed softly.

Well, fuck me sideways. The golden girl was still golden, and now I felt even more inferior to her, if that was possible, but I kept those inner thoughts completely locked away and checked my tone. "Wow, congratulations, Lily. Looks like you were born for this."

Lily beamed. "I love it. The pain was worth the gain."

"I'm still sorry about that," Jamie said. "It's an unfortunate requirement."

"Don't be. I've never been happier, and Allison's mending spell fixed my outfit." Lily crammed a dripping bite into her mouth.

I swallowed back a sigh. I was long overdue for some good news, and after that wallop to the self-esteem, right about now would be just awesome.

Allison addressed me. "Have you heard the news lately?"

Huh. Just maybe I finally got what I wished for. Had I known it was that easy, I would've just asked for good news. "Not in the last few days." I downed a juicy, dripping bite of my own. "I was at work lately, so I'm out of the loop. Why? What happened?"

Allison found the anti vampire-killing spell...please, please, please. Please?

"Then you responded to the call, right? The pile of bodies?"

And the sigh broke free. I stuffed another oversaturated bite into my mouth.

"People are talking," Allison continued. "A witness came forward and said a *woman* bit the people, drank their blood, and left. There was no weapon, and certainly no animal."

I remembered the familiar-looking figure walking away. I should've caught her. "So the public knows we have vampires running around?"

"In theory," Jamie said. "I'm not sure how much they believe. There are memes all over about Dracula right now."

Last thing we need is a repeat of 1871. Oliver's words echoed through my head again, which happened whenever danger was on the horizon. I couldn't imagine the horror he'd survived, considering how fearful he was of a repeat. Having people twist the truth and decide on disbelief was good news, of sorts. "It's best if they brush it off."

"Exactly. The last thing we need is another vampire bonfire," Jamie said, mirroring my thoughts. He stuffed his face with a fold of waffle too big to fit, and I held back a chuckle at his puffed-out cheeks.

"I think we can all agree with that," I said. For once, all our opinions matched. How strange.

Jamie swallowed twice with a wince. "Witness accounts can fade over time, but you never know which way the public will lean—belief and fear, or disbelief and apathy."

I didn't like where this was going.

"Now that I think about it, I'd better stock up on marshmallows," Jamie grinned.

"What?" I asked, but no one addressed me.

Allison chuckled. "I'll bring the graham crackers and chocolate bars. What about you, Daisy? Can we count on you to bring the roasting sticks?"

My lips parted in disbelief. This wasn't where I thought this conversation was headed.

"I can do the roasting sticks." Lily popped her hand up as if she were in class.

And the peace just blew to smithereens. I dropped my fork onto my plate, and it clattered purposefully. "Do you hear yourselves? You're talking about murder. Not just that, but torture, and you're planning snacks in anticipation of watching the public burn people alive."

Allison set her fork down. "They look like people, they blend in with people, but there's nothing human about them. People who eat others are charged with crimes. They're imprisoned and sometimes executed. Why does only drinking the blood give vampires a pass?"

I gritted my teeth. "In your example, people are choosing to kill and eat others. Vampires don't have that choice. So to survive, yes, they only drink blood, but they don't have to kill at all." After my first encounter with Soren, I never thought I'd defend vampires, but since then, he'd been redeemed in my eyes, and I loved Oliver more than anything. His soul was clean, a good man, and I'd defend him forever. "To me, there's a big difference."

"Well, not to be argumentative, but there's something else you should know that might change your mind," Allison said. I doubted it, but I humored her. It was my house, after all. "The witness to those four murders bought a commercial building on Main Street a few months ago, and he recognized the attacker. He *named* her," Allison said carefully, eyeing me and my sister.

I jumped to the vampires' defense again. "Whoever she is, she murdered four people. Vampires, like people, have good and bad among them. If the authorities identify her, and she's guilty of murder, then she deserves the consequences. I'm not sure how that changes anything."

"It's the 'who' that changes everything." Jamie mopped up the rest of the syrup on his plate with a final folded bite. He and his half-sister shared a look. My patience wore thin.

"Just spit it out." I pushed my empty plate away and leaned forward on the table's edge. The guilty party was a 'she', so it wasn't Soren or Oliver. I didn't know any other vampires in the area, so I wouldn't jump to defending her. But the way my roommates were eerily quiet and slow to release the information had me on edge.

Lily watched my roommates intently, quietly finishing her waffles.

"The witness named his real estate agent as the attacker," Jamie said, holding his fork. Tines out. "Stacey Barrett."

I frowned.

Lily's mouth popped open. "What?"

Allison got up and collected the plates.

One, that couldn't be true, and two, his lie only reinforced my point of view. "Our *human* mother died the day of my car accident. Soren confirmed he's the one who killed her, so the witness is wrong."

"Your boyfriend's brother murdered Mom? You knew all this time and didn't tell me?" Lily asked, voice lifting.

"Soren was under Newt's control, so if you want to blame anyone for Mom's death, it's Newt...the witch," I said, reinforcing that not all vampires were evil and deserved to be burned alive.

Lily slipped inside herself, processing the shocking information. No wonder my roommates were trying to be gentle. They truly believed our mother did this. I recalled the woman walking away from the gory scene. A tinge of familiarity had been there. A brunette woman in heels and a skirt suit—Mom's signature style.

No way. Just because I missed her so much—regardless of our dysfunctionality—I projected an image of Mom onto an innocent woman. And now my roommates were messing with me. I needed to reassure Lily as much as myself. "Lily, Mom's dead. Dad and I buried her months ago."

Lily remained tucked inside herself, likely fighting back tears. I didn't blame her. My anger boiled just under my skin—an anger I controlled, not the magic.

"Killing a person is required to turn them," Jamie said.

"You're forgetting the buried portion of the truth," I countered.

Jamie stood up, collected the glasses, and deposited them in the sink where Allison was washing and avoiding. He returned to the table but kept a healthy chunk of distance between us, and his posture was defensive. "The casket was empty."

I snorted a laugh in complete disbelief and rose. "I've heard enough."

"Daisy, Soren did kill her," Jamie said. "But she didn't stay dead."

And there was the punchline. "Are you saying he turned my mom into a vampire, and she never bothered to come home after all this time?" I shared a look with Lily.

Lily swiped at her eyes. "No way Mom would abandon us. If she were alive, she would've come home."

Exactly. She and I both faced Jamie and his lies.

Allison dried her hands and moved to Jamie's side. Cautiously, she said, "Your dad hated vampires, dedicated his life's work to their destruction. Why would she go anywhere near him?"

My mother wasn't that apathetic. Aloof, self-centered, and image-obsessed, absolutely, but cold and heartless? "She would've called to let us know."

Lily looked at me as if not believing my statement. The woman hadn't bothered to hunt down Lily while she was safely away from Dad, and when I needed her most, when I mourned her at her funeral, she'd avoided us both. Heat grew under my skin and pooled at my hands. This time, I wasn't choosing to wake the magic. It was my own anger feeding it. "Are you certain Stacey Barrett is a vampire?"

Allison dragged out her phone and swiped to the news article. Lily joined me in watching the video interviewing the witness. We watched as a stranger described our mother to a T, named her, and said which company she worked for. Her face was on local billboards, and he was adamant that her signature was on the documents as his agent. He'd never forget that face anywhere. Stacey Barrett killed those people.

Soren lied to me.

Anger burned my flesh until I couldn't take the pain any longer.

"Whoa, careful there," Jamie said, hands out in a placating gesture. "Everything's going to be okay. Just take it one day at a time."

Fire accumulated in my hands, painlessly licking at the flesh of my palms. I had to release it.

"Remember to swallow back the pain. Draw it back inside," Allison said, retreating to the broad framing between the kitchen and living room. She shouted around the corner, "Picture it sliding along your skin. You can do this."

Lily hid behind Allison as if she knew what was coming.

My hands trembled with the effort to contain the fury. "I can't."

"Homeowner's insurance doesn't cover random explosions," Jamie said, joining them in ducking behind the wall.

"Damn it." Sweat broke out on my brow, and I panted, trying to contain the magic furious at Soren's lie, whom I finally trusted, furious my own mother would keep herself hidden from me. How depraved was I for Mom to prefer I considered her dead? If Soren knew, Oliver had to have known. "They lied to me."

Heart pounding, I pictured my fists of flames flattening and sliding back up to my chest. The brightness of the raging rainbow burned. It burned worse than when it conjured, worse than the roof of my mouth after eating scalding pizza and chugging 192-proof alcohol. The burn was so intense it was like fire ate me from the inside. I fell to my knees on the kitchen floor and screamed.

Cabinet doors opened. Plates and glasses flew. Knives from the wood block hurled across the house and embedded in the living room wall. The faucet snapped, and water sprayed and rained down on me. Wet hair clung to my face, and a puddle formed beneath me. But the flames remained, dancing around the water in my palms. The minor release allowed me to swallow down the rest of the agony, but it festered and burned in my chest, kneading at me to come out and play, but I held it back.

Jamie rushed under the sink and shut off the valve, and the spraying water slowed to a trickle and stopped.

Allison peered around the edge of the wall. "That's why I keep the knives in the cabinet. One more layer of protection."

I glared at my curled hands. "I stopped it. There's so much more wanting to come out, but I stopped."

Allison rushed to my side and gripped my hands in hers, immune to the flame, and snuffed them out. "You did it. See? All you needed was to figure out how to control it. Now you're that much stronger. Safer. I knew you could do it." She met my pained gaze.

"What does it mean when the ultimate betrayal teaches me control?" Soaking wet, the heat spread across my skin like a hot spring, but my mouth was dry as the Arizona desert, and breathing became difficult.

"It means you're free. You've accepted the truth right before your eyes." Allison smiled. "I'm proud of you, but I can feel the unstable magic. Give it to me."

Free? I'd embedded knives into the wall and made spaghetti out of my plumbing. This wasn't a lighter's amount of power, nor a little green army guy's, not even a fireball's. This was a flaming wrecking ball, and as its name suggested, my house was in shambles. I didn't know how it still stood. "Are you sure you can handle it?"

"Do it."

I funneled the rest of the magic into Allison. She shivered and smiled. "Wow. Tingly. Better than a caffeinated jolt of coffee."

"You're welcome," I said, deadpan, relieved to feel a semblance of myself. Allison helped me to my feet, and I surveyed the rest of the damage. "Deductible, here I come."

Jamie was in the living room, ripping knives out of the drywall. "I can patch these holes. No big deal. And don't worry about the plumbing. I'm a master of the pipes." Jamie winked at me.

I wasn't sure whether to laugh at the innuendo or be utterly grossed out. "Great. Thanks, Jamie." I dried my face with a towel.

Lily approached me cautiously. "We're both witches now. We can do this together."

For the first time since I was a child, Lily and I had a chance to become friends, and there was no Dr. Greg Barrett to rip us apart. Maybe she was right. We could do this together. Soaking wet, I pulled my sister into a hug. Lily squeezed me back.

"I guess my schedule's been picked for me," I said, pulling away and lifting twisted pieces of utensils off the table.

"We'll work together, and this will all be cleaned up before you realize," Lily said, collecting a few herself.

Allison was already moping. Jamie appeared with a bucket of spackle, and I smiled in appreciation.

Thanks to good friends, I was thrilled I didn't need to file an insurance claim, but I was even more thrilled to have *some* magic control. I'd tossed an explosion smaller than the previous two, and I still held some magic back. With help and support from three directions, I could do this. I had a long way to go yet, and I didn't trust myself, but there was hope.

Oliver was at the end of my yellow brick road, and for the first time, I knew I would get there, eventually.

I couldn't wait to reach Oz.

IO
Deal Twisted

Oliver

Like my brother, I could smell the remnants of the gory aftermath of the previous homeowners. No matter how well the crime scene cleaners thought they covered everything, they didn't, especially not when grass and pebble landscaping were involved. In addition to the bodies left for the public to find, the authorities had found traces of blood inside the house, and I would bet an alarming amount in the basement torture room, where I recall bleeding profusely thanks to Evangeline. Stacey Barrett had broken my number two rule: keep the hidden world hidden at all costs.

Transitioning from a human to a vampire always led to heightened emotions humans were never prepared to experience. That had to explain this grievous misjudgment—a newly inflated sense of self-admiration and invisibility, causing her to ignore rationality and the danger humans posed to our kind. And perhaps this grievous misjudgment meant that having my brother come along was the equivalent of throwing oil on the fire.

At the front door of the suburban house with a rustic rowboat on the front lawn, I said to Soren, who stood at my shoulder, "Are you sure about this?"

"It'll be fine." Said the man about to face the woman he'd murdered and turned into an immortal being. Fine? Yeah, sure. Always went well for me.

I knocked on the door, fist between the crisscrossed crime scene tape affixed to the jambs.

"Come in," Stacey's voice lilted through the door.

With one last glance at my brother, I opened the door, and we both ducked under the crime scene tape and stepped inside. Stacey's gaze flashed at my brother in warning, but she didn't otherwise react.

"It's not wise to linger at your crime scene," I said.

Her focus rested on me. "I worked hard to procure this place. Until it goes through probate and the auction closes, it's mine. Like everything else in the world, I understand it's temporary, but I'm going to enjoy it while I have it." Stacey swung back toward the kitchen. "Don't be strangers. Come on in and get a drink."

Soren and I followed her into the kitchen. My brother plopped casually onto a stool, but I remained standing, on alert to the new vampire's lack of control. "A witness named you live on the news. The police are looking for you, so I'd be wary of how much you show yourself."

Stacey prepared a glass of Merlot for each of us. "I'm already dead. All thanks to you, Soren."

Her thanks wasn't genuine, and Soren picked up on that. "Newt ordered me to kill you, but I gave you the choice of staying dead or rejoining your family."

Stacey slid a glass to him, but he didn't touch it. "Getting fed another person's blood was quite...traumatizing, really. You need to work on your bedside manner."

"If I explained the process, would you have believed me?" Soren asked.

Stacey slid a glass toward me, but I didn't touch it either. "Water under the bridge and all that. Now, I'm not sure why you're worried about a witness. No one could trust their eyes if they saw me. I have the headstone to prove it."

Seemed like her death may have destroyed a few brain cells in the process—and that probably had something to do with how Soren made her. "You're not the first person on record to have faked their death, and the police frown upon using the system to avoid a murder charge. I recommend you change your look and avoid the public for a while until the case grows cold."

"I didn't do anything wrong." Stacey frowned and corked the Merlot. "Choosing not to correct their error isn't against the law."

"Killing four people is," Soren added.

"Pot and kettle, anyone?" Stacey placed her hands on her hips. "I can't believe this. Who are you to lecture me?"

Soren placed his palms out in surrender. "We came to warn you. Oli and I have many decades of experience covering our tracks. Considering your choice of hideout, I'd say you needed it."

"Then you've already forgotten my second-best weapon."

My brother and I waited, not expecting much.

Stacey tapped her temples, and I refrained from rolling my eyes.

"It's difficult to catch every witness, and people share. They'll figure it out. Trust me, it never ends well," I said.

"Never mind that. Now, let us celebrate the completion of your task." Stacey lifted her glass in a toast, a beaming grin spreading across her lips.

Soren and I left ours sitting on the island. We had no cause for celebration. Soren said, "Daisy is still a witch."

Stacey's brows lifted in surprise, and she lowered her glass next to ours. "She defended herself against the two of you? Well, that's why I sent you instead of attempting it myself, but I didn't expect her to be *that* powerful." She quickly added, "That compliment wasn't for either of you."

"No offense taken," Soren said.

"You're missing the point here," I said. "The witness named you on TV. How long before Daisy hears about this?"

Stacey snorted dismissively. "I'll wait for the next story confirming a gas leak."

"That's not amusing," I said. An out-of-control baby vampire was a horrible thing to have running around. A flippant, careless one capable of blending in was...worse.

"Don't be such a sourpuss. She hates her magic, and once she knows that I'm alive and what I am, she'll *want* to join us."

"You don't know her as well as you think you do," I said. Daisy would never go for it. If flattening two buildings didn't change her mind, the sudden appearance of her dead mother wasn't going to.

Stacey glared at me with contempt, the gears turning, shifting course, plotting her next move. There was nothing a few-month-old vampire could surprise me with.

Soren asked, as if trying to redirect the dangerous path the conversation headed, "Earlier you said your second-best weapon was your compulsion. What is the first-best?"

It worked. Stacey smiled at him, excited to explain. "Funny you should ask." Stacey ducked below the kitchen island again, but instead of lifting another bottle of wine, she brandished a black revolver.

Neither of us moved. Bullets weren't fatal unless made of wood, but the shooter needed perfect aim and inhuman reflexes to beat us. Stacey checked one of those boxes, but unlikely the other. Like her husband, she didn't appear to be the outdoorsy type.

"You know that won't hurt us," I said.

Stacey drew back the pistol's hammer nice and easy. "Can't you sniff out the famed vampire serum? You both had such...intimate experience with it."

Well, color me surprised, but I still wasn't concerned. Lily's blood was still the cure for the current iteration of the serum. "Soren and I took the last of the stock, made a point of destroying it, and your husband and Newt are dead. There was nothing left."

"Then I guess you know everything, don't you?"

I had a feeling she was going to explain.

Stacey shifted her weight and aimed the pistol at whomever she was speaking to at that moment. "Before you turned me, Soren, I knew all about this serum. I'd convinced Greg and Pierce that I fully supported them, which was how my elf bodyguard trusted me to leave the house alone that early morning. Neither Pierce nor I knew the true extent of Newt's reach." Stacey smirked at my brother.

Soren watched her intently, not moving a muscle. I wasn't sure how this story was going to end, so I stayed alert with that barrel waving at us.

"When I'd slipped my detail, I was heading out to pick up my divorce papers. After Daisy walked across that stage and received her degree, and we took pictures and shared in the congratulations, I'd planned to personally hand Greg our divorce papers. It was going to be a fantastic day for all of us. But I never got that far, did I, Soren?"

My brother shifted his weight. "You said you weren't complaining."

"I'm not sure which was worse: becoming collateral damage for my husband's ineptitude or becoming his lab rat for months while I grappled with my new reality. Nothing is sexier than my husband strapping me to a chair and stabbing me with needles, all the love in his eyes gone. I wasn't his wife anymore, just a subject to be studied, dissected, analyzed. No amount of pleading or tears worked on him. Playing the distraught widow, knowing I was going to kill him, was enough to keep me going, and because Greg had a bloated ego, and I had sensitive hearing, I learned where his hiding places were. The vampire serum is not gone, I assure you. But he is, and I have Daisy to thank for that. Now I don't have to pretend to grieve."

Soren and I exchanged a concerned glance, and I didn't doubt the truth of her words, but if she didn't still want something, she would've fired already. "What do you want from us?"

"Since you refused my polite request, this is my last offer. You have 48 hours to bring me Daisy as a vampire, or these bullets will be your long, slow, agonizing death sentence."

Now I wished I had that Merlot. "What's your endgame in this? Why Daisy? Why not Lily? None of this makes sense."

"I don't have to explain myself to you," Stacey said. "After an excessively long life, time doesn't mean much to either of you, but if you value being six feet above rather than six feet below, snap to it. Tick tock, tick tock."

I believed the woman, but I didn't trust her. Continuing to argue wouldn't give me the answers I wanted, only test her patience further. When words wouldn't suffice, she took action—a class-act salesperson—one of the traits I'd admired in her, until now.

My deal with Daisy would never waver just because her mother insisted, and I'd never force it on her. As she held her cards close to her chest, so did I. This was our opportunity to escape. "You win."

Stacey's brows lifted in approval. "Go on."

"Soren and I will turn her. We'll bring her to you when the job's done."

Stacey didn't lower the barrel. "I'm glad you were able to see reason. Get out of here."

Gladly.

II

The Truth Revealed

Daisy

Allison had insisted magic didn't react to humans, but I didn't believe her. I should be hunting through the grimoires for an answer, but my boss had granted me plenty of time off lately, and I couldn't come up with a reasonable excuse for more. I held a cup of coffee, cool in my hands, and I stared at the droning television in the breakroom. The clip of the witness claiming the perpetrator had been my dead mom was replayed, but my roommates had already told me my mom was a vampire, thankfully, so I didn't destroy another department in this building. I turned off the TV.

But someone wasn't going to tell me bad news away from the public forever. And at any moment, Kevin Fontaine, or any of the emergency department nurses, could walk through that door. None of them knew about the time bomb sitting alone, festering over these paper-thin walls, where sick and injured people recovered and qualified and educated people attended to them. Being near me, every single person was at risk...at all times.

I needed to focus on something before I accidentally triggered my magic. Remembering that breakfast with my roommates and sister, I snorted. I could hardly function as a human being, but Lily had floated a syrup bottle like it was as thoughtless as scratching an itch. I'm sure she had to endure some nasty pain to activate her witch gene, but Lily didn't have to watch the man she loved die in front of her or demolish a full department in a hospital and crumble a restaurant trying to learn control.

Why did everything turn up roses for my sister? Dad's favoritism aside, Lily had never struggled in school. She'd always been praised by Mom and Dad for her accomplishments, ranging from graduation to mastering a Rubik's cube. Now there was some true witchcraft.

Greg saw something different in Lily, and just because I didn't follow his cause didn't justify my killing him. People all over dealt with abusive parents, and they learned to manage without resorting to murder. I couldn't. I was weak, broken, deficient, worthy of his scorn. And I would carry that guilt for the rest of my life.

I loved my sister dearly, but I hated that everything was so easy for her, and those thoughts were yet another defect in myself I had to solve. Instead of trying to beat her at something, I only needed to become her equal. Become like Allison and Jamie—strong, in control, capable of having a conversation with Oliver and not killing him. I couldn't do it alone.

I missed him so much I could cry thinking of his sweet face, chiseled chest, and how he made me feel like a princess with just one steamy gaze. I needed him and his powerful arms, but I had to work for it—I had to deserve him. If he still lived. I slipped my phone out of my pocket. The messages I'd sent him were still unread, but Oliver was a Luddite, and I'd probably broken his phone when I'd exploded, so that didn't prove anything by itself. I had to beat this, and then I would be capable of handling the answer.

Returning my phone to my pocket with renewed motivation, I cradled my cool cup of coffee in both hands, concentrating, pooling the fresh emotions into my palms to heat the cup. The light brown liquid swirled, and steam lifted off the surface. I smiled proudly. Well, this dabble of magic didn't seem so hard. Excited to have a new and useful outlet for my magic, I watched the coffee continue to steam and heat—not too much magic, but not too little.

Oliver would be so proud, too.

In that instant, the coffee boiled in the cup, burning my palms. Instinctively, I dropped the cup, splashing hot liquid all over my hands and onto the couch and floor. Gritting my teeth against the pain, I rushed to the restroom and ran cool water over my burning skin. No matter how hard I tried, some cosmic force didn't want me to succeed. Well, the cosmos could shove its prejudice up its ass, because I wasn't giving up.

I ripped a wad of paper towels and shut off the water. I brought them over to my mess and scrubbed at the couch fabric. The leather-like fabric didn't take the heat well. With a sigh, I soaked the sticky liquid off the floor. I didn't want the nurses' boss to complain about their space being invaded by ants, and I didn't want pest control to poison the poor bastards on my account. I had enough murder on my hands for one lifetime.

Smearing the damp paper towels along the floor, heat ignited in my chest and spread to my fingertips. Since I wasn't focused on anything but friendly little dudes, it was a warning—my magic's defense system. Cautiously, I rose to my feet, and the person in the doorframe stole my breath and stopped my heart for a few beats. I couldn't move. I couldn't say anything. Oliver was alive.

And my magic was furious.

"Daisy, we need to talk," Oliver said carefully.

"You can't be here. I'm not safe."

"That's exactly why I'm here." Oliver stepped inside the breakroom and assessed the remains of my next failure.

With a shameful blush, I threw the wad of paper towels in the trash. My failure to do what my sister could easily, and his generosity toward my sad bank account, left me struggling to meet his intense gaze. "I found out what you did for me. I don't think you realize how life-changing that was, and I have no idea how I can ever thank you properly."

"I didn't do it for accolades, but if you insist—"

"I do," I interrupted. I had to do something—anything—to ease the guilt.

"You can give me a hug." Tears sparkled in his eyes.

A sob breached my lips, and I shook my head. He was so kind, so humble—sometimes—but I couldn't grant him that one simple request. Oh, I wanted to. I wanted so badly to be in his arms again, but my magic was heating, and sweat broke out on my skin. "Something's wrong with me. I still can't control this stupid magic."

Oliver stepped closer, and the magic swirled harder. "I will take whatever is necessary for a hug. I need to feel you."

Oliver pulled me into his arms, and I didn't stop him. I needed the hug as much as he did, and for that moment, I relished the familiar scent of whatever his fancy dry cleaners used on his fancy soft suit, and the firm muscle underneath. A perfect calm overtook my head and my heart as I listened to his steady heartbeat, but the magic had its own agenda. Oliver had to be feeling the painful coursing of magic through his body. I squeezed him closer desperately, clawing at him, needing his touch. His heart rate climbed rapidly. My hand pressed against the bare nape of his neck. His skin was hot. Blinking back tears, I whispered, "I don't want to hurt you."

"It's okay. A little longer." He rubbed my back in soothing circles, and I memorized the contour of every inch of his body against mine.

The burning sizzle hit my ears before my nose picked up the aroma of meat cooking. I dashed the tears from my eyes and gritted my teeth in a futile effort to stop the magic, to buy us more time. The sizzling continued. This wasn't fair.

Oliver released me. His singed skin healed itself before my eyes. I hated hurting him. "Soren is here, too. We have something you need to know."

The smoke detector wailed from Oliver's smoking flesh. Soren rushed inside, fisted a couch cushion, and waved it at the little ceiling-mounted unit before we all got an unwanted shower. So much anger in such a little device.

The detector quieted, and a nurse popped her head inside the breakroom. "Everything okay in here, or do we need to evac?"

I fibbed on the fly. "The microwave overcooked the popcorn, but the mess is all cleaned up. Sorry for the interruption."

The nurse nodded, gave Oliver and Soren dirty looks because they didn't belong in here, but she left.

Soren sniffed the cushion before tossing it back onto the couch. Thankfully, he didn't comment on my sticky mess. He grinned at me. "Next time we need smoked meat, I'll give you a call."

I frowned, and the swirl of my magic in the presence of *two* vampires—one of which was highly irritating—became almost too strong to hold back. A small release would be a welcome relief. "Come a little closer, and I'll give you a taste."

Soren held out his hands in surrender, displaying his amusement. "Point taken. We won't stay long, but you need to hear this." The smile vanished, and the serious faces on the brothers made me pause. Something was wrong.

Soren said, "Daisy, do you remember when I helped you break Pierce's compulsion when you were a prisoner in his house?"

He'd told me he'd killed my mom. Old news, but never forgotten. "Of course."

"After you figured out my intentions, you asked me whether what I said was true. Now I'm going to answer you." Soren leveled his intense gaze at me. "All of it."

While the conversation flitted through my mind, all of which I'd already come to terms with, my magic didn't like what my mind remembered. My hair fluttered in its own breeze. "You're running out of time."

A playful smile lifted Soren's lips. "Actually, all of it was true, *except* for preferring my prey to be afraid. That's just a fear-mongering tactic. The truth is, humans in love taste so much better. That endorphin rush is unlike—"

"Soren. Get to the point," Oliver interrupted.

"Hurry up, or you'll have that smoked meat sooner than you anticipated," I added, becoming concerned about the wall of heat I was desperately suppressing. Little strikes of magic—more than static discharges but far less than the little green army guy—were blasting out of me in all directions. So far, nothing was harmed.

"Maybe we should do this outside? Your track record isn't...the greatest...when it comes to receiving news while indoors," Soren said, once again delaying his news about the truth of my mother.

"Soren," I said, figuring out the secret they were petrified of telling me. "My mother's a vampire."

Soren and Oliver stared at me, uncannily still, awaiting what I was going to do with that information.

Oliver tilted his head. "Wait, you knew?"

"My roommates had told me, but I didn't know for sure." I stepped back and fell onto the couch with a bounce of the springs. I gripped the edge of the damaged cushion. Maybe I could make the rest of the couch match. I directed the massive amount of heat into my hands, and allowed a trickle to flow, so I didn't explode.

I'd already come to terms with my mother not wanting to see me, but hiding the truth hurt. I'd suffered through her funeral alone, and Oliver and Soren deliberately withheld her from me. The betrayal fed the magic like lighter fluid on a flame. I squeezed the cushion, focusing on the couch. "Why didn't you tell me all those months ago?"

Soren shifted uncomfortably. Oliver dropped his eyes. Damn right they should be ashamed, but that inkling of humanity wasn't enough to temper my magic. "Why come clean now?"

"Because she sent us for you," Oliver said.

The heat within kicked up. Blasts of static discharge now hit nearby furniture. A lamp turned itself on briefly. "Why didn't she come herself?"

"She's not strong enough to face you, Daisy." Soren wriggled his fingers in the shape of an explosion, while my raging magic was only moments from total destruction.

He and Oliver shared a look of worry.

"Get out of here, both of you. I'm getting stronger by the day, and I can't hold it back much longer." My hair flipped up around my shoulders, a torrential windstorm only affecting me. Every atom of my being wanted to throw my full force at these brothers and rid the world of two more vampires. My love for Oliver was winning that war in my blood, but only by a hair. Borealis Medical Center didn't need another remodel. How would I explain a second gas leak when new construction was still going on in our department?

Soren pressed Oliver's chest. "We have to go."

"We can't." Oliver's jaw flickered with tension.

My skin glowed, scaring me, but the magic took over, using me as a catalyst for something I didn't want. Freeing the couch from my wrath, my arms raised on their own to pool the strength into a mystical projectile.

"Now," Soren pleaded with his stubborn brother.

Oliver's features softened with a final thread of hope. "Daisy, you can fight this. I know you can."

That was a lie. He knew I couldn't, which was why he'd given me the onyx ring in the first place. Now there were no more onyx rings, and lying only made me angrier. Oliver never should've come here, and my heart broke knowing we'd never be together again.

I was an offensive system of magic designed to protect people against vampires. Right now, people were at risk, but my magic didn't care. I didn't have a choice. "Go now."

Still, they didn't move. I squeezed my eyes shut and forced myself to shift my aim. The blast of magic released, and I heard a rain of glass. Hissing. With the release, my magic eased, and my stomach sank. Reluctantly, I opened my eyes. I'd destroyed the coffeepot. Drops of scalding hot black coffee leaked onto the floor. Brown, scalding liquid had been sprayed all over. I looked for the brothers—they were faster than me—and they were gone.

"What's going on in here?" Kevin popped his head inside the breakroom and assessed the damage. "I heard you had trouble with the microwave, but now the coffee pot is giving you grief?"

And the couch. I smiled. "Just bad luck, I suppose."

"Don't try to clean it up. I'll call housekeeping. They have safety gloves, so they can get this sorted quickly." Kevin was so serious about it. Maybe his emergency training kicked in, wanting to prevent laceration injuries. This fancy breakroom didn't need people bleeding all over it.

"Sure thing." I backed away from the hazard I'd created.

Kevin sent me a caregiver smile and rushed out on a mission. Wanting to minimize the burden on others and reduce the chances for questions, I adjusted the roasted cushion and grabbed more toweling to swipe up the glass. When the breakroom door opened, it wasn't housekeeping. I dropped what I'd collected into the trash and straightened.

Wings of glory were folded neatly behind my ex. It was still weird as hell to see them.

"Daisy, what happened?" He inspected my kaleidoscope of damage. "Oh, did you...?" He gestured with his fingers in the shape of an explosion. No man around here could just say the damned phrase. Yes, I'd lost control again.

"Something like that."

The elf smiled. "On the bright side, you didn't drop half the department. You're getting better."

All I'd seen was failure, but of course Pierce, and likely my roommates and my sister, would see this as a big fat win. Was I getting better, or was it because Oliver and Soren left so quickly that I was able to prevent worse damage? That was a theory I wasn't willing to test.

"Who made you suicide the coffeepot?" he asked, coming closer.

With the excessive anger and murderous intent quieted, a relaxing peace settled in my head and body—almost as if I were normal. Even as Pierce approached, my thoughts remained level. I focused on him, a constant in my life, and despite my earlier issues with him, a friendly face was welcome right now. I had no one else. "Soren turned my mother into a vampire."

"And you believe him?" Pierce's brows furrowed. He was...angry, not in shock.

"She hasn't come to see me yet."

Pierce rubbed a hand down his face, drawing on the skin comically. "I was best friends with Greg. Why didn't she come to me?"

"You're an elf?" Obviously.

Pierce sent me a side-eye at my quip and relaxed. His hands rubbed my upper arms. "I'm so sorry, Daisy. Really, I am. I had no idea, or I would've gone straight to you. Are you sure you can handle a shift tonight?"

"Kevin needs his partner," I said without thinking. Was that it? My whole reason for working was so I wouldn't disappoint my new partner? I really had fallen.

"I can take your shift. Why don't you go home and take a breather?"

"You're going to work a double for me?"

Pierce smiled gently. "Go blow off some steam. I happen to hate how fancy the emergency department's breakroom is. I don't want them to get a remodel too."

I smiled gently. Truthfully, I couldn't handle holding my magic back from humans all night. "Thanks, Pierce. It means a lot."

He winked, and I collected my stuff, passing Kevin on my way out. Housekeeping was on his heels.

"Where are you going?" Kevin cocked his head.

My drained magic reignited at the idea of staying. "Pierce is taking my shift."

Kevin's brows lifted in surprise, but he reassessed my mess and smiled, as if understanding more than the obvious. "Get some rest, and I'll see you tomorrow."

"Good night, Kevin. I hope it's quiet for you." I swept through the department and out to the darkened parking lot, shaking out my limbs and exhaling deeply. Climbing into my now-paid-off car, I realized blowing off steam helped. Maybe I was getting better at this.

But I still couldn't be around vampires or humans. It was going to be a long road.

12
The Plan

Oliver

WITH A BLOOD BAG in hand, Soren leaned back against my couch, arm wide across the backrest. He tracked my steps across the open floor plan of my bed-and-breakfast, but at least this time he had the decency not to find entertainment in my distress. "Sit down and hang out. Watching you is giving me a crick in my neck."

I had too much energy to sit. "Your neck heals fast."

"Well, you can't pace forever, and Daisy needs her space right now, so instead of festering on something you won't change, sit with me. I think Makayla is going to find out who the father is tonight. I bet it's Kyle. It has to be. He was with her that night in the hot tub."

I paused my pacing and faced him. One word had caught my attention. "What do you mean 'won't?'"

"That's what I said. Where's the remote? I don't want to miss the show."

"Use your phone." But I wasn't done with the conversation. His dig still bothered me. "All I've been trying to do is find a way to help Daisy. Why do you say I *won't* change anything?"

Soren sipped. "Turn Daisy into a vampire. Her mother's happy, and you can be with her. Bonus points for no more magical explosions. It's win-win." Soren slipped his phone out of his pocket and lit up the screen.

"How could you decide that when it goes against everything you believe in? Evangeline isn't ancient history."

Soren looked at me, disappointment on his features. "I think we firmly established Daisy isn't Evangeline, and it's different this time. She has help with the transition—you, her mother...me."

I waited for Soren's punchline, but it wasn't coming. He was serious. "I'm not going back on my word, no matter who threatens her."

Soren turned back to his screen, opening an app. "Like I said, 'won't'. So, if you *won't* turn her into a vampire, gaining all the benefits but risking losing her from the betrayal, there's nothing else you can do. So, sit with me. Have a drink and relax."

Daisy hating me was worse than death. "You don't know what it feels like to have half of you missing. I won't give up on her."

"That's not an actionable stance, but noble, I suppose. I don't like having an unstable vampire threatening my life over a decision I don't get to make. Life isn't fair. Have a seat." He patted the cushion next to him.

I glared at my younger brother.

Soren shrugged at my silence. "Regardless of your heart's attachment to that new witch, she's stronger than you, and statistically speaking, long-distance relationships don't last. So unless you discover a way to teleport to her side, and you're okay with two-minute interactions..." Soren trailed off. "I can honestly say I've never considered this before, but if you're a member of the minute-man club..."

"Soren," I scolded. "This isn't the time for jokes."

"You didn't confirm or deny." Soren's lips lifted with his own amusement, and he sipped from the thin bag. "My condolences, dear brother."

I wanted to knock that blood bag out of his mouth, but I didn't want to stain my couch. "Are you really going there right now?"

"Relax," Soren said, drawing out the syllables. "Stacey isn't giving us time to make a choice here, so I'm trying to pry one from you. Unless...you're willing to kill your girlfriend's mother. Then we can go back to the wait-for-Daisy-to-figure-her-shit-out game. I'll admit, watching the news is far more entertaining these days."

I glared again, muscles tense, but I swallowed back the insane urge to rearrange his stupid straight teeth.

"Figured not."

There had to be an angle I hadn't considered yet. I raked a hand through my hair and frowned at the gel on my fingers. "Turning Daisy into a vampire is off the table. Non-negotiable. Killing her mother, likewise. And Stacey knows she's no match for Daisy's new power. So, my only problem to solve is why we can't be together."

"The serum is still in play. I prefer being undead rather than dead-dead, just for the record."

"And we have Lily. Get over it." I started to pace again, and Soren chuckled, so I stopped myself. "I've met more than a few witches in my day, and none of them struggled so hard to maintain their magic. Why can't Daisy control it yet?"

"Maybe she doesn't want to."

I flew at my brother and gripped the neckline of his T-shirt tightly in my gelled fist. "Don't ever suggest she's anything less than compassionate and sweet. I know Daisy. This isn't her. The magic has her twisted."

Soren's hands lifted in surrender. The bag's port was pinched between his teeth and bounced while he said, "I'm officially never dating a witch."

I squinted at him and released my grip, making sure all remnants of the gel cleanly transferred to his shirt. "Helpful, brother. Super helpful."

Soren slurped the last trails of blood from the clear plastic and set it on the coffee table. "We have what...twenty hours left on Stacey's countdown. It's great Lily can cure us, but where is she? Will she? I don't want to take that chance. If the vampire angle is completely out, do you know of a witch training facility? Something impatient, involuntary, with security...?" Soren trailed off.

Although I could wait however long Daisy needed to master her twisted magic, Stacey Barrett wouldn't, and I didn't know how far or what tricks she'd implement to get her way. So, the only answer was to fix Daisy's magic overload problem. Then I could hold her in my arms without her burning me alive, and Daisy could spend time with her mother, defending herself against being turned while not killing Stacey in the process. No one needed to die—temporarily or permanently. While there was no witch training facility, I happened to know two people who understood her and this situation best.

"She lives with a pair of powerful witches, who know the witch-in-training thing better than anyone, so they'll help me give her a semblance of a normal life." *With me.*

Soren pocketed his phone, apparently having given up on watching TV. "But let's say they don't. I mean, they don't like you, naturally."

"We all abide by rule number two: keep the hidden world hidden. The witches helping me solve Daisy's overwhelming magic aligns with that rule."

"I get your confidence, I do, but if they don't help, you need to warn Daisy of her mother's plan. That onyx ring came from Stacey, and she's more cunning than she looks. Then again...Daisy might be too pissed to listen to you."

"Why would she be upset with me?" I was perplexed.

"You knew her mother was not only alive but a vampire and failed to disclose that fact. I don't know. I'd be pissed if I found out Della or Sadie were still alive, wouldn't you?"

"Our sisters are dead. Feel better?"

There might be something in Soren's words. I'd be heartbroken if I'd discovered Sadie had survived her staking—she hadn't. Logonson was thorough—or if Della still ran free and I'd lost all this time with her. Daisy needed a deep groveling, as if those would be the last words I'd say to her. I spun on my heel to rush to her.

"Where are you going? Did we not just discuss how dangerous Daisy is? Send her a text."

I stopped briefly. "If I tell Daisy her mother plans to turn her into a vampire against her will—her worst nightmare—what do you think will happen if she's at the grocery store or the post office, or...refueling her car?"

"Big boom." Soren rose. "Do you want a distraction to tag along, buying you time to explain? It's been a while since I'd felt a little tingling."

I rolled my eyes. "No, and pick up your trash. This isn't a cave."

Soren said deadpan, "I know where the garbage goes."

I headed toward the back door to the garage, and Soren added for good measure, "Don't let the door hit you on the way out."

"Cliché," I called back.

"Just like you. Whipped with braided leather and a feather tickler."

"Your jealousy is showing." I hid my smile as I slipped into the garage. With my sensitive ears, I didn't hear any comeback from Soren. All his snark and playfulness hid the real loneliness deep within. If I couldn't repair things between me and Daisy, I'd be joining him in drowning my sorrows for the next few decades...or centuries.

I hopped into my Shelby. Cruising over to Daisy's house took only a handful of minutes, and I rushed up the porch steps and knocked. I straightened my suit sleeves and smoothed the lapels, wanting only to look my best for her. I should've brought flowers, but she needed an apology that flowers wouldn't fix. While waiting, I kneeled, willfully damaging my fabric, and I anticipated fully groveling until the sun rose.

The door opened, and I inhaled a breath to begin a deep, heartfelt apology for withholding that tremendous truth, but it wasn't Daisy.

Allison smirked down at me. "Have you finally decided to let me kill you? This is a great position." She gestured at my throat.

I climbed to my feet and brushed my clothing clean. "Where's Daisy?"

"She doesn't want to see you," Allison said, slowly starting to close the door.

Nonsense. I wanted to push right by her, but I was sure the barrier hadn't been released for me. Since I was desperate and willing to do anything, I swallowed my pride. "I need your help."

Allison grinned and leaned against the doorframe, thoroughly entertained. "A begging vampire. I could get used to this."

"Allison, I need to protect her, but I can't—"

The witch closed her eyes and interrupted me. "Hold on. I haven't finished absorbing this moment."

I needed the frustrating witch to listen, and that meant showing my hand. "Her mother wants to turn her into a vampire."

Allison dropped her levity. "Can't say I'm surprised. What do you want from me?"

Relief was palpable. "Her magic is overwhelming her. I'm sure you noticed. Can you diminish her strength or recharge the onyx ring?" Permanently would've been ideal, but at this point, I would be ecstatic for the two weeks we'd been promised.

A secret smile played on her lips. "It didn't last very long, did it?"

The tone she used set me on the defensive. "How did you know?"

The witch sent me a look of annoyance. "Do I really have to answer that?"

Witches knew witchy business. I refrained from sighing. "Is there anything I can do to help her control the magic?"

"Unfortunately, she has to power through it herself. We all do. It sucks, but I bet you kind of understand."

A vampire's transition wasn't a walk in the park either. That wasn't what I wanted to hear, but I had a plan of attack, so I moved on to the next problem. "Then I have to warn her. Where is she?"

Allison flicked her head to the side. "She went for a run, but I wouldn't get too close. The city park is flammable."

"Thanks, Allison."

"No problem. Hey, we're camping next weekend to celebrate Jamie's college graduation. It wouldn't be complete unless you were there. Invite your brother too."

I cocked an eyebrow.

She sensed my hesitation and continued, "I mean it. The four of us are on common ground—keeping Daisy fang-free and safe. And she'd want you there. We'll have a campfire, s'mores, a keg or two."

"That was the magic word." I smiled. Friends in weird places.

"Great." Allison gave me a friendly smile in return. "Go find Daisy...carefully. I don't think she'd appreciate barbecue squirrels." She closed the door softly.

I'd listened intently to the sounds inside the house, and I was certain Daisy wasn't home. Daisy wouldn't be at Fully Loaded without her, and she wasn't at work. So the witch had to be telling the truth. If only Daisy could control the urge to kill vampires like her roommate, all our problems would be solved.

13
The Grovel

Daisy

I DIDN'T KNOW WHY I always invited her, but Allison had declined to join me for a run. That was fine with me, honestly. I wasn't in the mood to hold a conversation, and I especially didn't want to talk about vampires or magic. A lifted pickup truck roared by with what sounded like holes in the muffler. I turned up the music. My sneakers pounded the pavement as I floated down the sidewalk, and I sang terribly and wonderfully. It felt good to belt out a tune.

The city was quiet at this time of night. A few people walked around or talked on their porches. I heard someone walking their dog a block over, but no one was close enough to care how awful I sounded. I moved around a corner, heading into the park. My ponytail swung with my steps, but strands stuck to my shoulders with sweat. My lungs pumped air in and out at a constant, controlled rhythm—the only thing I could control.

Piece had said I was improving, but I felt like I was only able to hold it back a little more, and the process hurt fiercely.

Everyone near me could see it on my face. Even worse, I had the urge to kill humans too. Allison had said that wasn't possible, but I know what I felt. I wanted my mom. I needed her to tell me everything was going to be okay, that I could fight through this, and that I wasn't and never would become a monster.

For months I missed her. I'd mourned. And when I'd needed her most, she chose to stay away from me. I hated to think Dad knew she was alive and kept it from me too. Seeing the shocked look on Lily's face, my sister must not have known either. We were equal there, at least.

So why did she choose to stay clear of me? Perhaps she had to adjust to her new life. Control took time... I sighed internally. But after that? Well, I killed her husband. Mom must've hated me for it. I didn't blame her. If someone took Oliver from me...so help me, God. That had to be the reason. So, she hated what I did, but she couldn't hate *me*...right?

I stopped and folded at the waist, panting. The music couldn't distract me. I removed my earbuds and listened to the frogs and crickets crooning in the night. The park was peaceful, dark, and only a few streetlights at the entrance and exit lit the path. My magic swirled, heating my skin with a built-in defense system, but I was alone.

I craned my neck around. Yep, completely alone. This was getting unbelievably frustrating. Was I going to start attacking squirrels now? What kind of monster attacked squirrels? Tears filled my eyelids. I couldn't do this anymore.

"Daisy?" It was Oliver's voice.

I spun to find him, relieved the squirrels were not in danger. His pale eyes glowed in the shadows of a bushy pine tree. I missed him so much my heart fluttered, but he'd hurt me. He lied to me by omission. "You can't be here."

"I know."

The music dangling around my neck was a shrill sound disrupting the peace. I tapped to turn off the music player app and waited for him to say something. My magic grew rapidly, and it was alarmingly strong. I wouldn't be able to hold it back for long.

He stepped forward, wanting to be near, but he kept some distance. Shame and anguish softened his features. I wanted to hear what he had to say, but silently I urged him to hurry. "Daisy, I should've told you she was alive, and I should've told you what Soren did, so you didn't have to hear it on the news." Heart pounding, I clung to his every word like a lifeline. "In trying to protect you, I made that choice for you. That was my mistake, and I'm so very sorry. I'll do whatever you wish to earn your trust again."

He paused, and I waited, processing his apology. It was honest and heartfelt. But without knowing everything about this hidden world, I didn't know what to ask or what to expect. It made me feel like a child, struggling through the rules of the world with snippets of useful information tossed my way like crumbs for a good dog. Frustration pooled rapidly.

"I was protecting you," he repeated.

I frowned and scoffed. "From what? No one can get near me." My hands burned with the emotions circling within, rapidly coalescing into orderly rows of rainbows ready for deployment.

"Stacey is not the mother you knew."

"That's good news." For once.

Oliver continued, "When a human becomes a vampire, it pulls out the dominant personality trait and amplifies it, and our emotions are exponentially increased."

I waited for the punchline.

"Including anger, hate, jealousy. All the bad stuff comes with the good. Mix in those traits with the natural urge to feed and kill, and it's a toxic mix you wouldn't want to be around."

So, *not* good news. All right then. "But you're none of those things, so why do you make her sound so awful?"

"You didn't know me back then. I've had decades to reel myself in, figure out how to function in society, and survive under the radar. Stacey is new, what I'd still call a baby vampire. They're unpredictable, dangerous, and always hungry."

A flash of anger tore through me. "You assumed my mother would feed and kill me instead of recognizing me as her daughter, and decided I wasn't capable of seeing her?" The magic coursing through me burned my skin, urging me to unleash.

"Not exactly."

"Then what?" My patience wore dangerously thin as a thousand needles all over my body pressed harder and harder to tear out through my skin.

"Soren and I worried you'd kill her by accident and regret it. We didn't want you to suffer through that. We thought if you were able—"

"You didn't trust me to control myself?" I interrupted. As the words popped out of my mouth, I realized how dumb the question was. Oliver was justified in his reservations. My magic pulled my arms up to aim. I couldn't stop it. And the voice that wasn't me popped out. "Well, you're right."

He stared pointedly, and the silence spoke for him.

"I'm only getting worse by the day. Get out of here while you still can," I warned him.

"We aren't finished."

Trying desperately to swallow back the burning magic, I was overwhelmed. "At least duck!" I managed to yell before a bolt of magic unleashed straight at him.

Oliver took the hit with grace, only his shoulder twisting back on him. He straightened quickly with a grimace.

The release helped ease the urge, but the relief was very temporary. "I'm not going to apologize for that, whether I controlled it or not, because I warned you, but yet you won't listen."

"I understand."

"You need to talk fast, because my magic will only get faster and harder the longer you stand there, and I'm getting tired of holding it back."

Oliver came closer. My magic reacted, and although I took a step back, magic rushed through my body and shot from my hands, surprising me. A direct hit to the abdomen caused

Oliver to curl to the ground and groan. I felt his pain, and tears filled my eyelids. I couldn't stop. I was a monster.

I couldn't find any spells to help me reduce this insane amount of magic flowing through me. But what I wanted more was a spell that Allison assured me was as likely to be found as a unicorn's hair at the top of Mount Everest. Oliver would be dead before then. Even if I somehow found the cure for vampirism, my magic still wouldn't let him be—it was threatening humans now, and I needed more data to determine its attraction to squirrels.

There was only one option left, and choosing it would put me back at square one in learning control. At the proposal dinner that I'd ruined, nothing Oliver had told me about his lifestyle was appealing, from attacking people with the urge to feed and kill or stealing from blood banks and drinking blood—like seriously, yuck—to the emotional overload. I was already a basket case—one minute about to bawl my eyes out and the next my magic steals it all, leaving me feeling like a zombie. Exchanging one form of monster for another sounded like the dumbest idea.

Except Oliver and I could have a future together, and I trusted him to help me through the worst of it and reclaim a semblance of myself. He'd only withheld the truth from me so I wouldn't accidentally kill my own mother. With my strong, nearly two-centuries-old Oliver writhing in pain at my feet, she wouldn't have survived my strike. He was right to protect me from myself.

Oliver climbed to his feet with a grunt. I couldn't hold the magic back, and I released another strike, but he stayed here, taking my blows, just to be near me, to talk to me. I never wanted to be with anyone else, and hurting him hurt me just as much. Could I do this to save people from my magic? Could I do this for Oliver?

I unleashed another bolt of magic at him, and Oliver collapsed onto the dirty trail, holding his middle and pinching his features. In a panic, I cried out, "Turn me."

"What?" His voice was hoarse, strained.

The series of releases relaxed my magic for a moment, and I rushed to his side. I swiped locks out of his beautiful face, and he panted with the pain I'd inflicted.

"I want you to turn me so we can be together. It's the only way to stop this insanity."

"I know you don't mean it." Oliver's face pinched, and he tried to sit up. "I need to tell you something. Stacey is planning—"

At the mention of my mother's name, my magic swirled again. I pressed against his shoulder. "Stay down. My magic is calmer when it thinks you're weakened. I promise I'll replace your suit." Now that I wasn't flat broke anymore, thanks to him.

"My tailor will send my measurements to you." A chuckle escaped his lips.

I smiled. "I already know your measurements."

Brief silence fell over our playfulness. I missed him so much.

As quickly as Oliver healed, my magic grew in response, no longer fooled. We didn't have time.

"Turn me, please," I repeated urgently. I couldn't handle killing him, so he had to stop me the only way that would work forever. Against my will, my hands pressed on his chest, pouring magic into him, burning him from the inside out. "I need to be with you. Oliver, I'm so sorry. I can't stop it."

Oliver's teeth clenched with the pain. "With the level of magic pouring through you, I don't think I could even if I wanted to. You'd melt my fangs out of my face and throw me across the park."

"You can't?" I asked in disbelief. Oliver was the oldest and strongest vampire I knew. If he wasn't capable, then turning wasn't an option for me. My magic turned me into a broken toy. Disfunctional. No longer useful. No longer...fixable.

"Know this. I love you, Daisy. You are my forever. We will get through this." His hand gripped mine, pulling it free from his chest, and like a current flowing through a completed path, heat surged through my body into his hand, and it glowed. His skin flaked away as if I were the sun, a source of endless energy.

My love grunted and shifted his weight to stand, and I squeezed his hand tightly, maintaining the connection while assisting him upright. I forced myself to release him to spare him additional pain. But my magic shot at him once more, knocking him clean off his feet.

I cupped both hands over my mouth, fighting back tears. "Oliver?"

My love wasn't moving, and I had to get out of here before I killed him. Then, our forever would've been far too short. With one last glance at Oliver's damaged body and singed suit resting on the ground, alone in the dark, I ran. Magic continued to blast its way out of me, and the streetlight at the end of the trail blinked out. More continued to shut down.

I brushed away tears so I wouldn't trip in the blackout.

14

She's Alive

Daisy

A DEAL WAS A deal, but that didn't mean I had to do hard manual labor. With the enormous task still ahead of me, I pushed out my lower lip and blew hair out of my face. Lily wasn't here right now. Otherwise, I'd ask her to do this, and she would've easily. I swallowed back the lump of jealousy. For all the horrible magic had brought to my life, there had to be some benefit, and a mop and a scrubber brush pulling a magic Mickey sounded amazing. I curved my palm over the stained washcloth and visualized what I wanted it to do, forcing energy down my fingers and shooting it into the ragged cloth.

Nothing happened.

Vampire speed would've been a second choice, but that meant giving up my dream forever—having kids someday, and curing Oliver to have that family. I didn't want to turn, and Oliver knew it and, thankfully, still respected it. At the time, I'd been reacting to the panic and desperation of hurting him again. I fingered the locket with a hidden vial of Oliver's blood. I'd never not wear it simply because he'd gifted it. But the wallop I'd learned was I couldn't be turned. I was too destructive for a vampire to get close enough, which left me no choice but to fight through this magic. Instead of going for a jog last night, and unintentionally harming Oliver again, I should've been spell hunting. The sooner I could get the cleaning supplies to do their job, the sooner I could return to working on my dream.

A knock at the front door peeled my attention from the disappointing task, and I sighed and stood up, stretching my aching back. I answered it, not expecting anyone, but my lips parted at the woman before me. I blinked at her long-layered brunette hair with blond highlights, skirt suit, and heels. She wore the familiar, if slightly fake, smile on her face I'd recognize anywhere. I blinked a few more times, not trusting my mind. "Mom? Is that really you?"

Stacey Barrett lifted a palm against the invisible force field, and it didn't let her through. My magic swirled at once, but it was much softer than when I was around Oliver or Soren, as if my magic grew to the strength needed to fight the opponent before me. Older vampires were much stronger than younger ones. I supposed that was one benefit—I could finally get close to a vampire.

"I'd heard you already knew I was still upright and walking, so I decided to try seeing you for myself. I have much to talk to you about, but I need an invitation into my own home, apparently." With a manicured nail, she tapped against the invisible barrier. A ripple in reality reverberated from her finger, but there was no sound.

"The house became mine and Lily's. We have to invite you."

Mom stared at me with big pleading green eyes, just where Lily got hers. "And you haven't exploded on me yet, so you're doing better with your magic, but we need to have a chat."

If I felt the need to hurt her, I could warn her away. "Come in, Mom," I said formally.

Stacey grinned and strolled inside, neck craning around like she hadn't seen the place in ages. "I need to get a cleaning company in here. Greg wasn't much of a housekeeper."

The only thing on my mind was why she'd rejected me, and I dreaded the answer, but I'd rather know than wonder. "Why did you wait all this time to see me?"

"Several reasons," Stacey said as she headed for the kitchen, high heels clomping on the hardwood. "Is the wine still stocked? I need a drink."

I followed her. "It's nine in the morning."

"You know they say—it's five o'clock somewhere." Jamie's line. Maybe it was more of a night-owl line. Mom ducked under the kitchen island at the wine fridge and lifted a bottle. She grinned at the label. "Sit down."

"I don't want one."

"That's not what I said." Mom reached for a single wineglass.

I dropped onto a bar stool at the island. My back needed a break from cleaning and packing, which maybe we didn't need to do any longer. How Lily would take that news—living with Mom again? The gentle warmth of my magic remained controllable...for now.

Mom sniffed and swirled the breathing wine. She sipped and groaned her enjoyment. "I missed the quality."

I watched. Mom's expected coolness, even after not seeing me for months and my having buried her, stung. "After I turned, I found myself in your father's lab."

I blinked and dug through her statement—and its date. Greg had always known. He'd been silent and calm during Mom's funeral—not because he'd tried to remain strong for us, but because he'd known she was still alive. He'd kept that from me and Lily. "I'm guessing you didn't wear a lab coat or clean the floors..."

"I'd called locked door number two my home for months. Evangeline Brant next door became my best friend. Through the walls, she told me all about her past with Oliver Rockwell. I'd heard about her dreamy escapades through Europe. In the end, Evangeline escaped, but she didn't free me." She scowled briefly. "Soren came to my rescue."

My mom was a victim of Greg's, just like my sister and me. A wave of relief washed over me—that he had been deserving of my magical wrath—but I was still confused. Mom had been in Greg's lab, tortured for months, but there was no fury. "Soren killed you, turned you, and delivered you to Greg. Aren't you...I don't know, angry about that?"

"Soren Rockwell," she said his name in admiration, "freed me from the constraints of aging and time. And when the opportunity arose, Soren freed me from the chains. He gave me a new life, and it's incredible. I haven't had time to properly thank him."

I didn't picture Soren Rockwell to be a hero, but more surprising things had happened. "Then why did you wait so long to return home?"

"I discovered you were a witch. Patience is its own skill set."

"But I'm still a witch." I looked at my hands, and the pulsing warmth grew at a steady pace, like when I was around Oliver, but the power knob had been turned down. "And we don't have much time before my magic gets destructive."

Mom slid her empty wineglass across the island. "Pour your magic's hatred for my kind into this glass."

"It'll explode." I wasn't in the mood for glass shards in the eye.

"Just do it."

Trusting Mom, I palmed the bulbous top of the glass and unleashed the gentle rumblings of magic. The glass vibrated and cracked in a spiderweb pattern. The relief, although minor, made me grin.

"And that's why you do what I tell you, when I tell you. Now, we're going to have ourselves a fun mother-daughter day."

I frowned, suspicious. "We've never done anything like that before, and Lily's not here."

"It's not Lily who deserves a special day."

None of this made sense unless she hadn't heard about my killing Greg. "I'm guessing you haven't heard."

"Heard what?" Mom's smile faded.

"Dad's dead."

Mom's hand rested on mine, and the magic warmed me again. She must've felt it because she pulled away like a hand to an open flame. "I know."

I stared at my palms. My stomach swirled. "Do you hate me for it?"

Mom laughed. "Hate is such a strong word. When you and your sister were little, I worked a lot."

Story time. "I remember."

"It wasn't because we needed the money. Do you understand?"

I met my mom's serious gaze. "He treated you like shit too, didn't he?"

"You saved me from a divorce. You know how humiliating those are? Now I have my freedom, and I get to keep everything." Mom glanced around the house as if seeing it for the first time. She smiled. "I've never felt better."

It was weird being at this end of the bad news train. "The estate's cash was bequeathed to the lab. All the money is gone. There's nothing left but the car, the house, and the stuff. You signed the will, Mom."

My mom flinched. "Then he forged my signature. That rat bastard. His lab needs to be shut down for good, not funded with my sacrifices." Mom glanced around again, this time with a different perspective. "Let me help you purge all your father's shit."

"That's a strange mother-daughter day, but...it works. Just realize we have a time limit on your visit."

Mom smiled. "I like having a reason to return."

I smiled in return. Maybe having Mom turned into a vampire was the best thing to happen to us. I collected my purse and dusted my hands partially clean, cooling off the warmth of the magic, and I pulled keys from my pocket with a jingle.

"Where are you going?" Mom asked, cocking a brow.

"Sacrificing the wineglass helped, but if we're going to spend the rest of the day together, my magic could use a break." I wriggled my fingers as if she couldn't figure it out. "And we need garbage bags. My order didn't come in yet."

"I've lost too much time with you, Daisy. Let me drive, and if it's too much to handle, I'll pull over." Mom grabbed Greg's keys dangling from the rack by the front door.

Slipping into the long-forgotten child's role, I let Mom lead the way to the garage with a lift of my lips. "Sounds like a date."

Mom opened the garage door, and we climbed into Greg's commuter car. I buckled in while paying attention to the music station Greg had last used. The jazzy, slow drone of a trumpet wasn't my cup of tea.

Mom backed the car down the driveway. "So, how was graduation?"

I glared at her question. I'd hated her for skipping it at the time. Now I knew her absence had been because she'd slipped Pierce's bodyguard detail and Soren had killed and turned her. I supposed she earned a pass for being busy that morning. "I never made it either. Marc crashed on the highway trying to avoid hitting Soren, by the way."

"I'd heard Greg and Soren talking. Such a shame." Her tone was lighter than I'd expected considering her sister-in-law, brother-in-law, and niece had died in a fiery wreck. "Do you know what happened to Marc's property?"

"I still have nightmares, thank you for asking," I said dryly.

"Sorry, honey. Your father experimented on me for months. Starvation was employed to keep me weak. His staff used so many needles. The scalpel, though. I'll never forget the scalpel, so pardon me if I missed some conversation through my cell door."

Greg was more horrible than I thought. I gritted my teeth in guilt over what she'd experienced. "Someone bought the house, but that's all I know about it. Aunt Lisa's family took over closing the estate, since Greg—I mean...Dad—had his nose in the lab, as always."

"You can call him Greg. I do." Mom focused on the road, so I took the opportunity to vent a little.

"You know, I used to make him microwavable meals since he wasn't home to cook, but he hardly ate those, either. I tried, Mom. I tried to be there for him, and I don't think he even cared. He never comforted me after the crash, and I dealt with serious survivor's guilt. While I'd mourned and moped about, all he did was check his watch and mumble stupid platitudes. It's like nothing in the world was as important as his work. Not even his own family."

"You're a smart woman, Daisy. I wish I could've figured it all out before it was too late." Mom steered us past Borealis Medical Center on our way to the sprawling mall area. "I'm sorry for what happened to you."

Her apologizing layered on the guilt with a trowel and spackle, because she'd suffered worse. "We want to trust the ones we love. None of it was your fault."

Mom patted my thigh, rings decorating her fingers as usual. The contact sent another wave of heat through me. "The past is over, and now the three of us get a fresh start. I want us to be a family again."

I wanted to share in her optimism. "I don't know how close we can be, with you as you are and Lily and me as witches."

Mom's brows popped. "You're sister's a witch?"

"She wanted it, and I couldn't talk her out of it."

"Huh," Mom said and withdrew into herself to contemplate.

Traffic was dense with cars zipping in and out of the store parking lots on both sides of the road. We passed all the major stores, heading for the busiest intersection in Marinette. A lump settled in my gut. "Garbage bags were back there."

Mom stopped at the light and turned on the blinker, heading south to Green Bay. "I know."

"Where are we going?" My magic began its swirl with my growing panic. I looked over my shoulder, disbelieving what my gut was telling me.

The light turned green, and Mom turned Greg's commuter car left onto Highway 41.

"You're not taking me to the lab, are you?" My skin heated.

Mom scoffed. "Of course not. I wouldn't subject a mouse to that treatment."

"Then where are we going?" I asked slowly.

The compact car's engine buzzed to reach highway speed. Mom swerved around slower traffic on some unspoken mission. "Just relax."

Fat chance. "Too late for that. Tell me where we're going. You're upsetting my magic. You know what happens when it takes over."

"Oh, yes. *Kaboom.*" Mom chuckled.

"And you're in a shoebox-sized car with me. Doesn't that concern you?" Vampires healed, but self-preservation much?

We sped along, heading toward the overpass where my aunt, uncle, cousin, and I had crashed. Having still never gotten over the accident, I trembled hard. My magic kicked up its defenses, swirling my hair. "Mom, what's going on?" I pressed urgently.

"I made a deal with your boyfriend and his brother."

My stomach twisted. Oliver and Soren hadn't mentioned anything of the sort. "What kind of deal?"

"I told them to turn you into a vampire."

"What? Why?"

The tires hummed over the road. "Daisy, remember when I told you to do as I say?"

"Yeah," I answered slowly, gut swirling in concern.

"This is where you drink the vampire blood."

I frowned. "I don't know what you're talking about. Mom, take the next exit and turn around. Please." My hand gripped the antique pendant Oliver had gifted me.

Mom followed my hand. "You think I can't smell that? It's Oliver's, isn't it? Drink the blood he gave you now."

But this wasn't an emergency. "You can't be serious."

"Oh, yes, I am. That overpass column was repaired after your crash, so now it's stronger than ever." Mom cruised along with a smile on her lips, gleefully passing slower motorists, and the column grew in the windshield.

"I'm not drinking his blood. Pull over and stop the car!"

"It's going to stop itself very soon."

My hair whipped into a frenzy as if I'd rolled the window down. Panic drove my words. "You can't take this decision from me. I'm not a child, and I don't want this. Stop the car and let me out." Despite my previous pleas, Oliver had always respected my carefully chosen stance to refuse, but my own mother was going to force me. She was going to take away my dream of a family with Oliver.

"That's not happening," my mom countered. "So, get on with it."

The longer I delayed, the longer she had to wait, or I'd simply die. I could reason with her. "You said you'd made a deal. What were the terms?"

"It's simple, really. In exchange for the Rockwell boys turning you into a vampire for me, they get to live."

I was still human, and that overpass was still coming. "And because they didn't turn me?"

"They refused because you didn't want it. Such honorable men." No matter how far things went between me and my dysfunctional family, at least I could trust Oliver and Soren. That was a massive relief, but it would be short-lived. "They'd argued if I tried it myself, you'd kill me, unable to control your magic. Well, those boys always forget I have tricks up my sleeve. Where do you think that onyx ring came from?"

My mom wriggled her fingers, and my eye caught on a ring similar to the one I'd worn and depleted. My magic wasn't matching the strength of my threat. She'd protected herself long enough to get close. To do this... Tears flooded my eyes. "What happened to them? What did you do?"

"Nothing yet. After I prove how inept they are, I will take care of them next."

I couldn't picture my mom trying to stake either Oliver or Soren, let alone the both of them together. "They're so much older than you. You'll never overpower them."

"I'm not stupid enough to take them on in a fair fight, so don't you worry about that."

"Then what? Hire a hitman? A hit-vampire?" This was ludicrous.

"I have your father's serum, and they know it, too. They might've done what I'd asked if they knew Lily no longer has the cure..."

I gasped. "What? How? The serum was destroyed."

"Says who?" Mom lilted, amused. The fateful concrete column came into view in the middle of the divided highway. "Now, drink up."

I leaned back in my seat, eyes wide, staring down the barrel of my death, terrified my own mother was going to hunt the two most important men in my life, and she could do it. The one thing that could destroy any vampire was in her possession. And the only way to survive the infection...was gone. I swiped away tears.

"Come now, Daisy. If you want to save the Rockwell boys, drink now. I promise everyone gets to live."

"If I refuse, you're still going to drive me into that overpass?"

"I was going to lose you to time, anyway. I'm just hitting the fast-forward button. Oliver and his brother will still be infected and die slowly. Otherwise, what's my word worth? The choice you make right now is permanent—live as a vampire with your boyfriend or die as a human, and your boyfriend dies too. The only thing I'm forcing is for you to make a choice. Make it now."

"Mom!" I pleaded, the overpass column growing rapidly. My skin burned with the pooling magic. This was what Oliver had come to warn me about, but he never got the chance.

"Tick tock, tick tock, Daisy. Look at yourself. You still can't control it. Your hair is flying wildly, and the magic's heat is radiating off you like an oven. You're a risk to my kind like this, one I cannot leave running free. Join me or die."

My stomach heaved. Memories of the crash, the fire, the blood spatter, and the shattered windshield kicked my heart into my throat. Aunt Lisa, hair matted with blood. Uncle Marc, asleep with razor cuts all over his face. Cousin Abby, swallowed by the car's side door, like a blanket of metal carefully draped over her. At a quick glance, they were peaceful, but only because they were dead. My magic swirled, spinning my hair in a cyclone of air. Would my magic save me? "You would be so flippant with my life?"

"I wasn't born a Barrett, so witchcraft isn't in my blood. The only way I could protect myself against your father was to turn, a lucky loophole. I asked Soren to do it, and I don't regret it, because now I'm stronger than humans. Daisy, I want the same for you. I see you, and you're miserable like this. Sometimes we need an extreme circumstance to force us into the right move."

She'd asked to turn, just as I had when I'd been panicking. If Mom had regrets, she wouldn't admit them now. This was a vampire removing a witch from the playing field, but like Soren, she was offering me a loophole.

The overpass loomed moments away. The wheels of the car drifted over the white line, beyond the rumble strip, and into the grassy divide. My fate filled the windshield. I panted. Even if I knew a protection spell, I didn't know how to do it. If I let my magic explode right now, Mom would lose control of the car and we'd crash, anyway.

I reached for my seat belt—my lifeline. I hadn't noticed before, but the lap belt, just behind the latch plate, was almost fully severed with a sharp implement. It would fail on purpose. I didn't know Allison's fabric-mending spell. I was a useless, broken witch! At our current speed, jumping out would kill me, too. There was no choice here.

Tears sprang to my eyes. "Don't do this. You can still stop the car. Step on the brake, Mom!"

"Drink, and I will."

The chance of my being conscious after the crash to drink the healing blood was beyond slim—impossible. I had to drink it now for a chance to survive, and my body would heal while emergency services arrived.

Please don't be Pierce.

The uneven grass caused the car to vibrate turbulently. I opened the locket around my neck and removed the tiny vial.

I uncapped it, hoping it wouldn't spill. Seconds remained before impact. I stared at the tiny volume. Please heal me. Please let me survive this. A clump of weeds thumping under the tires almost had me spilling it.

"Drink it now. There's no time."

"Step on the brake!" My cell phone rang in my pocket, but there was nothing I could do to answer it. The overpass column filled the windshield, shadowing the car's interior. With a panicked gasp, I downed the vial's contents and tried not to gag at the coppery, cold blood. I coughed and gripped the compromised belt with all my strength. With my magic's defenses and Oliver's healing blood, I should be fine.

The car hit the concrete with a sickening crunch.

15

The Big Bang

Oliver

THIS TIME I DIDN'T have an audience. I paced up and down the hallway of my bed-and-breakfast, calling Stacey Barrett's cell phone. I'd previously warned her to vacate the crime scene, and after she hadn't answered the fourth call, I'd checked her residence. Seemed like she'd finally listened, but her timing was terrible. Now my imagination was conjuring the worst possible scenarios. How was I supposed to meet her if she didn't answer the phone, and she wasn't home? I tapped my phone against my forehead.

Think, think, think.

Stacey had the serum. Soren and I refused to uphold her deal, so she should be coming after us. Instead, I'm trying to find her, and I hadn't seen, scented, or heard a peep from her. Like a ghost, she'd vanished. Were the threats empty?

Speaking of audience... Where was Soren? Had she gone after him first?

I entered the room he'd been staying in. The bed was made—likely by Nicole. Drawers were closed. Lights were off. It was like he'd never been here at all. When was the last time I'd seen him? I pulled up Soren's contact information in my cell phone and tapped his number. After a few rings, he picked up. I released an exaggerated breath of relief.

"What's got your panties in a twist, brother?"

"I wanted to make sure you were still upright and breathing."

Soren chuckled. "I wouldn't say entirely upright."

My features pinched, not wanting that visual. "I need to find Stacey. Any ideas where else she might be?"

"Ask the witch."

"I've already tried Daisy, but no answer from her either."

"I meant Allison. She's capable of not tearing off your head, and she can do locator spells, right?"

"You're a lifesaver. Thanks." I hung up before Soren could run with that praise. Knowing the witch was an ally, I called her immediately.

She didn't answer. What was the point of these stupid devices if no one used them! I called her again and again. The line finally connected, but I heard nothing. "Hello?" I prompted.

"Who's this?" Allison asked cautiously, clearly not recognizing my number.

"It's Oliver."

"You have a phone? Huh. Never would've guessed."

"I do now. Look, I'm trying to find Stacey. Have you heard from her or Daisy?"

"Daisy never came home after her run last night. She's been spending time at her parents' house, cleaning it out."

I'd needed time to recover from Daisy's attacks in the park, and by the time I was on my feet, she was gone. I'd needed to feed. If I could hardly take her licks, I couldn't imagine her mother getting the jump on her. But Stacey was crafty, and those nightmarish images only worsened. "Forget Stacey. I need a locator spell on Daisy right now."

"Sure, yeah," Allison said, concern rolling off her tongue. "I can do that. I have plenty of her things here. Give me a few minutes to set up, and I'll call you with her location." The line went dead.

Waiting was a game of patience. Typically, I was a master at the art, but with Stacey missing, Daisy not answering her phone, and not believing in coincidence, those nightmarish thoughts of what could be happening to Daisy had my head spinning, my teeth gritting, and my floors protesting my endless pacing.

Never in almost two centuries of roaming this planet had my heart ever been this sure of anything. I loved Daisy Barrett, and I would until my last breath. Until my spirit dissipated into a thin layer of mist to be drawn in by trees and plants and breathed by animals, my heart was hers. If the Other Side existed, I would love her even then—my spirit forever interwoven with hers. Having to remain apart from her was worse torture than being locked in the suburban house's dungeon with my grudge-holding ex wielding a knife and far more creativity than I'd given her credit for. That was a pleasant cruise in the Shelby down an empty highway on a summer night compared to this.

If I could hold Daisy in my arms again, I'd never let her go. I'd show her how much she meant to me and treat her as my queen deserved. I only wanted the chance, but her magic had other plans. Her mother had other plans.

"Testing the floors again, I see. What's the problem this time?" Nicole asked, leaning against the bar.

I'd always take pointers from my niece. With the damned phone in one hand, I had my car keys in the other, ready to roll at a second's notice. "Daisy's missing, and I'm waiting for a witch to give me her coordinates."

"You should bring extra blood with you."

"I carry plenty in my veins for her." Daisy would only need me to save her, and I only needed to find her.

"What if she's not alone?"

"Stacey can heal herself, but if she accomplishes the task she's been obsessing over, then healing is the opposite of what Stacey will be doing." I'd allowed Daisy the final word on what happened to her despicable father, but I didn't think I could show the same restraint for her mother.

Nicole settled herself on a stool and softly grunted. "Be careful now. Daisy wouldn't forgive you for killing her mom."

"I said healing was the opposite. I'll make her bleed, but I won't kill her." Although that would be an epic test of my restraint.

"If Stacey doesn't need your blood to heal, what if someone else does?"

If Soren had been in any danger, he would've said so. Who else—non-vampire—would Stacey go after? "I expect

Mother Barrett wants both of her daughters, but Daisy is harder to reach since she's a witch. Lily saved my life once, and I wouldn't hesitate to return the favor, but if I healed both women, I'd need a refill myself for full strength."

"And don't forget this ruse could be a trap."

"Stacey does plan to kill me and Soren, but if she infects me with the serum, I'd need Lily alive to heal myself. All vampires need Lily alive until that weapon is gone for good. Good point. Spare blood, it is."

Nicole smiled, and I zipped downstairs to my stocked fridge and poured a blood bag into my flask. No mixing it this time. As I discarded the empty container, my phone rang, and I answered Allison's call with lightning speed. "Talk to me."

"She's on Highway 41, and not currently moving. The closest I can tell is she's somewhere near where she crashed on her graduation day."

Daisy was terrified of that stretch of highway. If that's where she was, she must've been traumatized and in desperate need of help. "I'm on my way."

I used hyperspeed to get to my Shelby, and I fired up the engine and roared through town fast enough to earn me honks and middle fingers. I didn't care. And I stayed vigilant to avoid the authorities delaying me. Once I reached the highway, I shifted gears and roared with the full V8 under the hood, and within several gut-gnawing minutes, I reached the gruesome scene. My heart literally stopped as I swerved into the left lane and skidded to a stop over the rumble strip.

A car had pulled over and the driver, clearly distraught but keeping his distance, was on the phone. I paid him no mind. I was faster and better equipped than EMS. With my heart pounding in my chest, I rushed through the grassy median, following the tire tracks, to the scene. Greg's car had crumpled against the overpass column, and flames licked up the crunched hood. Flashbacks of Daisy's whole family dead sent a chill up my spine.

I checked the back seat first, but Daisy and Lily weren't there. I cupped my hands over the front window, and Stacey sat limply in the driver's seat, bleeding from the head, coddled by the deployed airbag. The front windshield on the passenger side was shattered. A passenger had been ejected, but Daisy was such a stickler for the seatbelt.

"Daisy!" I turned away from the car and followed the scent of blood. Yards away, her battered body rested in the grass, and she was unconscious. Daisy's softened face was sliced and bloodied from a thousand cuts of the windshield, and grass matted her hair. I dropped to my knees, and tears blurred my vision.

Without hesitation, I pulled Daisy onto my lap and bit open a vein in my wrist. Blood sprayed with the pressure pounding through my body. I pressed my wrist to her mouth, coaxing her to drink. She wasn't swallowing. I listened for a heartbeat, but I couldn't pick up the sound over the blood swishing in my own panicked ears, the crackles and pops of the fire, and the roars of the vehicles down the highway. I squeezed her against my chest, rocking her.

She still wore the necklace. Had she drunk the vial before losing consciousness? If she had, she'd be fine, eventually. But if not...I better not be too late.

"Drink, Daisy. Take a drink, and you're going to be fine...if...you just drink." I squeezed her tighter and whispered, "Please, Daisy. You can do this. I know you can."

Her head lolled on her shoulders. I moved my wrist away and massaged her lips to spur her into action. There was nothing more I could do. Her body had to heal and bring her back. Where was Lily? I reached out with my sharp sense of smell to pick up a blood trail, and I found something leaving the damaged vehicle and heading into the woods. If Lily was on her feet, she was in better shape than Daisy, but why wouldn't she stay for help? I was surprised Daisy's sister would leave her.

I picked up nothing else. No ambush, no threat of the serum and cold steel pointed at my neck, no immediate risk to my life at all. Knowing the cure was alive and well in Lily's veins, I calmed myself and listened to Daisy again.

There should've been signs by now—life restarting with the healing power of my blood. But still I heard and felt nothing—no heartbeat, no rising and lowering of her chest. Only silence. As long as she still had brain activity, she was alive, and my blood would repair the damage. I wouldn't give up.

My wrist had healed without her drinking to keep it open, so I tore it back open with a new spray, and I returned it to her mouth. "Daisy, you used to call me a god. Well, this god orders you to drink and come back to me."

The heat of the fire blew out a side window, and an explosion followed. I folded over Daisy, shielding her body with my own. Fiery debris rained down on my suit jacket, and I brushed it off. The car was fully engulfed. Her mother did this, and she could rot—or burn to ash—for all I cared. I couldn't imagine the depths of Stacey's depravity for a mother to want to kill her daughters, and so, I'd left Stacey in there, and for that, I'd take Daisy's wrath. I'd take anything from her.

Like a breath.

I continued rocking, trying to soothe Daisy, trying to coax her back to me, but she was still limp. I removed my healed wrist from her mouth and brushed the hair out of her face. Through tears wavering my vision, I kissed her unresponsive lips. An ambulance siren wailed in the distance, getting closer by the moment. Perhaps there was magic medicine could do that I couldn't. I had to hold on to hope. If Daisy died on me, I wouldn't survive it.

"Daisy, wake up. You have to wake up. Our forever isn't over yet." I pressed my face against hers as I curled around her.

The ambulance pulled off the road, and a pair of familiar medics rushed over, sharing the weight of a gurney and heavy bags on their shoulders.

"Daisy, come back to me. Otherwise, Pierce is going to see you like this." A friendly teasing didn't help. "Please come back, Daisy. I need you. I love you."

Pierce and Kevin approached, and when the elf recognized the patient, Pierce shouted, "Daisy!" He ran faster and collapsed next to me. At once, he stabilized Daisy's head with his thick, meaty hands and slid her out of my lap and flat onto the ground. "Don't disturb the c-spine. You could've paralyzed her."

As if I didn't feel awful enough already. Pierce was right. I wasn't thinking.

The pair of them checked her vitals and spoke in a medical code to each other, but I understood the sullen tone they used. Instead of giving up like I had, Pierce began compressions. With each violent shove, the elf's wings flicked as if they acted like a cat's tail for counterbalance. Kevin placed a bag over her nose and mouth. Why didn't I think of CPR? All this time, I could've been helping her instead of sobbing like a baby. Good thing I quit Borealis Medical Center. I wasn't cut out to be Daisy's paramedic partner. My healing vampire blood could only do so much, and beyond that, I was useless.

I'd failed to do anything for the one person I cared most about. So I made myself useful and collected her personal things from the grass. I pushed them back inside the purse slung across her shoulders, staying clear of the medics at work, and I dropped to my knees at her side.

Kevin squeezed air into her lungs and counted while the elf pushed against her chest. Three ribs cracked. She should've been in pain, pain that I could heal, but Daisy didn't flinch. Kevin asked, "What happened?"

I dragged my eyes from her soft face. Information would only help. I had to focus and give them facts. "Daisy was in the front passenger seat, and she was ejected upon impact. I believe Lily escaped from the back seat and ran off for some unknown reason. Their mom was driving."

"Stacey Barrett? That can't be," Pierce said, frowning.

"Stacey was a vampire." I looked over my shoulder at the smoking husk of a car. "Now she's ash."

Pierce widened his eyes at me in a silent message to watch my words in front of his partner. Huh. Pierce didn't know Kevin was a vampire. That was only mildly interesting.

Kevin made no indication that he heard what I said or cared in the slightest. "How long has Daisy been down?" Kevin asked. Tears pressed against his eyelids. They were colleagues. He was hurting too. They were trying to weigh the risk of brain damage and whether continuing was in her best interest.

"I arrived a few minutes ago. I don't know." But I could calm the worries plaguing me. I checked the locket around her throat. It had been opened. The vial was gone. I could only hope she'd used it, but her unresponsiveness said she hadn't. Had she forgotten about it? Was she stopped from using it? Had she chosen not to? The last theory was the most likely, but that meant she'd chosen to die instead of turn.

My fingers raked harshly through my hair. The future I'd envisioned for Daisy and me was over. She would always be my forever, but I expected Daisy to have me longer than this blink of a short life. It wasn't fair.

"I got something," Kevin said in a hopeful tone, the device next to him beeping steadily.

My heart leaped into my throat, and my breath flowed from my lungs in shaky spurts. Hope slithered out of the recesses of my toes and crawled into my dead heart.

Pierce stopped compressions and panted with the effort. The elf looked at me. "I'm going to get her all healed up."

Damned elf interfering again, but I couldn't muster the anger. If he could use his elf power to restore her human health, then I would be eternally in his debt. My Daisy would soon shoot me uncontrollably with magic again. I actually missed it. "Thank you, Evansson. I owe you."

Pierce nodded in acknowledgement. "Hang in there, Daisy. You're going to be right as rain in no time."

As expected, she didn't respond.

The medics lifted Daisy onto the stretcher and carried her across the lumpy grass. Moments later, as I watched the ambulance with my love rush off to the hospital, the police arrived.

I could at least take care of that. Thanking Nicole for her foresight, I freed my flask and drank down the blood contents. Compulsion could easily fail if a vampire wasn't at full strength, and after bleeding into Daisy's mouth, I was a pint low. I glanced through the driver's side window, confirming the evidence of the vampire was completely destroyed, and I compelled all the officers to report a young woman crashed after falling asleep at the wheel. They obediently copied my words, with only side glances at my bloody clothes. I got into my car and got the hell out of there.

16

A Short Reprieve

Daisy

IF I HAD TO guess how a pork shoulder felt squeezing through the grates of a meat grinder into a slick tube of sausage casing, I would say being ejected through a glass windshield, thrown into the grassy divide of a highway, tumbling like a rag doll, and having ribs broken was a tiny start.

I remembered the horrific sounds of shattering glass, crunching metal, and the bang of the driver's airbag. I'd caught a face full of grass, and then I remembered nothing until I awoke here in the hospital, connected by tubes to machines making annoying beeps. The vial of Oliver's blood healed me, but I shouldn't have needed it in the first place. If anything had gone wrong—too late to drink it, spilled it while trying to drink it—my own mother would've killed me. Truthfully, I didn't know if that was the vampire in her or just who she always had been.

My magic hadn't helped all that much. My chest ached, and breathing hurt. Where I'd punched a hole through the windshield with my skull hurt. Actually, everything just ached. But my self-esteem took the biggest hit. I'd already accepted a dad who didn't love me, but my own mom? She couldn't accept me as a witch. I hadn't done anything to deserve that. She'd rather I were dead. And since I'd survived, was she going to come after me again? And again? Until she finally made me turn or killed me?

I wanted my mom, but I got a monster. Tears welled in my lower eyelids. I had to keep my emotions in check or the machines helping me heal would be destroyed, and I didn't need to flatten another wing of his hospital. Focusing on the crushing pain in my heart, I pulled the emotion from my chest and drew it to my hand, but I couldn't sense the colors waiting to coalesce into a rainbow. Huh. I supposed being near dead would do that to a witch. I kept drawing and pulling and dragging, but...I didn't feel anything swirling inside. There was only calmness. Was that the answer all this time? A healthy dose of morphine to keep the killer magic away?

Puzzled, thrilled, worried—I'd called for witchy help.

"Are you sure there's nothing?" Allison set a vase of flowers near my head. No daisies. I smiled.

I reached my palm toward the beautiful arrangement, attempting to give the blooms a good breeze, but not even a quiver of movement happened. When I tried the fireball's amount of power, the flowers remained still as if behind glass. I was completely drained. Magically incapacitated. It was a relief not to be controlled by the urge to kill everyone around me. "There's nothing at all."

"It could be the morphine or maybe the accident knocked a few things loose. I'm sure it'll come back, but you need to focus on healing. Besides, I need you upright for Jamie's graduation party this weekend. I have s'mores waiting with your name on them."

"I wouldn't miss it." An unfamiliar scent caught my attention. Not the sweet nectar of flowers, nor the sterile astringent cleaners—this was something else. I couldn't pinpoint what it was, only that I wanted it like someone on a week's long fast who stumbled upon a free Thanksgiving feast. My stomach churned at the thought of roast turkey, and it wasn't s'mores I wanted either. "When's dinner? I'm starving."

"With the fluids and meds you're on, I don't know if you can have anything. I'll ask at the nursing station." Allison slipped out of my stifling and sterile room.

I tried using my hibernating magic to turn on the television, but nothing happened. With each test, I became more excited, more confident I'd been cured. I wanted to be a normal human so I could run into Oliver's arms and not feel the urge to kill him. I want to hug and kiss him without burning him alive. Maybe this accident was the best thing to happen to me in a long while. It was an odd feeling to think I owed my homicidal mother a wallop of gratitude. She gave me my freedom back, but I couldn't get my hopes up. As my body healed, the magic might too, and I didn't want to be let down. But I couldn't help myself. With a sly grin, I tried moving the bedside remote. Not a damn thing happened.

Allison returned with a pre-assembled food tray. "I don't know how good this sounds, but chilled vanilla pudding and a strawberry Popsicle are on your approved list. Chow down...or lick carefully?" She set the tray on a rolling table and pushed it in front of me.

The food looked like dirt to me—inedible and undesirable. And even with a glorious current of morphine numbing my body, my teeth still ached from that face full of grass and glass. But I needed sustenance to heal with. Begrudgingly, I unwrapped the Popsicle and stuck it in my mouth. The cold soothed my ache, but the flavor was disgusting, which was weird, because I usually loved strawberry-flavored treats.

"What's the matter? Not a strawberry fan?" Allison had only made small talk since arriving, and I was suspicious. She didn't once ask about the accident or give me any updates on what she knew.

"What happened to my mom?"

"What do you mean?" Allison tilted her head and furrowed her brow.

The tone she used felt like she was deliberately playing dumb. This wasn't where I wanted to drop the news, but I wasn't getting out of here right now, and I had questions. I sat up straighter and spoke quietly. "My mom is a vampire. She was driving when we crashed. Where is she? No one told me whether she'd survived."

"No one found, or at least mentioned, a body. Sorry. The car was flattened and burned to a husk. Are you sure she was a...?" Allison gestured with two fingers in a fang shape.

I should've done the same. We didn't have anyone available to compel the public to forget our conversation.

"She wasn't a zombie, risen from the dead to hunt brains. Yeah, I'm sure."

"Well, that would be the only way she survived, because, frankly, it's a miracle you're still breathing. I'm guessing Pierce had something to do with that."

I groaned, and my face burned with embarrassment. "Pierce was my medic?"

Allison's mouth formed a grim line. She remembered when my ex's hands had been on my unconscious body, and I wasn't a fan of it. "Unfortunately, it was necessary. Kevin was there, so I'm sure nothing nefarious happened."

My embarrassment couldn't get any deeper. Despite having the elf healing, my head stung, like a netting pulled tight over my brain, squeezing the soft tissue through the tight squares. My face hurt too. With a grimace, I pressed the button on my morphine pump, and I relaxed once more.

"How are you feeling?" Allison asked with a hint of concern.

Like I'd been hit by a train, obviously. "How do I look?"

"Like yourself. But the nurses missed some blood smeared on your face."

"I'm not all purple and swollen like I did five rounds with a heavyweight?"

Allison chuckled. "You look healed. A little dirty here and there. I don't think the nurses got all the grass, either." Allison pinched a wad of debris from my hair and dropped it into the nearby waste bin. "But presentable. I'd say Pierce's magic worked. Speaking of which, any improvement in yours?"

I certainly didn't feel new again, and I was actually grateful. How would I explain being perfectly healed hours after a nasty car accident? "Still nothing, honestly. I couldn't deal with it acting up right now, anyway." I squeezed my eyelids closed against the blinding sterile overhead lights. Hunger gnawed at me, but the unappetizing food wouldn't satisfy.

"You've been through a harrowing ordeal. I'm going to let you get some rest. I'm sure you'll be back to normal soon, but don't black out the hospital." Allison patted my arm, and her soft footsteps retreated out of my room.

It was awkward enough being a patient where I was an employee, but this uncomfortable mattress and the five-times-daily vital checks weren't helping any. I also felt a hunger I couldn't ignore, and the cafeteria food was not going to do it. As long as I remained in this bed, there would be no rest. For proper healing and the safety of this building, I needed to be home, where a vampire couldn't enter. I pushed the call button for the nurse.

Several minutes later, a nurse popped her head inside. "Daisy, can I get you anything?"

"Yeah." I leaned forward, faking pain-free health with what I hoped was a bright, gleaming smile. "I want to leave AMA." That was official-speak for requesting a form to sign that released the hospital of liability should I die after walking out of here. If I were going to die, it would be from staying here where my mother could finish her task.

The nurse approached my bedside and checked the morphine pump. She turned to face me and touched her hand to mine. "Daisy, I know the doctor hasn't been by to explain what happened, but I must insist you stay. This pump is all that's keeping the pain at bay, and you're actively using it." While she talked, I noticed the vibration of her throat—something I had never once noticed outside of a professional capacity before. "I can get you a warm blanket."

"I don't need a blanket. I'm fine. I just want to go home." I swung my legs over the side of the bed, and my face throbbed again. Where was it coming from? I focused, following the ache to my teeth, near the front, but not my incisors. I pressed my lips, pinpointing the tender spots. The canines—not the standard area of impact in a car crash.

"Normally, I'd rush you the form, but the paramedics said you were down for a few minutes, and we need to monitor you for brain swelling. It's protocol. Let us help you through the worst of your healing." The nurse offered me a motherly smile.

Something about her words snagged in my head. I replayed her statement and processed it more slowly than usual. "I was *down*? You mean I died?"

Her smile slid away. "Your heart stopped beating for only a few minutes, but don't worry, you're going to be okay, as long as you stay here." The nurse's carotid artery pulsed close to the surface of her thin frame, like it was taunting me. That explained why Pierce's healing didn't make me feel like new.

Because I wasn't new.

I was different.

Just before the crash, I drank Oliver's vial of blood—both by my mother's orders, but also to heal me in case I wasn't conscious enough to drink it afterward. But if I died with his blood in my system...I was in transition. My headaches, the aching teeth, the inhuman hunger—none of it would be solved with hospital care.

My breathing became shallow, and my heart rate kicked up a level. When Oliver and I went out to eat last, when I'd exploded on him and nearly flattened a restaurant, he had explained briefly how transition felt. I tried to recall the series of things he'd mentioned, but what popped into my head was the most worrisome. I was on a timer to satisfy the uncontrollable hunger, or I'd die forever.

How could my own mother do this to me?

While watching me, the nurse's artery pumped harder. She was nervous, worried. I shouldn't have known these things, and that gnawing hunger drew me to her throat no matter how much I didn't want it. I was a danger to everyone here. As a witch, I'd never mastered the ability to be safe around others. Now there was a whole other set of rules to learn. I had a feeling I was just shoved off a cliff against my will, and I was going to take out everyone in my path on the way down. "I have to insist on that form, please."

The nurse frowned. "It's your decision." She turned and walked out.

I rolled my IV pole across the tight room and found my clothes and battered purse in the closet at the foot of the bed. Constrained by IV lines, I hastily dressed my lower half, and paced the claustrophobic room like a caged animal, waiting for the nurse's return, and seriously regretting the condition of my torn clothing. I needed a damn shower.

The nurse returned, holding a clipboard with the standard form on it. I signed, and she unhooked me from the pump without a word. "Thanks," I said, reaching for my shirt.

"Be careful." The nurse left.

I ducked into my shirt, collected my purse, and stepped outside the hospital. I breathed in the fresh air and squinted. It was cloudy, but still, I hardly tolerated the light. I shielded my eyes with my hand and crossed the surface lot toward my car. In my usual parking space, my car wasn't there. I'd forgotten Mom was driving Greg's commuter car—a flattened pancake. My car was at home.

I didn't want to bother Allison or Jamie because of the requisite tongue-lashing and what would happen if they discovered I was in transition, and I didn't want to call Oliver and risk my magic waking up. Then my problems would be twofold.

Priority one: shower. Priority two: figuring out what to do next, after I was clean and feeling somewhat human again.

Apps to request a ride weren't readily available in our small town, so with my beaten-up, screen-cracked cell phone, I called the local cab company. While waiting for the driver to arrive at the curb, I wished I had sunglasses, and I almost headed back inside to the gift shop to look for some. A late-model Honda pulled to the patient pickup area, and the driver rolled down his window and called my name. I climbed into the back seat. At once a pleasant scent overwhelmed me, but I couldn't name it. Not cologne, not one of those pine tree air fresheners either. In fact, it was...tasty.

My driver, a dark-haired man in his twenties, pulled away from the curb, heading toward the address I'd given him. "What happened to you?"

I looked down at my clothes. "I had a bad day."

"I can see that. I hope you're feeling better. Don't bleed on my seat or barf on the floor, otherwise there's a fee."

I rolled my eyes and said deadpan, "I'll try not to." The tasty scent filled my nose again, and my stomach growled. I had no idea when I'd last eaten, and a few licks of a Popsicle didn't count. "What food do you have in the car?"

The driver frowned at me in the rearview mirror.

So I wouldn't look like I planned to steal it or complain if it was microwaved fish, I added, "It smells really good. I'm just hungry."

"I get that hospital food sucks, but I don't have any on me. This is leather, and I have payments on it. No eating allowed."

So much for requesting a visit to the drive-thru. If he had no food, what was the delicious scent drawing me? I couldn't place the culture of the dish, but it was warm, inviting, and my stomach rumbled. I was starved. I had to have it. The driver turned the wheel, his head following his path. The artery popped on the side of his neck, and I fixated on it. *That* was calling me. I needed to feed on him. I needed to complete the transition.

Repulsed by my own thoughts, I reeled back in my seat and stared out the side window. No way. I couldn't bite a person. I couldn't drink their blood. I'd been bitten by a vampire.

It was painful and terrifying. I was a healer, not someone who deliberately hurt others. This wasn't me. I didn't want to think about this right now. I needed to focus on getting home...safe...clean.

We turned down a side street, out of the main congestion of traffic, and my stomach grumbled. Like a knife that stabbed my stomach over and over, I had to ease the pain. I needed to satisfy the urge. My body demanded food now. I had an unknown number of hours left to choose between going against everything I stood for or dying forever.

I wanted those hours.

The driver's scent called to me like a Thanksgiving spread all over again. The savory, the sweet, whatever scent drew me, I could smell it. It would be whatever I needed it to be. The change within showed me what I needed, guided me to the buffet.

I shook my head. I wasn't a slave to some blood disease.

"Are you okay back there?" The driver glanced at me in the rearview mirror with furrowed brows.

"I'm just hungry."

"Well, you know my rule—no eating in the car, and if you insist on a detour, then you'll have to wait to eat it until you get home. If you had a bag of fresh food, could you hold out?"

I stared at my driver's neck and spoke honestly, "I don't think I can."

He added, ignoring the danger behind him, "Alright then. Plus, there's an extra charge for the time and distance. I suggest you hold tight. We're almost at your destination."

This moment was more than a turning point in my life—it was a literal turning point in my death. Feed on blood or die. As a vampire in transition, returning to a normal human life was off the table forever. I would no longer be a paramedic, saving lives, helping the vulnerable, rushing with sirens blaring to comfort the ill and injured, reducing their fear. No, now I would take advantage of people, make them ill and injured, give them fear, and torment them with nightmares of monsters feeding on their throats and the horrible paralysis that accompanied it. The hunger made the choice easy, but my head and my heart fought.

I never wanted it, and I wasn't going to give in. When I'd been levelheaded and human, I'd determined I'd never take the change. I'd already been a monster as a witch. I didn't want an eternity of being a worse one. Remembering Soren's and Evangeline's glowing eyes and fearsome fangs as they each attacked me indiscriminately sent a shiver down my spine. That wasn't me.

But I wasn't me any longer. I needed to eat. I had to eat. Now. "Pull over."

"What? We're not there yet." The driver turned another corner, now on a quiet residential street, a few blocks from my house.

My eyes burned as the sun clawed its way through the hazy clouds. "Just do it. I'll pay the full fare."

"You got yourself a deal then." The driver slowed the Honda and rolled us to a stop at the curb under the shadow of a large maple tree. He shifted into park and waited for payment. "Whenever you're ready."

This was it. Was I strong enough to fight the demanding instincts of this disease coursing through me? If my failure to control my magic was any indication, I absolutely wasn't. I would never be strong enough to control myself, and right now I was hungry.

At the impatient glare of my driver, I fished my wallet out of my purse. Luckily, I carried a few bucks with me, because my eyes hurt too much to look at the cracked screen. I thumbed through the bills and pinched the right amount. I freed them from my wallet, and my teeth throbbed. My hand froze in the air.

My driver craned his neck around to extract the payment from my fingers. His neck twisted, and I salivated. I wouldn't last hours. I needed this gnawing ache to go away now. Oliver had learned to live with regret. No better day than today to start mine. I unbuckled. "I'm sorry about this, but it's my life or yours, and I choose to live."

"What are you talking about? What do you mean?" The driver hastily reached for his phone and unbuckled.

A growl deep in my throat passed my lips. I couldn't let my prey escape. He would never escape. I was too hungry. My driver's heart rate soared, pulsing the delicious scent into the air, and I licked my lips. As his hand fumbled with the door handle, he dropped the money. I launched myself forward.

In a flash, I gripped his jaw and wrenched his head to the side, exposing the strongest and easiest place to feed. My driver whimpered, but he was no match for my new strength. My mouth fastened on his throat before he could beg for his life. How was I supposed to bite? As the thought rolled through my head, my upper teeth burned as if someone had yanked on them with pliers. I winced, but the hunger overrode the pain. At once, my shifting, sore canines punctured his skin.

Sweet, luscious blood squirted into my mouth, and I drank it down. Swallow after swallow. Like a chilled icy on a hot day, or a steaming coffee on a cold winter's night, it glided down and hit the spot perfectly. I groaned with ecstasy. My driver didn't protest, and even if he had, I couldn't stop. As the spray lost its vigor, I sucked desperately, dragging in more until the tap suddenly stopped like a spigot turned off. What the hell? I pulled back. My driver was asleep.

I picked up the payment and dropped it onto his lap, leaving him a few extra bucks for the hassle—and the dry-cleaning bill. I double-checked I had all my things and climbed out of the car. My head spun and pounded. My eyes burned. I glanced at my reflection in the car window. Blood ran down my face, and my mouth popped open in horror. I backed away from the gruesome monster staring back at me.

"No, no, no, no." I shook my head, hoping the images would be swept away, leaving behind my real face again. It didn't work. I continued stepping back, out of the shade of the tree, and sizzles fried my skin. I lurched back under the shade.

Not knowing where else to go but unable to stay here, I broke into a desperate run toward home, and moments later, I leaped up onto my covered porch. With the current angle of the sun, from my shins to my feet were exposed to the hazy sun, but the rest of my body healed quickly.

I opened my front door, but an invisible field stopped me from going inside. "What? No! Allison?" My fist pounded against the barrier. What was this? World's worst timing award. My lower legs continued to sizzle and smoke, burning as if I rested too close to an open flame.

I turned, looking for shelter. My car was still at Greg's house. My fence and gate were decorative—not private—so there was no shade. All I had was the shade provided by my young maple tree. I rushed to the trunk and curled up under it. Sweet relief. While the pain eased, I scrubbed my monstrous face clear of blood using my shirt. After the accident, no one could tell the difference.

The breeze swayed the branches and shimmied the leaves. Rays of light sneaked through and burned me, like an ant caught under a magnifying glass. I yelped and leaped to my feet. I pressed myself flat against the tree trunk to minimize exposure.

I needed real help.

I had only two people in the world I could trust, and sleeping magic or not, I didn't have a choice. Squinting against the brilliant but cracked screen, I called Oliver.

17

The Struggle is Real

Oliver

THE STENCH OF SICKNESS coated in sterility and the beeps of machines monitoring the statuses of ill and injured humans always made my skin crawl—an array of food, feeble and unable to fight, should be a vampire's buffet. But to me, sickness always tasted off, like spoiled meat, and most of these patients dined on hospital food—generally including a selection of dairy products. In desperation, disgusting, regrettable food was better than none, but thankfully, I wasn't hungry. My focus was entirely on Daisy.

I approached the nurse's desk with a vase of flowers in hand—a summer collection of pinks, purples, and yellows, with sprigs of forget-me-nots. Daisy would love them, and I looked forward to her cheerful smile. Hell, they cheered me up from the torment of her slack face while the elf violently pounded on her chest in desperation to draw life back into her. I'd paid the florist top dollar for the most stunning mix she could craft. Anything for the woman who survived her greatest fear—a terrifying repeat of her fatal car accident. And having to relive her mother's death again, I couldn't imagine the anguish crushing her now.

The nurse ignored me, busy with her work. These people needed a desk bell. Not that I would want to touch it in a place like this.

I cleared my throat loudly. "Excuse me, I'm looking for Daisy Barrett."

The nurse's head snapped up, and she assessed me, searching my suit for official identification. She wouldn't find any. The nurse smiled gently. "Barrett, you said?"

"Correct."

"One second." The nurse typed on her keyboard, focusing on her screen, and she frowned. "Daisy left."

"What do you mean 'she left'?" Daisy had been revived in a way that had broken bones after flying through a windshield. She should've been wrapped in a cast from the neck down.

But the elf...

"She signed an AMA, but no matter how much we tried to convince her, she was capable of walking on her own, so we let her go. According to the timestamp, you just missed her."

Pierce must've healed her completely, but I didn't trust him to leave her be while she was so vulnerable. "Was anyone with her?"

"Not that I saw."

"What about Lily Barrett?"

The nurse checked her screen again. "No one here by that name. Sorry."

I patted the counter, confused. "Thanks."

Where would Daisy go, and why did she go alone? Where was her sister? It made no sense that Daisy ejected from the car while Lily ran off into the woods and their mother turned to ash in the blaze. I should've gone after Lily when I'd finished with the police—if for no other reason than to figure out what was going on. I couldn't change the past, and my present and future were Daisy.

I was just so damn thankful she was up on her feet.

After being in an accident, she'd want a shower and a set of fresh clothes. I folded into my Shelby and headed for her house. Blocks away from her neighborhood, I picked up the scent of blood. It grew as I approached a car resting at the curb. I double-parked next to it. Through the side windows, the driver's head was slumped over. Blood ran down his throat. I didn't need a medical license to diagnose this guy as dead by a vampire attack. Plus, the silence from lack of heartbeat was a dead giveaway. Pun entirely intended.

Soren better not be drunk drinking.

My cell phone rang. I slipped it out of my pocket and saw Daisy's name filling my screen. I answered in a hurry. "Daisy, where are you?"

"I need help." Her voice was terrified. My heart thundered in my chest.

"Tell me where you are, and I'll be there." My feet itched to shift gears, waiting for her answer.

"I'm trapped in my front yard."

"I'm on my way." I tossed the phone onto the passenger seat and shifted. My wheels spun out as I sped the last few blocks to her house, knocking the vase over in the process, and

I pulled into the empty driveway. Daisy pressed herself against the trunk of the tree. I jumped out of my car, puzzled. "Daisy? What are you doing there?"

"It was the only place I could think of."

In her sliced, bloodied, and dirty clothing, with lumps of grass still caught in her locks of hair, and terrified, blood-streaked face, she should never have left the hospital. They were getting a firm letter from me about the condition in which they allowed Daisy to leave. "Come with me. I'm going to take you back to Borealis."

"I can't. It hurts."

No kidding, a car accident would make everything hurt for weeks...but the elf's healing should've taken that away, and why wasn't she attacking me with magic... "Come here. We need to go." I held out my hand for her to take, but she trembled against the tree, refusing to come close. She trembled as if she were fighting an internal battle. "Is it your magic?"

Daisy reached toward me. I braced myself for a strike. As the tree swayed in the breeze, a spot of sunlight pierced the canopy, and Daisy's flesh burned. She yelped and pulled back, face crumpling with the pain.

My heart stopped.

I'd blamed my brother for someone else's handiwork...again, but in my defense, he'd been guilty more often than not. Soren didn't attack that driver a few blocks away. Daisy did. Her mother had succeeded. Thankfully, Mother Barrett burned up in that car—a convenient case of karma—or I'd be casting her from her earthly body myself.

Whether Daisy understood or not, she was a vampire, having already completed the first feed. Standing out here without a sun ring, she was at monumental risk of burning to ash. She needed guidance and protection—not just from elves and witches, but from herself. Once an out-of-control witch who I couldn't go near, now she was a baby vampire with an insatiable appetite and a cascade of overwhelming emotions. She needed me now more than ever.

And I could be there for her.

We were both immortal, and we could be together forever. I wanted to cheer. I wanted to shout to relieve the ecstatic buzz flooding my veins, but there were still dangers around, including her own roommates. Daisy needed to understand her new form and control herself before the pitchforks came after us.

This changed everything.

"We need to move fast. I'm taking you to my house. We have much to discuss."

Daisy nodded, and I shrugged out of my suit jacket and flipped it over her head and shoulders. "Looks like it's clouding over, so that'll help a little. Get ready to move, and don't worry, I won't stick you in the trunk."

Daisy gave me a look as if not understand what I'd meant, but we had no time for fun. I ushered her to my Shelby and set her into the passenger seat. The flowers were on the floorboards.

"What are those?"

"A gift for you, but don't worry about it right now." I moved the vase out of her way and closed the door. The tinted windows would help a little, but the UV rays still penetrated the glass. I rushed to the driver's seat. Even under the cloudy sky, Daisy whimpered at the rays frying her skin, and she frantically patted at her legs with my suit jacket. I unbuttoned my dress shirt and shrugged out of it. The white fabric wouldn't help much, but it was better than nothing. I tossed it onto her lap, and she calmed, breathing deeply through the pain.

"I can't reach an arm out. Buckle me in, please."

"We're only going a few blocks." I started the car.

"My mom crashed me into a concrete column. Forgive me for not wanting to be without a seatbelt."

I leaned over, pulled the strap across her shoulders, and clicked it into place. And in doing so, wasted precious time.

"We need to move fast. You won't get hurt, I assure you, but hang tight." I drove recklessly, speeding down every street and rolling through stop signs. Thankfully, I didn't get pulled over—more precious time I couldn't waste. I rolled up my driveway, under the porte-cochere, and curved around, drumming my steering wheel, waiting for the garage door to amble open. "We're almost inside. Just another moment."

The clatter of the rising door ended, and the garage swallowed us in darkness. I removed the coat from Daisy's head. "You're safe now."

Her face was bloodied and tear-streaked, and her clothes were damaged beyond repair. She looked like she'd survived a month in the jungle, and her burned skin healed before my eyes. Despite all that, she smiled. "This is a view I could get used to."

I blushed and took my shirt off her lap and pulled my arms into it. "We'll have time for that later." Still buttoning, I rushed around to the passenger seat and opened the door for her.

Daisy held the vase of expensive flowers in her hand. "These are beautiful." She took a deep inhale of their scent.

I smiled proudly and offered a hand of assistance. She accepted, and the soft, warm touch of her hand had me sighing in relief. She was here. She was safe. I would take care of her every day of my life. I pulled her into my arms and closed my eyes for just a moment, relishing being this close to my love for the first time in far too long. "Those flowers are nothing compared to how I feel right now."

Daisy set them down on the car's roof, and her hands pressed me closer, as if she couldn't believe she was here in my arms either. She inhaled my scent and sighed with contentment. I could stay here like this forever.

Daisy drew back first. "I was so afraid my touch was going to burn you. When I was young and dumb, I'd been sunburned so badly that being in the sun the next day hurt. But nothing compared to today. The sunlight felt I was being sprayed with scalding water. I bet that's what my magic felt like to you. I'm so sorry."

"Do you understand what you are?" I asked softly, still enjoying the fact that she was in a good mood, until reality settled in.

Daisy's gaze landed on my throat. "I think I want to suck your blood."

I paused, confused, waiting for her to lunge at me or laugh. "Daisy?"

She playfully punched my upper arm, and it actually hurt. She was much stronger than she used to be. I sent her my best comforting smile, trying to contain my excitement at her high spirits. I took her hand in mine and rubbed along her thumb. This was a dream come true for me.

"I converted. My face still hurts."

I needed to tread lightly, but I had so many questions. "I know you didn't want this, and I tried so hard to prevent it. Daisy, I'm so sorry. Can you tell me about it? What about Lily?"

Daisy's face scrunched in confusion. "Lily wasn't with us."

My turn to be confused. "Why wouldn't she want both of her daughters to become vampires? Unless...with the serum still in play, she wants to preserve the cure in case her plan didn't go accordingly." Since I last saw Stacey dead in the driver's seat before the car exploded in a ball of fire, I suspect it hadn't.

"You haven't heard." Daisy looked at the smooth floor of my clean garage, avoiding something she didn't want to tell me.

"Clearly not. What is it?"

Daisy met my gaze. "Lily's a witch. She wanted it, and even worse, she's good at it. Great even. She never struggled like I do...did. Not that I'm jealous or anything," Daisy said dryly. "She's...she's scary."

Witches didn't concern me, but Lily's change had me pause. If Stacey did in fact have the vampire serum, then that threat was still out there, and now there was no cure. Maybe the secret stash of serum died with Stacey. "The sun is only one of many enemies to you. Come inside, let me get you a drink, and I bet you'd like a shower."

"At least I won't drown this time."

I tipped my face to her, confused.

Daisy chuckled. "Never mind. A shower sounds wonderful. Why did you think my sister was in the car?"

"I scented a trail of blood leaving the car. I thought your sister escaped."

"And you didn't go after her?"

"Daisy, you were dying in my arms. I was trying to heal you, and I wasn't leaving your side for anything but a pair of medics with equipment." I led Daisy up to the doorway, but as I entered, her hand was forced from mine. How could I forget? She had to be invited. I swallowed back an expletive of frustration. "Cover your ears."

"Why?"

"I need to find Nicole," I explained at a normal volume. I turned my head down the hallway and shouted, "Nicole, I need you in the garage."

Daisy's hands clapped over her ears a little too late, and she grimaced.

When I finished calling my niece, I pulled her hands down. "Welcome to your new sensitive hearing."

Daisy looked at her hands again. A solemn wave dragged her spirits down. I touched a finger to her chin and tilted her face to meet mine. She could joke and smile on the outside, but she was hurting deeply. "Talk to me."

"I did this." Daisy pointed to the leftovers on her shirt, hands trembling. "I attacked a man, an innocent man, helping me with a ride home. He trusted me to behave, and I...I didn't. I was so hungry." Her sad eyes met mine. "I didn't want to die, so I chose my life over his."

I collected her hands in mine. "This isn't the life I would've chosen for you, and you know that, but sometimes things are out of our control. You made a choice, one you will struggle with for a long time, but I'm glad you made it, and I'm going to make you believe it was the right one."

Tears of gratitude shimmered on her eyelids. I gave her a hug despite her mess and kissed her forehead. She squeezed me back in desperation. Daisy was a vampire, my vampire, and we had all of eternity together. Except...I had to make sure she didn't take after Evangeline and turn homicidal, negligently leaving a trail of bodies in her wake, risking both my first and second rules. No time like the present to test her. "When Nicole gets up here, I need you to stay put. Can you do that for me?"

Daisy frowned. "Of course. Why wouldn't I?"

"A new vampire needs time to control the powerful urge to feed. Your body is generating its supernatural strength while all your senses are being pounded by things you previously couldn't perceive. In a nutshell, you're a mess—an emotional, strung out, starving mess."

"So, PMS on steroids? I have plenty of experience with that." She chuckled and grabbed the vase from the hood of the car. When she returned to my side, her face fell, and her pupils dilated. That was the moment she picked up Nicole's scent.

I smiled gently. "It gets better with time and booze. Lots of booze helps." At least, it would help me.

"What's the matter out here?" Nicole asked.

I stiffened, prepared to counter Daisy's reaction. But like she said, she stood still, hugging the vase. She didn't tense in my arms. She didn't shudder with a quaking need to feed. Perhaps her recent fill helped stymie the hunger. "Invite Daisy inside, please."

"Invite her?" Nicole's gaze bounced between me and Daisy. "Are you...? Is she...?"

"She is."

Daisy only watched Nicole.

"Daisy, come inside. You look like you could use a shower." Nicole smiled, wrinkling the corners of her eyes.

Daisy chuckled, seemingly broken from her trance. "No kidding. The floral aroma is all that masks my own stink."

I assisted Daisy inside and brought her to the bar. She sat heavily on a stool and set the flowers where she preferred to look at them. Her fingers straightened the leaves and fussed with the blooms. I circled around to mix our drinks. I kept my eye on her for signs that threatened Nicole, but so far, nothing concerned me. "What would you like to drink?"

"I've spent a long time trying to figure that out, and I think I want a tequila neat. Hold the lime."

"Coming right up." I mixed a pair of the drinks, chest puffed with a little pride that she'd chosen my signature flavor.

"Is there anything else you need from me?" Nicole asked.

"Not right now. Thank you, Nicole."

My niece nodded and returned to whatever I had interrupted her from.

Daisy didn't even watch her leave. She slumped forward, hand holding her head above the bar, hair a disheveled mess, clothing torn and stained from the accident, made worse by the driver she'd feasted on. I wanted to wash every inch of her skin and dress her in the finest materials.

I set the glass on a coaster and slid it to her.

Daisy didn't move.

"What's wrong?"

A quiet sob came from her lips. She lifted her dirty face. "I've dedicated myself to helping people and saving lives. I'm not supposed to hurt others."

"It's not your fault; you couldn't help yourself."

"That's just it. I *liked* it. My face shocked me when I saw it, but I relished the feed. I'm dealing with a combination of the world's worst hangover and feeling like I was hit by a truck, and the need to feed is the only thing keeping me on my feet. I want more, but it's not so strong I can't function."

"I know you do. I have plenty here to tide you over. Stay put, because as your transition completes, the sun will burn you very quickly, and I don't have a spare sun ring for you."

Daisy hugged the glass between her palms. "Last time we spoke, I asked you to turn me. It was the plea of a desperate woman in love, but I didn't truly want to become something else, a thing that attacks and hurts people, but my mother forced me to drink your blood before she crashed us into the same column where my family died on my graduation day. I begged her not to, but she did it anyway. I hate her for it." She looked up at me. "Where is my mom?"

I collected Daisy's hands in mine. I figured her mother burned to ash in the car, but since Lily wasn't with them, the blood trail had to be hers. "Your mother must've escaped into the woods."

"She left me?" Sad eyes gazed up at me.

"That appears to be the case." My heart broke for her. Daisy's own mother was willing to kill me and Soren to have Daisy turned. Stacey did it herself, and instead of gloating in her success, she abandoned her daughter at the worst possible time. It made no sense.

Daisy released a long, slow breath. She snorted back tears. "She wanted us to be a family again, of strong, ageless vampires. Why wouldn't she help me through it?"

"I don't know, but there's a bright side here." I smiled at her.

"What's that?"

"You haven't spared a glance at Nicole's throat."

Daisy's lips lifted briefly. She stared at the drink I made her, and she slipped inside herself for a moment before facing me with a gentle smile. "There's another bright side here."

"What's that?"

"I haven't attacked you either. The magic is gone, and it hasn't come back. I fed and I'm strong, but the magic isn't there."

I reached for Daisy's hand and stood her up. I cradled her against me. "That's the best news I've heard in a while. We need to celebrate. Kiss me." I leaned toward her lips, but her index finger stopped me.

Daisy cringed. "Wait. I'm a mess. I need a shower. I need clean clothes, but I couldn't get into my house. How am I supposed to get into my own house?"

"You can't. Not without some creativity with the deed. Don't worry about it now. You have a home here, and we'll get this all straightened out. In my closet you can pick whatever you want to wear, and after dark, I'll take you shopping for all new clothes."

"Why dark?"

"Evil sun." I reminded her.

"Right. That's going to take a while to get used to."

"But it only takes a split second to remind you." I gave her a sly smile.

"That's not funny."

I grinned anyway. "Go clean up. I'm getting you a meal."

Daisy's face twisted with uncertainty. "It's not live, is it?"

"I'm glad you asked. Already dead food it is." I winked at her. I wasn't going to bring her a compelled human to drink from—not this early and probably never—but teasing her entertained me greatly.

Daisy smiled and took the stairs up to my private bathroom. I headed to the basement and collected a stack of blood bags. While I was thrilled I could be with her again and how well she'd handled the transition so far, I had to be careful. I locked away my hope—a sneaky and dangerous little thing just prancing at the corners of my heart, eager to come out and play—and rip my chest open.

If Daisy turned out like Evangeline, I would have to stake her, and I couldn't allow Daisy a century of murders before I gathered the strength to do the job right. I doubted I'd be able to do it at all, but until I could trust her, tonight's date would be a test.

Could Daisy become the vampire of my dreams, or would she become the nightmare haunting me for centuries?

18
Hidden Treasure

Daisy

I WAS A MESS, not a hot mess, but a legit catastrophe, like I'd fallen down a ravine and clawed my way back up while playing Russian roulette with random berries while fighting off hordes of cat-sized mosquitoes. Nothing a four-headed shower drowning me in a waterfall couldn't fix. Grass clippings missed by the nursing staff fell down the drain. Blood streaks from attacking the helpful driver slipped away, washed into nothing as if it had never happened. His face was permanently etched into my memory, forever haunting my dreams with his terrified eyes, the blood leaking down his throat, and his vacant gaze. I attacked him like an animal, and I didn't even know his name. Even worse, I didn't stay to erase his memory of it—not that I knew how to.

I didn't want to hurt him, but I couldn't fight my baser need any longer, and for that I was sorry. If I could find out who he was, I owed him a cheese gift basket at a minimum.

I turned off the water and wrapped a fluffy towel around me. Inside Oliver's vast closet were racks of shiny shoes, suit jackets, and pants clipped to hangers—sorted by color. What would fit me in here?

I picked a folded white T-shirt off the stack and a pair of boxers. The shirt could've been a minidress, and the boxers fit my hips loosely. This would have to do until I could get my stuff, but I couldn't get into my house without some kind of deed manipulation. I braided my wet hair and realized I didn't have an elastic, and I couldn't go shopping dressed like this.

Since witches could sense vampires, I didn't think it was wise to ask Allison, Jamie, or even my own sister for help. From personal experience, witches can kick vampires' asses, and I wasn't a willing practice dummy until I had a chance to explain and gauge their reactions. As Oliver said, I couldn't be too cautious.

I could ask Pierce. A rock settled in my gut at the thought of involving him. Perhaps I feared how he'd judge me, but I couldn't think of any other option. I collected my half-broken phone and typed out a text. My finger hovered over the 'send' button. If he helped, I would instigate another fight between the elf and Oliver. If he didn't, I pictured complete humiliation trying to buy clothing while dressed in Oliver's underwear. My only other option was Kevin, but I didn't know him well enough to be comfortable asking him to pack my underwear from my bedroom. Pierce was my only hope. I tapped the button to send the message. *'Pierce, I need your help.'*

Only a moment passed before he responded. *'Anything.'*

'Can you go to my house and get some T-shirts, jeans, underwear, and bras for me? And a set of my work uniform?

Also, in the bottom drawer of my dresser, there's a box with witch symbols on it. I need that too.'

Little dots bounced with his reply. *'Where do you want them?'*

I bit my lip, hoping he wouldn't bail on me now. *'Oliver's house.'*

I waited for those dots to reappear, but as seconds of agony stretched, they didn't. "Come on, come on, please don't let me down."

'Give me ten minutes.'

'Thank you, Pierce.'

Despite our differences and rocky history, I appreciated his loyal help. He didn't even ask why or say anything snarky about the location, and I appreciated that. I brushed out my feeble attempt at braids and went downstairs to wait.

Nicole vacuumed the common room rug, wearing slacks and a blouse. I was wholly underdressed. My cheeks heated as if I were a kid who had shown up naked at school. In a silly attempt to hide myself, I sat at the bar, curling myself on a barstool. When the host of the house spotted me, Nicole turned off the machine and smiled. "There you are. Everyone's been worried about you." She gave me a motherly once-over and frowned. "That won't do at all. Don't you have anything to wear?"

"I have it covered, thanks."

She approached and smiled. "If you need anything, and my big lug of an uncle hasn't gotten it for you, just give me a holler."

It was weird this gray-streaked older woman called my boyfriend her uncle, but technically that was accurate. Her heartbeat thumped in my ears. I gazed at her throat, hungry again. She stood too close. The craving wasn't so strong I was a threat to her, but I didn't know how long my previous meal would last, and I didn't like being alone with her. "I appreciate the offer."

Nicole followed my eyes, and she stepped back, nervous. "Are you feeling okay?"

"I'm fine, really." It was mostly true.

"Are you sure?"

Her insistence made me realize she was afraid of me. I stood up, palms out. "I won't hurt you, I swear."

But apparently my words meant nothing to her. She shouted, "Oliver!"

My sexy vampire appeared in the doorframe instantly. He assessed me quickly while carrying a frilly-lidded picnic basket, likely Nicole's. "What's going on?"

"I wasn't going to do anything, I swear," I repeated, hands still hanging out in surrender.

Oliver set the basket on the bar. He collected my hands in his. "Are you sure you're feeling well?"

"I'm fine. Why do you keep asking me that?"

"Because a baby vampire isn't in control. The fact that you haven't tried escaping, even during the daylight, and you haven't attacked Nicole is...unusual."

I frowned—a compliment at exceeding his expectations, but also an insult that I couldn't be trusted. "Then why did you leave me alone with her?"

"She's full of vervain, and I'm staying close."

Cool. His niece was poison to me. Good to know.

"I would never leave you in a compromising situation alone. Not until we know for sure you can handle yourself." Oliver smiled warmly at me. He was only looking out for my safety, and that of his loved ones. As much as I appreciated it, being treated like a child annoyed me. I didn't need a babysitter...except when I'd been alone with the driver in his car.

But that was different.

"Daisy can handle herself, and if you doubt her, you're an idiot." Pierce's voice came from the foyer. The elf strolled in casually, carrying a tote bag in his meaty fist. It was easy to forget he wasn't human.

My jaw dropped at my new sight of his wings—even more glorious than when I'd been at the elf clan—full, vivid color and gold flecks that glistened under the lights, almost glowed. And those elongated ears were something out of a storybook. His true elf form—bumped in contrast and saturation—was beautiful, absolutely ethereal and stunning. His movements made a soft rustle like a bird's that no human could hear. He looked like...honest to God...an angel. How could vampires stop themselves from staring?

Oliver frowned. "What are you doing here?"

I shook my head to clear my shock. Pierce didn't know about me...yet.

Pierce approached me with a secretive smile. "Just doing as the lady asked."

He held out the tote, and I grabbed it, sighing audibly in relief. "Thank you, thank you, thank you. Now I can get dressed. Be right back."

I zipped into the nearby bathroom and fished through the options Pierce had brought me. Their conversation penetrated the walls as if the house had surround sound speakers. That would take some getting used to—as well as everything else about being a vampire.

"You're not welcome here, elf," Oliver said in a dark tone.

"Well, if Daisy didn't need me, I wouldn't be." Smugness radiated off Pierce, and since he'd pulled through for me, I wasn't judging him. But no matter what happened, the two of them would never be cordial.

I slipped into underwear and jeans, wet hair sliding into my face. I should've asked for hair ties, but I didn't know if Pierce would've found them. We'd dated for a while, but we never lived together.

"You're not needed anymore, so get out," Oliver said.

Digging in the tote bag again, I found a perfectly comfortable and properly fitted T-shirt, and I eagerly pulled it over my head. Buried at the bottom was the ring box with the witch symbols on it. The idea was entirely a hunch, but what did I have to lose? I picked it up, and my hand burned as if I'd stuck my palm over the open flame on a gas stove. I gritted my teeth against the pain. Okay, so several layers of skin just fried away. At least I healed easily. I tried to open the box again, but with my pain tolerance, I couldn't and I yelped loudly. The ring box tumbled to the floor intact, and the tote toppled over, spilling my remaining clothes.

"Daisy, is everything okay in there?" Oliver asked, voice loud enough to be just on the other side of the door. "What did Pierce do?"

I would've rolled my eyes at the elf being blamed, but he couldn't see me. I flung the bathroom door wide. "He didn't do anything. My ring box burned me." I pointed to it resting on the floor.

Pierce appeared in the doorway. He bent and lifted the box. "This burned you?"

"Can you open it for me, please?" I asked in my sweetest voice. It didn't take a genius to figure out the symbols were meant to keep vampires out, so there was no point in asking Oliver.

"You're a vampire, aren't you?" Pierce sent a burning blaze of hatred toward Oliver.

I answered his unspoken question. "He didn't do it, but yes, I am."

Anger radiated from Pierce as he opened the box and held it out to me.

Not one to waste an opportunity, I shifted out the false bottom and collected three rings. They didn't burn me, which gave me hope.

"Then who did?" Pierce demanded. The elf closed the box and set it on the bathroom vanity.

I hated the tone he used, almost as if I were his property. He didn't need a reason to hate even more vampires. "It's none of your business. Thank you for your help, but like Oliver said, I don't need anything else."

At my dismissal, his anger vanished. "Daisy, I don't mind that you're a vampire. I was surprised, that's all. Forgive me for my bone-headed reaction?"

That was an easy request. He accepted I was a vampire much better than I'd accepted his elf status. A pang of guilt rang through me, and I wasn't angry at him at all. "I thought you and Oliver would fight, but it was a necessary risk. So I'm sorry for involving you. Forgiveness isn't needed."

Pierce smiled and glanced at a steaming Oliver before returning his attention to me. "You're still coming to Jamie's graduation party at the campground down by the river, right?"

"Yeah, I'll be there."

"Bring Oliver too. You'll need someone to keep me in check." Pierce winked.

"I was already invited, elf. I'll gladly keep you in check." Oliver's dark tone was ignored by Pierce.

I gripped Oliver around his thick arm. "We will both be there. Thanks again, Pierce."

"Oh, I brought you a polo and khakis like you asked, but in your new condition, you can't go to work."

After dying in a car accident, coming back to life as a vampire, and attacking a man, all I wanted was to pretend my life was normal. Anger sparked in my chest. "I appreciate your help, but don't tell me what I can and can't do."

Oliver placed his hand over mine. "I hate to admit it, but he's right. Until you can control this new form of yours, you can't be around people by yourself. You're fully aware of what happens without it."

I'd wrecked a hospital department, a restaurant, my living room, and several city streetlights. I looked at my hands, the ones responsible for so much damage. That destructive magic still hadn't come back. I flipped my palm upright and back for any sign of the mystical force within. I listened for the buzz of magic, but all I heard were the flutters of delicate wings outside. A bird whooshed nearby. The tumble of water from the dam. Wayward droplets slipped along the rocky shore and trickled off. A car's tires hummed, and the transmission clicked as it changed gears. Pierce's thick heart slowly and steadily pumped, but Oliver's heart pounded in his chest, awaiting my answer. The sounds were beautiful, magical all on their own. "I couldn't control the magic, but it's gone now."

"I'm not talking about magic," Oliver said, steadying his gaze on me.

The nameless driver I'd eaten. I sighed. I could hardly keep my eyes off a human throat. What if my patient were bleeding? How would I explain a compound fracture of the fibula *and* a pair of fang punctures? It wasn't a risk I could take. "All right, fine. I won't go to work. Okay? Both of you, I won't."

Oliver's heart rate settled. "Tonight, I'm taking you out to celebrate."

This time, if anything bad happened, Oliver could stop me because I was no longer hindered by homicidal magic. That was a comfort I didn't realize I needed. Heat of appreciation bloomed in my chest for him.

"Really?" Pierce asked dryly. "You're going to celebrate her turning into a vampire?"

"Not exactly," I said, grinning as I thought of our proposal dinner if the magic hadn't been there. Now I didn't have to worry about hurting Oliver or innocent bystanders. I was free to live my life with Oliver at my side.

And we had forever.

I wrapped my arms around Oliver and squeezed his firm body tightly. I sent an apologetic look to Pierce for the awkwardness. He must've thought the same thing. "I'll be heading out. Bye, Daisy."

I lifted some fingers to wave, and Pierce left without further incident.

"Why did you call him for help?" Oliver asked.

Still holding the rings from the witch box, I opened my palm, displaying them. "I don't expect you two will ever coexist peacefully, but I found these a while ago, and they reminded me of your ring. If one of them works, then it was worth it. Don't you think so?"

Oliver's eyes popped wide. He gripped my palm in disbelief. "You have *three* sun rings?"

"Looks like it."

His lips pulled into a full grin, displaying his perfect pearly whites. "I've searched for so long for these, and you had all of them this whole time." Oliver slipped off his ring. Under the setting was a circular mark. I didn't know how rings were made, but I figured some manufacturing had to be visible. "See this?" He pointed.

"It's a circle."

Oliver slipped the ring back on his finger, excitement growing, and he took one from my palm. He turned it to show me the underside of this setting. "And what's that?"

"An 'S'." It was an engraving. "For Soren?"

"This ring is smaller. I'd say this was Sadie's."

He shifted the other one. "This thicker one is Soren's, and this last one has to be...Della's." Oliver showed me the engraved 'D' on it.

I couldn't believe it. The family's rings, engraved just for them. "My ring really was yours all this time."

"You thought I was lying?"

"Not exactly, but it was a far-fetched tale and hard for me to believe."

"But you believe me now?"

"I have for a long while." I smiled at him.

"Well, this ring has your name on it...sort of." Oliver selected a delicate ring with an 'S' and slipped it up my finger.

"Sadie's?" I asked.

"She won't need it anymore." A sadness pulled at Oliver's beautiful face. His sister was dead, thanks to Pierce's dad, and even though he'd gotten his revenge, it hadn't brought his sister back. As if pulling himself from a dark place, he sent me a crooked smile. "How much do you trust it?" he asked, repeating the question I'd asked him when I first gave him his sun ring.

"Enough to allow you to take me outside," I repeated his same answer back. I set Soren's and Della's rings on the vanity.

Oliver took my hand. "Perfect. I have a promise to uphold before our date tonight."

19

Get in the Car

Oliver

Light glinted off Daisy's cascade of dark hair. The sun ring had proved to be authentic, and since she didn't have an out-of-body existential crisis like I had, it was a five-second ordeal. For a baby vampire, she seemed level, in control, but I couldn't trust that yet. While I worked on gauging her cravings, I had an old promise to fulfill now that she no longer wanted to kill me.

At the curb in front of the bed-and-breakfast, I opened the driver's side door of my Shelby and rested my arm on top, a casual display to ease her nerves.

Daisy still hesitated, worry creasing her brow. "Are you sure this is a good idea?"

"There's no better way to learn than to jump into the saddle." I gestured for her to take command of the driver's seat.

"Yeah, but this is an *expensive* car. Couldn't we borrow a practice car for me, some kind of junker?"

"If the junker has a bad clutch, it won't help you learn, and with your new reflexes, my Shelby will be fine." Repairs needed or not. Things were replaceable, and I'd give her anything she wanted. Paying off all her debt wasn't even a drop in the bucket for my well-endowed accounts. Had I known how much she struggled, I would've done it sooner.

Daisy eyed me warily, but she slipped into the seat, and I closed the door for her. I dropped into the passenger seat next to her. Was I nervous about her driving? I'd be lying if I answered in the negative, but if I admitted that, her performance would be hindered, risking my bumpers and fenders. I had her start the vehicle.

Daisy buckled in and glared at me expectantly.

"What's the matter?"

"Buckle."

"That's unnecessary."

"This car isn't moving until you're buckled. There's no reason to risk your life. I'm a student driver, remember?"

I would've loved to rib her for the easy opening, but banter wouldn't get us down the road. "We both heal. An accident won't kill us."

"Would you rather walk out of the car, your suit intact, or scrape yourself painfully off the road and heal slowly, dealing with the police and accident reports?"

"Good point." I buckled in. Instead of arguing, I should've just done it. Daisy's trauma was still fresh. She needed time to adjust to the new her.

Daisy beamed, and I'd do anything to see her that happy. I instructed her on how to use the pedals, and she placed her feet appropriately. I had her shift into first and release the clutch. The car jerked, and she punched the brake.

"Slowly. Very carefully."

A pair of women strolled down the sidewalk with their tiny dogs pulling the leashes taut. During Soren's useless attempt to become vegetarian, and my attempt to assist him, I'd encountered rabbits larger than those dogs. Daisy focused on the people, and her pupils dilated. I knew the look in her eyes very intimately. She was hungry.

"Daisy?"

She licked her lips and shifted into neutral. Daisy's hand reached for the emergency brake.

I captured hers with mine. "Daisy, we're in the Shelby. We're going for a drive. Listen to the rumble of the engine. Feel the power vibrating under you."

She shook her head as if clearing her thoughts, and her eyes returned to me. "That was weird. I don't know what got into me."

I reached behind my lapel and retrieved my flask. It was spiked, but not enough to concern me with vampire metabolism. I offered it to her. "Anytime you're craving blood, let me know, and I'll get you a drink before you do something you'll regret."

"Like attacking that driver?" Ignoring my offering, she fixated on the pedestrians.

"Exactly."

In a flash, faster than I could've predicted, Daisy yanked up on the e-brake and dashed from the car. Gritting my teeth and swearing under my breath, I tore after her.

Daisy stopped before the pair of pedestrians, dogs barking wildly. The startled women backed up, tugging on the leashes.

"Stay still, and don't say anything. I'm not going to hurt you," Daisy said, gazing into their eyes.

The women nodded.

My mouth dropped open. Did she...? She just... Damn. She'd mastered compulsion without learning how to do it. Look me years to figure out I could do it and then several more weeks of testing to learn how I did it. I was equally impressed and worried. "Daisy, don't do this. Let them go."

Daisy didn't look at me. She licked her lips. "But I'm so hungry."

I pushed the flask into her hands. "Drink this. It'll take the edge off, and there's a refrigerator full of food in the house."

"But this is fresher, warmer."

"Actually, the flask stays pleasantly warm in my inner breast pocket..." I trailed off as Daisy stepped forward, focused on the first one's throat. The women were both puzzled and scared, but they obeyed.

"But I'm hungry *now*." Daisy dropped the flask. With hyper-reflexes, I caught it before the sidewalk damaged it. She stepped forward again, slowly, as if fighting her instincts.

In a city of this small size, bite marks like ours were hard to hide. The dog excuse only worked for so long. I'd rather go on the run with her, permanently relocating from town to town as suspicious winds blew through the citizens, but Daisy wouldn't go for that. Her home was here. Her life was here, as was mine now, but staying in one place required a constant watch, and it never worked. Routines were memorized. Lies were crafted. People were manipulated. Distractions were orchestrated, reiterating that if she couldn't pull herself together, I'd have to stake her. The mere thought of performing such a heinous act rent my heart in pieces. I had to do whatever it took to stop her from becoming Evangeline. And that started with preventing the slaughter of two more people in broad daylight. "Remember the cab driver?"

"He was tasty," Daisy said absently. "But not enough."

I'd done some digging on the man for just this situation. "His name was Bryan Olsen."

"That doesn't matter now." Daisy rested her hands on the first woman's shoulders.

"You don't want more of those on your conscience. Trust me." I had plenty, but the nature of feeding back in my day wasn't as easy as it was now, and I had over a century to process my actions and live with them. I also had that long to learn to control my basic instincts. Daisy was green as a cucumber. Many decades had passed since I had last encountered a baby vampire. I believed I was more nervous than she was.

"More of what?" Daisy's gaze remained fixed on the first woman she'd chosen as a meal. Both women caught in her compulsion swallowed thick lumps. Sweat broke out on their wrinkled brows. I needed to get these humans out of here before they had heart attacks.

"More deaths. It doesn't get easier, taking lives. After enough decades, the individuals start to fade from memory, but you know they're hovering in your mind, just out of reach, tormenting you with their cries and fears." It was the truth, but tequila helped suppress their voices.

"More deaths? The driver is dead?" Daisy finally looked at me.

I was getting through to her. Hope dug its claws into my chest and hung on for dear life. "There wasn't much left of him. You must try to ignore the call of the blood. Focus on something else. In my day, a missing traveler or wandering child was easy to explain away, but in this modern world, you don't want the police investigating you. If you want to have a home and a life, you must be careful."

"You sound like you have lots of experience."

I didn't want to force her. I didn't want to lock her up and implement a half-cocked feeding therapy regimen. Daisy needed to choose for herself, but I could reason with her. "More than a century's worth. I'm only telling you this to help you. Bryan's family was devastated by their loss. His little brother Maverick cried, falling into his mother's arms when he heard the news."

Daisy faced me. "He had a little brother?"

I nodded. "And divorced parents, but they came together in grief. Little Maverick will now grow up without the memories of the family he deserved."

Sadness tugged at her features. The open doors of the baby vampire's wild desires were closing, constricting, hiding those instincts. I wanted so badly for Daisy to reign in the hunger. And I was so close, I kept piling it on. "Maverick was robbed of his big brother. Daisy, leave these women alone. They could have spouses, children, grandchildren of their own. You don't want more grieving kids on your shoulders. You don't want their cries haunting your dreams."

Daisy blinked away tears and met the women's gazes. "Go. Get out of here and forget you saw me."

The women tore off with their dogs excitedly charging away. I sagged in relief, and Daisy turned to me.

"This is harder than I thought." Her hands slipped up my chest, and I cradled her against me, sighing in relief. "But thank you for saving me from more regrets."

I kissed the top of her head, hiding my tears. She was stronger than I'd ever expected. Stronger than I'd been myself. I wanted to rush her back into my house and tear off her clothes and show her just how much fun sex could be with an equal distribution of strength, but I had promises to keep. "We have forever ahead of us. You'll get through this."

"How long does it take before I can face humans without losing myself to the cravings?"

"It varies, but a few weeks is a fair estimate. I'll be here to support you and make sure you stay full. And on that note, let's go inside and raid the refrigerator before we work on lesson two."

Daisy cocked her head up at me. "What was the first lesson?"

I smiled. "The importance of buckling up."

Daisy laughed. "Then what's lesson two?"

"Lesson two is placing your hands on the stick and making sure the engine is warmed and purring." Only after I said it did I wonder whether I meant it literally. I'd let Daisy choose.

"For the sake of public exposure, I recommend we begin lesson two behind closed doors then," Daisy said.

I closed my eyes, picturing all the things I wanted to do to her new vampire body. I'd always dreamed of a blood bond ceremony, and with her permission, it was possible, but there was no point in asking until I knew she would get through this change.

Switching off my roaring cylinders, I used my better judgment—my words had been in the literal sense. "We'll save that for later. I still have my promise to keep, and with your rough reaction on the clutch, I'm concerned you'd rip the door off the hinges if you spot another tasty meal."

Daisy's playfulness suddenly stopped. "You were being serious?"

I grinned, joining her in the tease. "I have a feeling that mastering the stick will take a long while, into the small hours of the night, perhaps." My fingers caught a stray lock sliding in her face, and I tucked it behind her ear. A twitch in my pants had me yearning to strip her naked right here.

Daisy caressed my chest with her fingers, playing with the buttons. "I thought I had a good handle on it already."

"You're a vampire now. Driving is different, and I might add, much more durable...harder, faster, rougher." I repeated her phrase when we'd first met.

"Okay, now I know you're not talking about the Shelby." Her fingers unfastened my first button.

In a flash, I gripped both of her hands together at the wrists. "Get in the car."

"But...we were having fun." The disappointment was palpable.

"Lesson three will take place inside my bedroom, sans car." I released her hands.

Daisy bit her lower lip in a grin. She gripped my tie and pulled me close. "Only if I get to drive the stick."

"That's the idea," I growled, and I captured her lips, not wanting to think of how catastrophic this encounter would've been had I not been here. If I had to stake her, I wouldn't survive it, but if Daisy tackled this change like a champ, then I was going to propose the biggest question of our lives. I deepened the kiss, and Daisy responded, pressing against me. My breathing became shallow with desire.

Eternity stretched before me, but I wouldn't waste a moment of it, because I carried enough regrets in my pocket for several lifetimes. "The sooner you master that stick, the sooner mine gets attention."

"I'm ready for you to teach me new tricks," she whispered in my ear.

"Woman, you're killing me."

"And I'm just getting started."

Redirecting her wasn't working. Redirecting the throb in my pants wasn't either. A car putted down the road and honked at our display. "That's our cue. Get in the car."

20
Dangerous Temptation

Daisy

Oliver and I strolled hand-in-hand along the marina on First Street in Menominee. Since I was not yet a master of the stick, he'd driven the Shelby, and that also meant we hadn't proceeded to lesson three. As much as I was very much looking forward to releasing lots of pent-up energy, I was just happy to be with him tonight.

Like the vibrant change in Pierce, the world around me was different, bolder, more detailed. The waters within the wave attenuators remained calm enough to see fish swimming near the surface, even under the moonlight and streetlights dotting the marina. Having this new vision was amazing, but it also meant I could see every stray hair clinging to my shirt and specks of dust on Oliver's suit. Not only was this new world more beautiful, it was also louder. Beyond the docks, droplets from soft whitecaps pattered the water's surface as the gentle waves appeared and disappeared. The empty masts of the resting sailboats greeted me with their halyard slaps. A gull flapped overhead, the rustling of its feathers a new sound.

A smile pulled at my lips, but the relaxing sounds of nature fell from my attention as we approached the Bandshell in the park.

People filled the space, listening to the evening's live band. I wore jeans and a clean T-shirt, and Oliver wore his usual custom-tailored suit, as usual. It looked fabulous on him, but sometimes a little out of place. Most of the audience wore stretchy pants and sat on folding camp chairs for the casual free concert. And Oliver turned heads, also as usual. Possessively, I gripped his hand.

The audience was mostly old ladies, laughing, sipping from disposable water bottles, and talking, but the most interesting...the rhythmic thumps of their fresh pumping blood. As a human, grocery stores were always available. Restaurants speckled the area with enticing smells. And fast-food establishments snuggled up in high-traffic areas. But this was different. This was as if every person pushed a food cart with a sign that said, "Free!"

The literal buffet was everywhere, and free was very hard to resist.

Oliver squeezed my hand as if reading my thoughts. "If you're feeling the urge too strongly, we can turn around."

"Why would you think that?" I was enjoying myself, and I didn't plan on causing a stampede. I was new to my form, but I wasn't stupid. Oliver's grim story about my first and last uncontrolled meal, Bryan Olson and little Maverick, was enough to dissuade me whenever the cravings seized my focus.

"I can hear your heartbeat, but I trust you to tell me if it becomes too much."

"I can do that." While I was still taking in this new world, he was only trying to help me remain functional. I was grateful for the help, even though I didn't really need it.

Oliver rubbed his thumb along my hand, and we continued closer to the main crowd. Upbeat jazz reached the gently swaying listeners.

"Dance with me," he whispered in my ear.

I wore sneakers on the grass. This time I wouldn't sink in and fall. "I thought you'd never ask."

"Liar."

I chuckled.

Oliver pulled me into his frame and led the steps. His hands and hips guided my movements, and he made me look like I knew was I was doing. Oliver was a shining light in the darkness. A beacon, a ray of sun. My immortal protector, and a damn fine dancer.

"What are you thinking about?" he asked.

My cheeks heated. "You."

"Of course, that's the truth."

I squeezed his hand playfully. "You know you look hot in a suit dancing to jazz in the park under the moonlight. And I'm underdressed."

"As usual." He sighed, lightly making fun.

"There's more elastic in any three audience members' outfits than however much wool your suit is made from."

"I suspect you're right." Oliver chuckled. "Besides, if you wore heels, I'd be catching your missteps and preventing a twisted ankle instead of showing you off to the crowd."

Nice recovery. "No one's watching us."

"Is that so?"

I glanced over his shoulder, and the audience continued swaying, but many of them watched us with adoration or even nostalgic smiles. I squeezed Oliver's hand tighter and gripped his shoulder harder, a new possessive instinct. I was never going to let him go.

"I heard that." A deep chuckle rumbled in his chest. Oliver twirled me around, and when I stopped, my hair fanned over my face. Oliver spun me back against his hard chest, against something else hard.

"Is that a gun in your pocket, or are you just happy to see me?"

Oliver panted against my ear, and a shiver ran down my spine. His fingers dragged the locks away from my neck, and he kissed my throat. I groaned.

"Does that answer your question?"

"Stop. You have to stop," I begged, stifling a chuckle at the tickles of his lips.

"Or else what?" Oliver's smile brushed my throat, and he kissed the sensitive skin again.

"Or I'm going to strip you naked in front of all these old ladies, and I think they're going to like it."

"We can charge them five bucks to watch."

I smacked his arm playfully. "Entrepreneurship has its time and place."

"I think it could be quite lucrative." He kissed my throat again.

Murmurs of delight floated over from the audience. Soon we'd steal all the attention from the band. I groaned softly, unable to resist his touch. "I didn't say the proper time and place wasn't here and now." A silly, fun idea came to me, something I wouldn't mind seeing myself. "Instead of something that would bring the police, I think you and Jamie should dance. Change up the music. He takes the lead, but skip the glitter—environmental hazard. Between the two of you, I could charge twenty."

Oliver laughed. "First, Jamie isn't necessary."

"You are hot enough all by yourself," I agreed.

"And two, I don't need help to raise funds." Oliver's eyes flashed red for me. The lust was palpable.

"I think the Shelby's future repair fund will need it."

Oliver mulled it over. "You do have a point."

I laughed at my own expense, and Oliver leaned down for another seductive kiss on the throat.

An old lady nearby catcalled Oliver. In light of our teasing conversation, I should've laughed it off or reiterated the business plan, but I couldn't. Oliver was mine. My instincts locked onto her at once.

"Daisy." Oliver's warning tone went ignored.

I zeroed in on her fingers as she brought them to her face, wriggling in a tease. Her heart thundered in her chest. Sweet blood pumped hard through her arteries. Someone needed a cold shower...or a drop in blood pressure. I volunteered to assist a patient in need. With vampire speed, I flew to her side and gripped her shoulder.

"Daisy!" Oliver shouted sternly. He closed the distance and whispered, "B.M."

"I don't care if she wears diapers."

"B.M.," he repeated, enunciating the letters in a warning tone.

Not bowel movement—the initials of the brothers whose lives I'd destroyed, Bryan and Maverick. The women around us cringed at my words, and my flirtatious future-patient frowned. Not so cute now, was it? She could scream bloody murder for all I cared, but the man I'd killed and his mourning little brother had me pause. She attempted to shrug out of my grip, but she was no match for my new strength.

"Get your hands off me."

Oliver leaned in toward my catch and made eye contact. His irises glowed. "Stay calm. This is all an act."

The woman nodded absently. Her friends watched suspiciously at first, and as their friend relaxed, they did as well.

Oliver gripped my wrist and pulled it off the not-so-flirty woman. Over the loud music, no one else could hear him but me. "You're overreacting to jealousy. Your emotions are driving you, weakening you to the hunger. Rein in those feelings. Find yourself and return to me."

Oliver was mine and only mine. A hollow ache grew. My muscles trembled, begging for strength, and my eyes stung. There were so many oblivious humans here, sitting around like food carts with their steamers opened, scent wafting straight to me, calling me to sample the flavors, "Free" signs blinking, begging. My fangs extended, pleading with me, demanding I fulfill the noise. I had to teach this walking blood bag a lesson. Anticipation drove my heart rate, and I salivated.

"Daisy, you can do this. I need you to do this for me." Oliver's voice wasn't as stern this time. It wasn't a warning tone either—he was worried, and this was a plea. Oliver tucked a hand into his pants pocket. For what, I didn't know, and I didn't care.

My lulled victim turned in surprise to find me still inside her comfort zone. "What kind of act...?" She abruptly cut off, and her mouth popped open in horror at the fangs protruding from my mouth. Others in the audience nearby whispered to each other and pointed at me.

I wondered, not so briefly, how much more fun it would be to chase. So weak, so feeble. Such was human nature. But...their faces. The horror stretching their faces reminded me of the reflection I'd seen in Bryan's car window after I'd mauled him. I withdrew my fangs. I was a monster.

Oliver leaned down to the woman once more and compelled her to forget everything she'd seen. He gripped my wrist and whispered, "Time to go."

He swiftly walked me back down to the sidewalk along the marina, and I struggled to keep up, feeling almost like I was being dragged. "Can you slow down a little?"

He didn't, and he also didn't say anything.

"Oliver, stop. Are you mad at me?"

Away from the crowd, Oliver spun to face me. "That was too close. I shouldn't have let it get that far. I shouldn't have brought you here, but I trusted you to give me a warning. Nevertheless, I should've expected it. That was a misjudgment on my part."

"I didn't have any warning myself," I countered, hating feeling like a failure. "One second, this old lady flirted with you, and the next..."

"You must recognize your emotional surges and prevent yourself from losing control," he interrupted.

Anger swelled through me. "I spent the last few weeks trying not to kill every vampire I encountered, some I care about, and some I love." I paused for a second to let that sink in. It was one thing to hunt strangers for survival. It was another entirely to try killing those you loved and the guilt that followed. "I didn't choose to become a witch, and the urge to kill grew so much, I started getting the itch to kill humans. But sure, go ahead and lecture me about controlling myself as a vampire. I didn't hurt anyone. That old lady is fine."

"Because I stopped you—" Oliver's mouth opened to continue, but nothing else came out. I almost countered with the fact that I'd stopped myself when his brows knitted, and he added, "You wanted to kill humans?"

"Yeah, and squirrels, but that turned out to be you hiding in the bushes."

Oliver's posture shifted immediately. No longer upset, he was deeply concerned, and he took my hands in his. "Daisy, I've known more witches than I care to admit, but never has one felt the urge to kill humans. Ever."

That was what Allison had said.

"If I didn't know any better..." he trailed off, leaving me in the lurch.

"What?" I prompted.

"It almost sounds like someone cursed you."

I frowned, speechless. Who would want to hurt me?

Oliver squeezed my hands. "Thankfully, you're not a witch any longer, and I'm sorry for snapping at you. I thought bringing you here would be a good gauge of your progress, and I wanted to see that sparkle in your eye as I twirled you around. Since I had fun with you, I don't regret the close-call. Forgive me?"

He was only protecting me from exposure, and his lashing out was in judgment of his own err, not mine. I smiled warmly. "I understand. There's nothing to forgive."

"But you're not ready for Jamie's party."

I pulled my hands free of his. "I am not skipping the party. He's one of my best friends, and despite what you are and what I am, he still invited us—an olive branch. I have to be there for him, so I need you to help me beat this."

I would do anything to be able to go, because all I wanted was to be normal, to have the man I loved next to me, and not want to kill him or anyone else by magic or fangs. I wanted to sit with my friends around a campfire and eat s'mores...

Scratch the s'mores.

Oliver gave me a gentle smile. "Of course, I'll help you. I already have something special planned for tomorrow night."

"Will I be underdressed again?"

"Not this time."

21

I Tip Well

Oliver

I'D CALLED MY TAILOR for a custom-fit dress for Daisy, but he'd insisted no amount of money could get it done in a day. After offering a five-fold raise, the tailor apologized, claiming time was the limiting constraint. Frustrated, I insisted on taking Daisy to Green Bay to find a high-end boutique worthy of her body, but she'd pleaded that another trip down Highway 41 so soon after a second fatal accident was too much to bear. Yielding to her request, I'd questioned the couple of dress shops in the area and picked one capable of meeting my expectations. Connie closed the store to give Daisy her undivided attention—the level of service I'd expected.

Daisy stood on a raised platform in front of a folding mirror. The gimbal lights above shined on her, as if the woman I love were radiating her beauty for an audience. But I was the only judge. She twirled to seek my approval of this particular blush-colored cocktail dress. I watched the layers for movement as she twirled, assessing the quality of the craftsmanship.

"You look like you're searching for rust on the undercarriage," Daisy said impatiently. "It's just a dress for drinks and dancing, as you said. What's wrong with it?"

A special kind of drinks and dancing to accompany a special question. Everything had to be perfect. Daisy turned once more, wearing the sweetheart neckline with a loose, asymmetric skirt that ended halfway up one thigh and curved lower to the other thigh, all layered with an intricate patterned lace. It complemented her shape perfectly. "The blush doesn't suit your complexion. Connie, do you have this dress in navy?"

Connie, a plump woman in her forties with a cloth tape measure hanging around her neck, screwed up her lips in thought. "I think I just might. Hold on a second." The dressmaker dashed away without hesitation.

Daisy narrowed her eyes at me. "Did you compel her?"

The corners of my lips twitched. "Something far simpler can have the same effect: I tip well."

Daisy gripped the tag dangling from the dress, and her eyes widened. "I hope your tip includes the price of the dress, because until I get paid, this is out of my budget."

I rose out of the plush armchair and approached the beautiful love of my life. "When we're together, never concern yourself with the price of anything. Money is not an issue."

Daisy looked at the floor and bit her lip.

"Does that make you uncomfortable?"

"Honestly, a little. I was never showered with money, and it seems so...frivolous? No offense."

I gazed into her eyes. "This dress isn't frivolous. Anything I want you to have is for a reason, and anything I'm willing to offer isn't a burden. I want you to understand that."

Daisy rubbed a hand over her bare arm. "I just wanted to make sure. You paid off my debts, and I'm eternally grateful, but I'm not out of the poorhouse yet."

My brows knit together in confusion. "You don't have enough money?"

"By your definition of enough, not by a long shot." Daisy snorted. "But I'm doing okay—just not at-this-level-of-dress okay."

I didn't like her worrying over something as easy as money, but I hadn't always been this comfortable. The days before I'd attained my standard of living were a long way off but still clear in my memory, as was the fresh bathwater in our single-room cabin that our whole family had shared. "You might think I don't understand what it's like to be broke, as you call it."

"It's hard to imagine you any other way."

"When I say it's my pleasure to feed you, to clothe you, to treat you, I mean it. When I was young, I'd sacrificed many meals to make sure my little sisters and brother could eat."

"Sadie," Daisy said and touched my arm softly. She gazed into my eyes. "But you said 'sisters'...plural. The ring with the 'D' inscribed on it. Who's your other sister?"

I tried to hide a smile in memory of my high-spirited sister. "Della. You don't want to meet her, and even if you insisted, I haven't seen or heard from her in about forty years."

"Lily is my only sister, and since Greg made it his life's mission to pit us against each other, we've never been as close as I wanted to be." A wistfulness settled on her beautiful face. My Daisy was lonely, and my heart ached for her. "My family is so small. I'd still love to meet her someday."

I pressed my lips into a thin line, wishing I could take away all her troubles and worries. I nestled her face in my palm. "If I ever see her again, I'll introduce you."

"Why didn't you want me to meet her?"

I pictured my sister's blood-smeared face, her hair unkempt with snarls and her torn clothing. "Imagine Soren while under the witch's spell and toss him in a cave for a few months without feeding."

Daisy grimaced.

"Della had never gained control, and, like Evangeline, I hadn't the strength to do what was necessary. I suppose my weakness is beautiful women." Every time Della's name resurfaced, I remembered her smirking, blood-streaked face as she ran off into the night, never to be seen or heard from again. I had to assume after all this time she was dead, because she'd never been spotted and I never received any further reports of unexplained mass murders. But my weakness couldn't rule me this time. I discreetly touched my pants pocket where I'd carried a stake ever since Daisy had turned.

Daisy flinched, and I settled any unnecessary jealousy before it returned. "You are the only woman for me. You are my forever, and I'll do anything to keep you safe and make you happy." I captured her hand and kissed her knuckles.

I heard the footsteps returning, and that reminded me of this minor test. "How do you feel with our helper so close?"

As if my question reminded her, Daisy's pupils dilated, and she licked her lips. "Like I've been living on broth for weeks and she's a juicy, flame-grilled bacon cheeseburger. I'm hungry, but I'm handling it."

I slipped my flask out of my interior breast pocket, unscrewed the cap, and offered it to her.

Daisy sniffed the air and took it. "You carry some on you?" She drank a few sips at first, but then faster and faster as the hunger took over. Better she got her fill from my flask than Connie's throat.

"Always."

Daisy licked her lips and returned my empty flask. "I always thought it had tequila."

I winked at her. She missed a spot of blood on her lip, and I swiped it away with my thumb. I stuck the smear into my mouth to clean it, and Daisy's eyes tracked my sensual movements with lust warming her eyes.

Connie reappeared, carrying the dress in her arms as if it were a fragile baby. "You're in luck. I have one in her size."

I nodded my approval, and Connie assisted Daisy in changing into the new color, which was fun to watch all on its own. After the dressmaker zipped her up, Daisy twirled for me. "What do you think?"

Utterly, breathlessly stunning. "Navy is your color. We'll take it." I embraced her, my body pressing against her soft curves. I worried the stake would be mistaken for my excitement again, so I shifted my hips and whispered into her ear, "You are simply divine. Let's have dinner."

"We have reservations?" Daisy asked, puzzled now that neither of us could eat human food.

"Not exactly." My lips quirked up in a sly smile.

I was a confident man, assured of myself in all my decisions, until tonight. So many things had changed so quickly. I had only one test left for her—the graduation party. A lot could change that night. Until then, I had a question to ask, one that I wasn't certain of the answer. I was left with an unfamiliar flutter of nerves in my stomach.

I needed a drink.

Daisy

For all his insistence on an extravagant dress just for tonight, I couldn't help a twinge of disappointment as Oliver brought us back to the bed-and-breakfast. I'd seen his whole house—with and without clothes on, so I didn't understand the significance of the effort. And since this dress was far more expensive than I was comfortable with, I was even more confused.

Oliver assisted me out of the car and inside, with my arm wrapped formally over his. I was looking forward to lesson number three, but I thought we were having dinner. I teasingly asked, "All dressed up just to get naked?"

Oliver sent me a sly smile as he pulled me through his bedroom and onto the balcony overlooking the river. White string lights and hanging lanterns decorated the expansive balcony like a fairy tale garden. In the center was a table with a white cloth and flickering candles casting soft light.

Not a stressful, stiff location, but a beautiful front yard date. Tears sprang to my eyes.

"Is something wrong?" Oliver asked, gripping my hand.

I brushed the tears aside. "It's beautiful. It reminds me of Abby's wedding—the happiest night of my life up until that point. I just wish Pierce would've let me remember you."

Oliver puffed out his chest and gestured over himself as if showcasing a prize. "You know why he didn't."

I laughed.

"You can thank Nicole and Soren for most of the heavy lifting here."

Nicole I expected, but I tilted my head in surprise. "Soren? Your little brother helped?"

"Of course."

"I didn't think he was the type." Like at all. There wasn't a domestic bone in his body. I tried to picture him on a ladder, hanging paper lanterns around the ceiling with clips between his lips, and I...couldn't.

"He's easy to bribe," Oliver explained, and I frowned. "Don't worry, I promised him something you were already giving him."

That could be only one thing. "His sun ring? But it's his. He didn't need to work for it."

Oliver playfully shushed me, and I snorted.

"Let's eat." Oliver gestured toward the table, and he assisted me into my seat. On the table rested a set of sparkling glasses, white cloth napkins, and a series of flickering candles. Music, a classic easy flow of notes, filled the area. I craned my neck and found Nicole in the shadows of the bedroom door. She waved, and I smiled, returning the friendly gesture. Nicole disappeared into the hallway.

Before taking his own seat, Oliver leaned over and opened the frilly basket lid he'd had earlier. He popped the port on the first bag and poured it expertly into a pair of wineglasses. Next, he retrieved a bottle of red wine from a bucket of ice. "I know this isn't as fancy as I typically prefer, but I thought you'd feel more comfortable here."

Thankfully, I wouldn't have to worry about the temptation of scores of humans in an enclosed space. Oliver was the most thoughtful person I knew. "It's perfect. Thank you."

He poured the wine, grapes mixing invisibly with the blood, and he sat across from me. "You had direct contact with Connie, and no witnesses but me, and while the hunger was there, never once did I sense you were going to attack. I'm proud of you."

I blushed fiercely, but it was hidden by the warm light of the lanterns and candles. I wasn't used to so many compliments...to not failing.

"I've spent more years as a vampire than a human, and sometimes I forget what it's like to be weak, with muffled senses and a frustratingly slow speed of movement. But I would've walked to the ends of the world with you, no matter how slowly we got there."

Blushing harder. My heart thundered in my chest.

Oliver leaned forward and collected my hands in his. "We don't always get to choose the road we take in life. Being a vampire comes with its benefits and drawbacks, just like being human. But now that you and I are the same, we can hit the open road together as equals. And I want to show you the world."

"I don't know what to say." I smiled awkwardly. His speeches were always so sweet, and the words on his tongue were a melody to my ears. "The Louvre sounds amazing. I pronounced that right, didn't I? The...Louvre?"

Oliver's lips pressed together as if trying to hold back a laugh. "A museum?"

I shrugged. "It sounds sophisticated and exotic."

"My love, you have all the sophisticated and exotic right here, but I'd be delighted to bring you. And now that you know where I stand on our current situation, I want you to know I'm not sorry you became a vampire. The events surrounding your transition were unfortunate—horrific, really. I would've chosen something far more romantic and painless for you. I wanted to be there."

I cast my eyes aside, wishing never to think about my mother's terribly selfish act again.

"Regardless of what may happen from this point forward, you are my forever, and I love you." He squeezed my hand.

Tears sprang to my eyes, and I smiled. "I love you too."

Oliver lifted off his chair and kneeled before me. My hand pressed against my chest to slow the wild galloping of my heart. I thought I knew what this was, but I didn't want to get my hopes up. Still, the excitement pulsed through me, waiting for just those words.

"Daisy." Oliver retrieved a ring-sized jewelry box from his suit coat.

Knowing what was coming, I gasped and grinned and blinked away tears of happiness. "Yes, Oliver. Yes!"

"I didn't open the box," Oliver said, slightly disappointed I'd ruined his second proposal.

I was too damned excited to wait. Besides, I'd already seen the gem the size of my thumbnail when I'd flattened Schooner's Landing. This time, no one was exploding in the literal sense. "It doesn't matter what's in the box. I absolutely want to marry you." I gripped his face and pulled his lips to mine. I grasped at him, pulling him close, and Oliver squeezed me back. I couldn't have been happier than at this moment, one I would remember for the rest of my life.

And I felt just how excited—and hard—he was for me.

Oliver released me. "Now that I know where you stand on the matter, allow me to introduce the jewelry to adorn your finger." He lifted the lid, and the gem sparkled under the soft glowing lanterns.

No longer under the thrall of furious magic, I could finally see it. The oval center diamond was bigger than my thumbnail, and whimsical vines in platinum curled around smaller marquise diamonds—a little garden worth more than my car, probably more than my house. And on that note, I hoped he'd insured it.

My vampire pulled the ring free from the velvet supports. "It will be the greatest honor of my life to be your husband. But realize marriage, till death do us part, is a very, *very* long time." He smiled warmly.

I laughed. "That sounds perfect."

With a gleaming smile on his face, Oliver slipped the ring up my finger, next to the ruby sun ring. As he stood, he scooped me up into his arms and spun me around. I squeezed him against me, never wanting to be apart again.

Oliver slowed our spin and set me on my feet. He gazed longingly into my eyes and said, "Kiss me."

My balance shifted, and my shoe's narrow heel wobbled my ankle, toppling me over. Oliver caught me in a low dip, supporting the nape of my neck, and he brought his lips to mine. The firm length of his erection pressed against my hip. "That rod in your pocket has been extra happy to see me lately."

"You haven't mastered lesson two yet."

"You're going to make me wait?" I asked, incredulous. "What if I never figure out how to drive a stick shift?"

"You make a very persuasive argument, my bride to be."

Oh yeah, I won.

22

A Different Proposal

Oliver

I HAD TO BE careful of the stake in my pocket, because I couldn't bear her knowing the painful truth. As much as I loved her progress, I still couldn't trust her yet. Until then, I had to carry it on me to keep humans safe—to keep our hidden world hidden at all costs.

With the vigorous flood of desire driving my need, I took Daisy's lips slowly at first, and quickly I deepened the kiss. I pressed her hips against mine, showing her how much I loved her, and how much I wanted to be inside her. I wanted to please her until she cried out my name—or called me a god again. Either one was fully satisfying.

Riding on the same wavelength, Daisy leaped up and wrapped her legs around my hips. My pants tightened, and I moved us into my bedroom. I had every intention of getting naked, but I had one minor problem to fix. While Daisy's mouth was busy with mine, I slipped a hand into my pocket, captured the stake, and tossed it under my bed. It clattered as it rolled off the rug. I groaned with pleasure to hide the sound.

"What was that?"

"We may have just given Nicole a heart attack." I insinuated my niece had heard us and dropped something in shock. It was a plausible claim.

"Then we need to invest in a set of noise-canceling earmuffs for her."

Relieved, I smiled. "That's a good idea."

"I have another good idea." Daisy kissed my throat.

I groaned for real this time. "You're just full of surprises tonight."

"You haven't seen anything yet." Her fingers made quick work of the buttons on my suit jacket, giving me time to admire the navy blue asymmetrical cocktail dress. It was truly perfect for her. My hands slipped along her smooth shoulders and followed them with kisses.

As I was about to unzip the layers decorating my queen, I was overcome with a realization. This was our first time together—as vampires. Despite my pressing concerns for the future, there was a chance I could fulfill a dream I'd always wished for, but never thought possible. Now that I knew she accepted me forever in the tradition of her culture—that we had a forever to speak of—it was my turn.

"What's wrong?" she asked. "You're shaking."

"Nothing. Absolutely nothing." I cleared the clog out of my throat. "When I asked you to marry me, I meant I wanted to be with you forever, but there's another superseding layer of forever I want to offer you."

"What's that?" Daisy smiled and slipped her hands along my chest and dragged her nails gently down to my belt. She was still a little distracted with undressing me. I couldn't blame her.

"It's called a blood bond." I held my breath as she accepted or declined.

Daisy reeled back. "What's that?"

I exhaled. She hadn't been a vampire long enough to know about the sacred ritual. "I don't want to diminish the importance of the ceremonial bond of a human wedding, but in truth, human traditions aren't...relevant...to vampires. Humans have an out called divorce, where they can disentangle their lives forever. A blood bond is a permanent connection created between two vampires. I'll be able to sense you, and you can feel me."

"You want me to forge a magical bond with you?" Daisy cocked a brow.

With her use of that adjective, I suspected she wasn't thrilled, and those once-rare nerves fluttered in my stomach again. I cracked open my heart and soul for her. "Every day that passes without a blood bond, for me, is like a gummed-up spark plug, a misfiring piston, a death rattle from a broken spring suspension. I can cruise the streets, shiny and clean, but the rumbling under the hood is a little off. No one notices. But I can feel it—a long, restless life with a piece missing from my heart, and that hollow leaves me paralyzed by an ache I can't fill. When I tell you that you are my forever, I mean it literally. You're it for me, and with you, my Daisy Lynn Barrett, I can have that bond making me whole, if you'll have me for both our immortal lives." I swallowed back tears, awaiting her answer. To me, this was the only answer. The rest was pomp and fluff.

"No matter where I go, I'll always be able to find you, sense your presence, and I'll never feel alone?" Her tone shifted, became lighter, and hope sparked like the flick of a lighter's flint. I swallowed thickly. "And I'd get to keep those magic fingers of yours and that snake in your pants forever?"

Aware of the favorable direction this conversation headed, I smiled, and a wave of warm relief washed through me. "My fingers and my snake are yours, however and whenever you want them."

Daisy beamed with a radiance that swelled my chest. "If I want that snake in your pants now?"

"It's yours."

"What happened to lesson two: placing my hands on the stick and making sure that the engine is warmed and purring?" Daisy's teasing smile had my engine already roaring.

"Today's lesson is sometimes I'm literal and sometimes I'm figurative."

"And this time?"

"The stick and the engine are entirely literal." Daisy's face fell. "But not located in the garage."

Daisy grinned. "I'm already going to marry you. To me, that is permanent, and I expected nothing less when I accepted your proposal. You are my forever, right?"

And there it was. "You are my forever." I tilted her lips up to meet mine, and I kissed her softly.

Daisy pulled back, excitement glittering in her eyes. "Then let's do it."

"As my lady wishes." I kissed her throat, trailing from her earlobe down to her collarbone. I unzipped the first few inches of her dress and freed the navy straps from her smooth shoulders. Daisy tilted her head back in silent pleasure and invitation. In eager anticipation, my fangs descended, and I dragged them along her flesh in a tease.

Daisy stiffened under my touch.

Alarmed, I pulled back. "What is it?"

"What exactly happens during this ritual?"

I'd forgotten to explain, and now I hoped she wouldn't change her mind. "We take turns feeding from each other until our blood is one and the same, and our bodies circulate the same life-giving force."

Her hand covered her throat where I'd left dainty marks that had already healed. "Is paralysis part of it?"

I hadn't performed the ritual before, obviously, but I had good information about it. "According to my brother-in-law, Jesse—"

"Who...? Who's married? Soren?" Daisy blinked in surprise.

I laughed at the ridiculous guess. "Soren requires a special flavor to tame his ass. Sadie was before she'd died."

"Sadie was *married*?" Daisy's face fell in heartbreak for my sister, and that was one of many reasons why I loved her. That compassion was unmatched. "How awful."

My hand cupped her jaw. "They were bloodbonded. Despite the strong link between them, Jesse couldn't save her in time."

"I'm so sorry."

"So am I."

We took a moment of silence for my sister.

"Why haven't I met him?" Daisy asked.

"I got to Logonson before he did. He's still salty about it, and having your bloodmate taken from you is eternally devastating. He may never be functional again. I know that if I lost you, I would choose the sun over the pain of never feeling you again."

Daisy's eyes glistened with tears. "The whole thing is terrible."

"We can wait until another time, if you wish."

Daisy's gaze took me in from disheveled hair, thanks to her hands, down to my shiny leather shoes. "I've waited long enough for lesson three, and I don't want to waste another moment without you permanently bonded to me. Tell me about the steps."

I smiled softly and eased her concerns. "According to Jesse, as a vampire, a bite from another vampire is quite exciting—not scary or painful at all. But if you feel any hesitation or pain or anything at all, just tell me, and we'll stop."

Daisy tilted her head and dragged her hair back. Clinical, perfunctory. She trembled at my touch. I collected her hand, dropping her hair. "Not like this."

"Then how do we...clean the spark plug?"

I could've exploded in my pants. Instead, I brought my lips to hers in a sensual tease, and I unzipped the rest of her form-hugging sexy cocktail dress. Using the palms of my hands, I slowly slipped it down to pool at her ankles. I picked her up, lifting her free of the material, and I rested her on the bed. I kneeled before her, kicked off my shoes, and shucked my suit jacket.

"I think I like this already," she said, watching me.

"You haven't seen anything yet." I climbed over her magnificent body, quivering for my attention. It had no idea what was in store for it.

Daisy's panting increased with anticipation, and she pulled at my pants, eager to free my throbbing length. I dropped down, brushing against her in a tease, and I trailed kisses over every inch of the body I worshipped. As I worked her deeper and deeper into the throes of passion, the quivering of fear slipped away, and the trembling of desire took over.

Now we were on the right track.

Daisy unlatched my belt buckle, forcibly pulled it free, and tossed it to the floor with a metallic clatter. I reached behind her, and Daisy arched under my touch, allowing me to unfasten her lacy black bra. I ducked low to kiss those mounds of neglected flesh, but Daisy stopped me.

"What is it?" I asked.

"Too slow. I need faster." She panted, and my erection twitched in my pants in full agreement.

I chuckled. "Hard, fast, and rough?"

"You got it." Her hands tore my shirt open, exposing my bare chest. Buttons rattled on the hardwood. I shrugged out of the material and flung it aside.

"You know that has new meaning now, right?" My voice was gravelly with the surge of lust and anticipation of the blood bond. I could hardly speak.

"It does?" Daisy panted with need.

I couldn't wait to give her what she wanted. "Here's the real lesson three: as a human, you were breakable, and I had to be so gentle. But now..." I trailed off and grinned mischievously.

"Wait. You were holding out on me?"

"Unless you wanted a shattered spine, multiple rib fractures, and so many contusions you looked like something from a Halloween party, I had to." Waiting to give in to my animalistic full potential had me gritting my teeth with hardly restrained patience.

"That's a graphic way of saying I would've died. First rule of almost married life, no more holding back."

"As my lady wishes." I hooked a pinkie around her lacy underwear, and she raised her hips. I slipped them free, gliding my open palms along her smooth legs. Her fully naked form never disappointed.

I unbuttoned and unzipped my pants while my future wife and bloodmate watched. The hungry stare in her eyes almost sent me over the edge. Slipping free of the restrictive clothing, I finally leaned over her quivering body and captured her lips. Her legs wrapped around me as if unwilling to let me go.

I had no such intention.

Daisy's hands slid along my thick arms, down my ribs, and gripped my hips before she squeezed my ass.

A groan slipped from my lips. I lifted her to a sitting position, and I spun us, settling her onto my lap, but I didn't thrust into her yet. "Ready?"

Her hands gripped my erection. "I have been."

I rose up in her grasp, unable to help myself. The surge of an organism tingled and climbed, but I stopped it. Not yet. I kissed her throat to mark the spot. Extending my fangs, I punctured the soft flesh, and Daisy gasped.

But she didn't tense.

Warm blood spurted into my mouth, and Daisy groaned in pleasure. Her fingers raked my hair, and she gripped my locks, freezing my head in place. Her hips rocked in my lap. I drank and drank until I couldn't take in anymore. I released her throat and licked at the wounds. Heat surged through me with a power I'd never felt before.

Daisy's eyelids fluttered, and her face relaxed with pleasure. "I had no idea. It's like getting drunk without the room spinning. It's...euphoric."

"It gets better. Now bite me."

Daisy leaned forward and bit my throat. While she took in her first swallow, I lifted her onto my erection, fully seating her in one slick thrust. With her first swallow, Daisy cried out in ecstasy. And I shuddered, focusing on not exploding in her too soon, and my eyes rolled with the warmth coursing through me.

As soon as she sucked, I exhaled, fighting back my own release. I lifted her up, and I thrust over and over, pounding into her, bouncing her and those luscious breasts of hers. Each pull of her mouth sent a wave of heat surging through my body, and I tried to focus on banging her lights out. Daisy cried out again, and hot blood leaked down my neck.

My love leaned back with a drunken grin on her lips, a single blood trickle sliding down her chin. "Don't stop. Oh God, don't stop," she begged.

I rose while holding her in place, and I leaned her against the wall. Her arms wrapped over my shoulders, and I thrust into her as fast and hard as a vampire could. Sweat broke out on my brow, and I panted. Plaster cracked, broke, and fell at our feet. My art rattled on the sturdy walls. The wooden furniture nearby shifted under the vibrations. Daisy's vocals had me panting to hold out.

I shifted away from the wall to change positions, and Daisy climbed down off me. She shoved me by the shoulders against the bed and climbed over me. My fingers found her fleshy clit, and I stroked her. My love settled herself onto me.

I pleaded, "Come here."

"I'm definitely coming somewhere."

I chuckled. "I mean closer. Come closer."

Daisy leaned down, but I kept my pace. I whispered, "Bite me again."

"Are you sure? I took a lot."

"Do it."

Daisy bit down and drank. My breath sucked in, and I arched my hips up. The climax had approached again, and I couldn't hold it back. I didn't want to break her drink to switch positions again.

"Daisy, I'm coming." I exploded inside her, filling her tight cavity like a garden hose, but I kept rubbing her clit while she rocked me—the only muscles still functioning.

The drawing on my veins was a shot of tequila to the brain, relaxing me fully until I couldn't lift more than my hand. I let her continue drinking me down, lost in the drunken stupor. Daisy's drinking became erratic as her climax approached. Wanting to pass out from blood loss, I fought against the head swim and brought her to the cliff's edge. She retracted her fangs from my throat and sat up, throwing her head back, and she cried out in pleasure. Spent, I exhaled in relief and slowed my strokes to a stop. My hand tumbled over.

Daisy panted with a broad grin on her lips. "That was..." she trailed off and looked at me. Daisy, my baby vampire, had taken too much. Her smile faded. "Oliver?"

I was too weak to answer her, but I was in a delirium of pleasure unlike anything I'd ever experienced. My whole body tingled, and I could sense her presence with my eyes closed, but it faded quickly.

"Oliver! What do I do? Oh, shit." She looked around the room for a solution.

"Feed," I hoarsely answered, perfectly content to stay between her naked thighs.

"What?" Daisy leaned down by my ear.

"Feed me."

She pulled her hair back and pressed her throat against my mouth. I bit down and drank until I could function. Within a few seconds, I was sated, and I released her and spun her onto her back with vampire speed.

"I'm so sorry," Daisy said, fingers touching my face. "I didn't realize how fast I could drink a person. Is it weird I just said that? It sounds weird."

"Vampires are efficient in everything. I need a little more, and the bond will be completed."

"Take what you need." She leaned down and offered her throat to me, and I nuzzled her neck while I sank my teeth in.

I drank until the bond flooded me, like standing in the warm summer sun. My skin heated, and the bond flowed throughout my body, filling every crevice, and settled in my chest. My heart was full. I released Daisy. "Do you feel that?"

"I do," she said with a drunken grin.

"You're mine forever." I sat up and lifted her off my spent erection, settling her on her feet. She was woozy, and I stabilized her.

"Let's get some bags downstairs." I craned my neck around my bedroom at the damage. "Look at that. Nicole doesn't have to replace the furniture. Some spackle and everything's like new."

"You sound amazed."

"Let's get some robes. We'd managed to spare her extensive repair work, and now we need to spare her a heart attack. And Daisy?"

"Mmmm?" she mumbled while I slipped a fluffy robe over her shoulders.

"You called me a god again."

Daisy laughed—the second greatest sound on earth.

23

Apologies, Apologies

Daisy

I floated. With each step, I walked on a cloud, unable to feel the tug of gravity on my knees or the pressure of the floor against the soles of my feet. I supposed that could be post-sex numbness, but I'd prefer to think of it as the greatest shot of endorphins in my life, making my body feel like it was invincible. Except one region. The lower hip soreness was very much real, but I couldn't erase the smile from my face while we both sucked down bags of blood.

Bloodbonded to my vampire. Oliver was right about being able to sense each other. From the bathroom, I couldn't see him, but I could feel him, even through walls, as if I had my own X-ray machine built in. I was curious what the range was.

Assuming Pierce had already blabbed the news about my new immortal form, I texted my roommate, worried about how she had reacted. But if he hadn't told her, I wanted the opportunity in person, in public. *'Alli, I need to tell you something heavy, and I don't want to do it over text. Can you meet me at Fully Loaded?'*

'Sure. When?'

'Now would be good.' I ducked out of the bathroom and glanced at Oliver, who'd crashed on his bed, sheets tangled all around him, with his bare ass showing to the world. I grinned. We were both satisfied, but even as a vampire, a massive orgasm still knocked him out.

'Give me ten minutes.'

After my shower, I'd changed into a set of casual clothes, ready to go, but I didn't have my car here. I smacked Oliver's firm, rounded, perky, naked ass. He grunted, still half asleep.

"Can I borrow a car?"

He waved and mumbled something in the affirmative.

"Thanks." I collected his keys off the dresser by the bathroom, shouldered my battered purse, and headed out. I probably could've walked, but I didn't want to backtrack from the next place I wanted to go, assuming this meeting at the bar went well.

With only half of lesson number two under my belt, because of my hunger for the dog walkers, I didn't want to destroy the clutch in his Shelby. In the garage, I slipped behind the wheel of his automatic Mercedes. To replace the grill on this car would gobble more than my whole paycheck, so I motored carefully and pulled into the parking lot at the bar, leaving extra empty spaces in case of door dings. I strode inside, and there were only a few people here. Allison was already at the bar, talking shop with the bartender on duty. I approached and touched her shoulder. "Hey."

Allison stopped mid-sip, composed herself, and set the drink down. "So it's true."

She'd sensed me. "I hope that doesn't change anything between us."

My nervous roommate gestured to the stool next to her. She hadn't yet made eye contact with me. "Have a drink. This isn't a conversation I can have sober, and I don't want to drink alone." Allison called to her colleague to bring me a drink without asking my preference.

"Alli," I said carefully, "for next time, tequila neat is my favorite."

For years she'd been making me drinks, encouraging me to sample all the varieties, but when the time finally came that I'd made a choice, I thought my best friend would've been more excited. Granted, I'd dropped a massive ball on her, and she needed time to process.

Ignoring my comment, Allison turned to face me, mouth set grimly. "What did you want to discuss?"

I waved my sparkly ring, grinning wildly with the blood bond still fresh in my system. "Oliver and I are getting married."

Greg would've been disappointed, and likely retreated to his cave, planning to kill Oliver again. My mom probably would've celebrated, but she'd disappeared after the accident she'd caused, and I still had no desire to find her. Pierce would've cursed himself for failing to dupe me with his compulsion and then threatened Oliver with a staking again. They were all easy and predictable responses, but I wasn't sure how Allison was going to react. Although she didn't outright gush over Pierce, she didn't discourage it until he'd made a few mistakes, and I didn't know where she stood now.

Allison's brows popped. "I don't know what to say."

That stung, and awkwardness settled between us. I said quietly, "The word chosen most often is 'congrats', but hey, we're free to make our own choices."

I got up to leave, torn apart by my best friend's rejection, but Allison stopped me with a hand on my arm. The electric shock from witch to vampire blasted through me, and I yelped and reeled back in pain. Guilt over what I'd done to Oliver and how much he'd endured, settled in hard. I rubbed my arm.

"I'm sorry. I'm still in shock at the new you. Let's toast."

Cautiously excited about my roommate's understanding, I resettled on the stool and raised my glass.

Allison cleared her throat. "Roller coasters are meant to be five minutes of thrill, not months of drama."

I suspected this was the beginning of another strange story, like when she and Jamie had chased an extremely quick lizard, but she tapped her glass against mine and sipped.

"I think I'm missing something."

Allison drank her glass down and set it harshly on the napkin. "Look, you know my stance on vampires. I'm still learning to coexist with them, and honestly, you're the closest I've ever been to one, so pardon me while it messes with my *vamp-dar*. Changing the viewpoint I was raised with, and the magic ingrained within, isn't going to happen in a blink. I *can* control my urge, but not without effort."

If our situation were reversed, I would've leveled this bar already, so I ignored the tiny insult.

My roommate spun in her seat to face me, excitement growing. "You know what? Just to prove to you I'm turning over a new leaf, you and Oliver can invite Soren to Jamie's party. Why not? Now that you can't eat, we won't run out of...s'mores. Damn it, Daisy. Now you're going to miss out on Jamie's s'mores."

I smiled warmly and offered the apology without hesitation. "Sorry."

"Besides, the three of you are strong as hell, and we could use extra hands to move the kegs and picnic tables."

My Allison was back, and I blinked back tears of gratitude. "I know how hard this is for you, so thank you. Can I ask for a favor?"

Allison snorted in exaggerated playfulness. "First you want me to accept you're dating a vampire, and then you want me to accept you *are* a vampire, leaving me in the dust with our witchcraft lessons." Allison sent me a sly smile, but the friendliness remained. "You're my best friend, and we have a weird history, but I'm not going to leave you hanging. What is it?"

"I was wondering if I could announce our engagement at Jamie's party." As soon as the words popped out of my mouth, I regretted it. It was a tacky idea. And I'd already put too much on Allison's shoulders.

My roommate stared at me, lips pressed into a thin line while she considered. After a few agonizing beats, a heavy sigh lifted and lowered her shoulders. "I'm going to need an extra keg for that."

A surge of excitement pulsed through me. "So that's a 'yes'?"

My contagious excitement reached Allison, and she beamed. "Of course! We're getting drunk in a campground and burning marshmallows to celebrate Jamie's being all grown up, so why not? It's going to be a night to remember."

I couldn't wait for a crowd full of cheers, for Oliver's sensuous lips, and for more excuses to drink. A night to remember for sure. "I'm living out of a tote bag, and I need clothes. Can you invite me into my house?"

"That's another favor," Allison said. "Show me the ring."

I held out my adorned finger, and Allison rolled her eyes at it. "Figures, Mr. Moneybags. It's beautiful. Let's go."

Daisy

I brought Oliver's car to my house and parked in my driveway, and Allison pulled to the curb seconds later. Last time I was here, I ran for the door with the sun scalding my body, and in desperation to get inside, my legs nearly caught fire. I was trapped under my maple tree until Oliver rescued me. How things changed in just a few days.

Allison and I both exited our vehicles and met on the porch. I opened the front door of my own house and felt for the barrier. It was still in place, refusing me entrance.

Allison said, "Daisy, you are invited inside."

I touched the barrier, but it was still there. "Uh, it didn't work."

Allison went inside the house and faced me. "Daisy, please come in."

This time, the barrier dropped for me, proving any human who lived in the home could invite someone inside since it was their home, too. Now I was thankful I had roommates.

I stepped inside. With my vampire hearing, I confirmed Allison and I were the only ones here, and I relaxed a little. When I'd heard my mother was alive and I'd magically exploded in emotional overload, I'd damaged the drywall with knives and overall made a complete mess. Everything had been patched, painted over, and repaired. Jamie did a great job cleaning up my destruction. I owed him a discount on rent. "Feels like forever since I've been home. Have you talked to Lily lately? From my experience, I'm afraid of seeing her like this."

Allison settled her purse on the kitchen island. "Don't worry about your sister. She mastered the basics quickly, but I placed a throttling spell on her, just in case."

I tilted my head, not reassured. "Like the one you did for me? Because it definitely didn't work."

Allison shifted nervously. "You know everyone's different. Speaking of your sister, I thought I should warn you that I invited Lily to the party this weekend, too. She'll tell me at once if she's struggling, and I'll help her out. We're there to have fond memories of friends, family, and booze, not an accidental slaughter." Allison chuckled.

Yeah, funny. I sent her a closed-lip smile. "I can't wait to see her. This weekend is going to be great." I hoped her throttling spell worked, or there would be nothing accidental about the slaughter.

"Oh, and I'm sorry about your mom. She shouldn't have done that to you. She really shouldn't."

"Thanks. I'm sorry too." Or I used to be. Becoming a vampire had its pluses and minuses, but now I was firmly on the affirmative side. Mom did me a favor, but I still harbored anger at how she handled it.

Allison's face shifted.

"What is it?" I asked her.

She turned toward the front door, and I followed her gaze. A dirty, disheveled woman appeared at the entryway, and her fine clothing was torn. I almost didn't recognize her. I squinted and stepped closer. "Mom?"

Allison blinked twice. "Mrs. Barrett?"

She leaned against the door frame, exhausted, and swiped a dirty hand across her smeared forehead. "Do you know how humbling it is to catch a bunny? Those little shits move fast."

I folded my arms across my chest, unable to garner sympathy for her plight in the woods. "You killed me, and you left me to die."

"Right to the point, I see. I'm a mess. Can I come inside?"

I silently scowled. Thankfully, Allison had my back, and she remained mum on the request, too.

"Fine." Mom sighed. "I saved you, dear. I saved you from this pathetic existence." My mom looked at Allison. "No offense, sweetheart."

Allison didn't respond. As a witch, she'd never consider vampirism an upgrade, and I didn't judge her for it.

"Daisy, don't you see? Now you're free of humanity's chains, unburdened by time eroding your looks, capable of endless choices and discoveries. You have a free-range buffet surrounding you all the time."

Now Allison joined me in scowling.

"I don't feed on people," I said.

"You're a vampire. Yes, you do." Mom attempted to smooth the wrinkles in her skirt suit, but it didn't work.

"Like Oliver, I drink out of bags, and I don't hurt people." I said that for Mom's sake, but also for Allison's. Anything to help cement my case for peace between us. Allison was my best friend, and I didn't want a wedge between us ever again.

Mom smirked. "Look, I'm tired, I'm dirty, and I'm hungry, but I want to talk to you. You are my priority, Daisy. Can I come inside?"

I exchanged a glance with Allison that pleaded with her to have my back if my mom tried anything tricky. Allison nodded.

"Yeah, Mom. Come in."

Stacey stepped forward, but she bounced against the invisible barrier. Even though it was my house, I was invited inside, and I was on the deed. But I wasn't human. Allison had to do it. "Alli, can you invite her in?"

"Sure," Allison said slowly. "Come inside, Mrs. Barrett."

My mom entered and smirked again. "It's Ms. Barrett now."

"I don't have anything for you to eat," I said. "But you can borrow some of my clothes and take a shower."

Mom looked down her nose at my wrinkled clothes from the tote Pierce had brought me. So he didn't pack an iron—I didn't need one, nor care. "Oh, honey, no offense, but I wouldn't be caught dead wearing your clothes." She paused. "Well, I suppose I intended that pun."

I looked down at myself. "What's wrong with a T-shirt and jeans?"

"Clothing choices aside, I didn't leave you to die alone. I smashed out the driver's side window and escaped the burning car before it exploded. Oliver already tended to you, and as a healthy and fully healed vampire, he was more capable than I was at the time. To avoid his wrath, I dragged myself to the woods to heal. Since I had no blood and humans didn't wander through the woods, I had to subsist on animals to heal enough to drag myself here days later. But believe me when I tell you that wasn't the worst I've survived."

I remembered why our relationship was strained. Mom was selfish and vain, and put everything else above her own children. I regretted allowing her inside. "I'm not in the mood for a sob story. You severed my seat belt, intending to kill me, and while I was still alive, you left me to die. Then you dragged yourself over here only to insult my clothing, my lifestyle, and my choice of friends. Pardon me for not sympathizing with your broken fingernails and torn skirt."

Mom sniffed. "I turned you for a good reason."

It didn't matter anymore, but curiosity and manners got the better of me.

Mom added, "After Soren began my transition, giving me the choice of living as a vampire, or dying at the orders of a witch..." Mom paused and glanced at Allison. My roommate didn't move, just watched and listened with a critical eye. "I chose to live. For my children, I chose this life, and for that selfless choice, your father placed me in a prison cell. Greg would've found the papers in my possession. Did he tell you that?"

"No," I said softly, captivated by secrets revealed.

"Every day, the only thing keeping me going was dreaming of getting revenge. After Soren freed me from the lab, I returned to town to finish the divorce and fight dirty with my attorney, but I found out you had already destroyed him. Heart attack—clever."

My brows popped in surprise. She already knew my secret.

Mom laughed. "After that, I knew you were on my side, but I needed you to become like me, a higher being, stronger than men like Greg, and we could be a family again."

I didn't get it. "If you wanted us to be a family, why didn't you turn Lily, too?"

"Lily would never agree to us destroying your father."

My sister always did favor Greg. I couldn't even stomach calling him 'Dad' any longer. Not that he'd argue from the grave.

"Now that we're all caught up, I need to make myself presentable."

"Hey, Ms. Barrett," Allison said with a light tone on her tongue. "We're having a party this weekend. I'm sure Jamie would like to see you."

Mom lit up. "I miss that boy. How's he doing?"

"Graduating college," Allison said, beaming proudly. "And I want you to come too."

"Would he be okay with that? I'm not exactly in the hip club these days." Mom patted her legs and looked down at herself.

"Witches, vampires, and humans are going. Everyone understands it's a neutral territory party, and no fights are allowed. Peace, beer, a bonfire, and a few people will bring weed too, if you're into that." Allison glowed warmly, a hint of nostalgia wafting from her. All of us women hadn't all been together since Aunt Lisa and my cousin Abby were still alive.

"That sounds lovely. I hope I'm not the oldest one there." Mom winked.

"You won't be." Allison laughed. "Other than Daisy, I think you're the youngest vampire I've invited."

"Well, if you don't mind, honey, I could really use some fun, if you know what I mean." My mom gave me a look that burned my cheeks in embarrassment.

I closed my eyes and scrubbed that painful thought out of my head. "Yeah, Mom. I get it. Have all the fun you want. Just don't let me see it."

"Perfect," Allison said. "Lily will be there too. Everyone's invited. It'll be the party of the century."

My family was going to be together for the first time in years. My boyfriend and his brother were coming. My best friends would be there. It sure sounded like the party of the century. I would never miss it.

But I didn't trust my mother.

24

Sister Bond

Daisy

I'D FORGOTTEN TO ASK my mom about her plans for her marital home. Since she'd offered to dispose of Greg's stuff, I'd texted her for cleaning help, but she hadn't replied. With a resigned sigh, I'd resumed the duties of clearing it out for Lily. The two of them could decide who was going to live in it.

I dropped an armful of garbage bags onto the kitchen island. My phone chimed with a text, and I swiped a sweaty brow. As a vampire, I could move so fast humans thought it was teleportation. I could carry multiples of my body weight, and I had more energy than the cumulative caffeine from a dozen cups of coffee, but I still sweated, however that worked. With a pinch of the front of my shirt, I fanned my chest and grabbed my phone from my back pocket.

'Five more minutes,' Lily had texted.

I needed to talk to her in person, but still I was nervous to see her—a new witch and a baby vampire in close quarters was never a great idea, but she needed to hear this from me first. *'Sounds good.'*

I'd brought a couple of bags of blood from Oliver's basement refrigerator to tide me over. He had every flavor, like an ice cream store, and with amusement, I tasted the red rainbow. The blood types swayed either nutty or fruity. I didn't know if that had to do with what the donor ate before donating, but I liked the strawberry hints in the type B-positive, and I avoided the nuttiness of the A-positive. As a human, I used to be A-positive, and nuttiness summed me up right.

I popped and punctured a port and sipped from the bag, reminding me of a child's juice box. That was a bad image. I sucked it down fast and tossed the empty bag into the full trash. I carried the bag outside and dropped it into the bin. Lily pulled into the driveway, and I approached the car to test her resolve against vampires. If she felt the need to take a few magical shots at me, at least we could spare the house, and I wouldn't be trapped.

Lily waved through the driver's window as she shifted into park and shut off the vehicle. I opened her door for her. "Hey, how's it going?"

"Good. Take these." Lily passed me a plastic shopping bag, and I took the handles. So far, so good. "I picked up some gloves and more bleach. There are corners of the house Dad never cleaned. The dust bunnies have dust bunnies."

Mom had mentioned chasing a bunny to drink in the woods. I shivered. "Well, looks like you're prepared."

Lily handed me a gallon of bleach and climbed out of the car, carrying another pair of bags herself. While she moved toward the house, I stayed put. "Lily, how do you feel around me?"

Lily turned, surprised I didn't follow her. "You mean the urge to kill vampires?"

"Say it a little louder for the neighbors in the back. I don't think they heard you."

"Oh, sorry," Lily said quieter and stepped closer. "I mean, it's there, like an annoying buzzing you want to swat away. Sometimes it's only annoying. Other times it can be angering, depending on my mood, but mostly I actively choose to ignore it. It takes effort."

Effort? I had been a raging homicidal monster with my magic. Lily simply called me a pest. I was annoyed at her ease with magic and what she compared me to. "Great, I'm a pestering bee."

Lily smiled. "More like a mosquito."

Even better. My snark lashed out. "Awesome. I'm the most hated bug on the planet."

Lily backed up. "I didn't mean it like that. But what about you? Feeling any intense hunger or drive for something like my throat?"

"I indulged recently. I'm okay."

Lily headed toward the house, and this time I followed. "Let's get to work. This place won't empty and clean itself."

"I wish." Unless... I remembered my magical Mickey idea. "Is there a spell to animate cleaning equipment? You know, sweep, mop, scrub?"

Lily snorted and stopped at the front door. "I saw that clip, and it didn't end well. Besides, Mickey magic isn't real magic."

"That's a shame." Since she hadn't taken any shots at me, I figured the house was safe. I opened the door for her, and Lily went inside ahead of me. "Nothing like hard physical labor to appreciate your magic more."

Lily swept her gaze around the open floor plan. "What the hell happened in here, and what's that smell?"

Boxes of new garbage bags piled on the island, opened garbage bags were scattered around as I went from area to area but quit when I wasn't sure what to do with an item. The further I dug, the more dust and dirt appeared out of nowhere, so footprints tracked around. "It's always worse before it gets better, and the smell was my empty blood bag. Sorry."

Lily made a noise of disgust and wrinkled her nose. She unpacked her shopping bags, and I watched her, proud of the woman she'd become. My sister handled being tossed from her home and left on the run, and she'd handled Greg's death well, or so I saw. Now she handled my change from a witch to a vampire with grace. Lily was strong, more so than I realized, and now I had news that would cheer her up, but I wanted to be careful since she was actively holding her anti-vampire magic at bay. "Lily, there's something I need to tell you."

"You changed your mind about my keeping the house?" Lily paused in the emptying of her purchases, as if that was her greatest worry.

"No, uh, not at all." *Hell no* was more like it. "But it's probably not our decision anymore. Have a seat."

Lily frowned and settled on a stool. "What do you mean?"

"I don't know how else to tell you this, so I'm just going to come right out with it. Please don't shoot me with magic." Lily waited, concern pulling her eyebrows. I exhaled slowly. "Mom's still alive."

Lily's hand moved to cover her open mouth. She stared at me. "She survived the crash? You said she was dead."

"I said they never found a body."

"And a dead vampire, separated from its sun ring, would be ash, therefore no body," Lily added.

"That's what I thought, but she's okay, still rough around the edges. Alli invited her to the party this weekend, and she told me you were coming. For the first time, we'll all be together."

"Except Dad," Lily said sharply.

I didn't have anything to say to that without upsetting her more, and now that she'd brought up that wrecking ball, I wanted to change the subject. "Is there anyone you're hoping to see at the party?"

"Well, there is this one guy."

I smiled, happy for my sister and excited for some old-fashioned girl-talk. "You have to spill. Who's the guy who caught your eye?"

Lily bit her lip. "I don't want to say because you're going to laugh."

"I promise I won't." I smiled at her encouragingly. I couldn't even guess because she'd never mentioned an interest in anyone.

"Jamie." Lily's cheeks flushed pink.

"Jamie...?" I dragged out, prodding for a last name. How many Jamies did I know?

"Harris. Jamie Harris, duh. Who else?" Lily's anger bubbled.

My stripper, college grad, witch roommate? I pinched the bridge of my nose, not wanting to explore the details, but I had to know one thing, and I had to ask carefully so she wouldn't flatten me. "Have you...? Have you watched his show?"

Lily bit her lower lip. "Only a few times. Why?"

My mouth popped open in shock, a little disgust, and a lot of horror at the loss of innocence of my little sister. Yeah, she was a grown adult, but I'd seen Jamie's shows. Most recently at Fully Loaded, fully by accident, and I needed eye bleach afterward.

"What? Come on, he's hot, and I'm not a kid anymore. You trust him, and so do I. We've known him for a long time."

"Precisely. He's like a friend to us, almost like...family."

"Well, I don't see him as a brother, but I'm glad if you do. We spent a lot of time together while he taught me witchcraft, and he invited me to a show at the bar not long ago. I helped him apply glitter—"

"That's enough." I held out my palm to stop her.

Lily laughed.

Now that she'd mentioned it, Jamie was like a brother to me, and I couldn't see him the way she did. "I don't need details. Does he know you have a thing for him? I mean, is this thing between you mutual?"

"Rubbing oiled glitter onto his bare skin didn't feel entirely platonic—"

"Lily," I warned.

She chuckled at my embarrassment. "I was hoping to talk to him soon and figure out where we stand, you know?"

If my sister was interested, then I was happy to play a little matchmaker. I smiled slyly. "I think I can arrange something, but you have to agree to keep the details to yourself."

Lily beamed with excitement. "I promise I won't tell you any details that I wouldn't want to read about in public. But don't...don't say too much. Having my sister put in a good word for me... I don't know. Just don't embarrass me, okay?"

"Let's get this house cleaned, so you have somewhere to take him after the party."

Lily slapped me playfully on the shoulder. "Shut up."

She needed to bring him here, because there was no way I could sleep in my house knowing my sister and Jamie shared a bed. *Nope, nope, nope.* I was energized with excitement on her behalf, so I used vampire speed to get this place cleaned up on time. I'd honestly do anything to make her happy.

Even scrub Greg's toilets.

25

Careful What You Wish For

Daisy

I OWED SOREN HIS sun ring, and it was long overdue for him to receive it, regardless of whether he'd helped with the storybook proposal. I'd gotten to experience Oliver's shock and awe when he'd put on his ring, so I was giddy with anticipation at Soren's reaction. Despite how late to the party we were already going to be, and that it was already nighttime, I intercepted the younger brother before he ducked into the Shelby.

"If you want the back seat, it's all yours," Soren said, gesturing his invitation. "With the way my brother drives, I prefer the security of the bucket seat."

While fighting back a smile, I held out my fist and opened my fingers. "I believe this is yours."

With a knowing smile on his lips, Oliver dropped into the driver's seat.

Soren's lips parted. His hand covered his mouth, and he stared in utter shock for several beats. "You really have it?"

The ring remained on my palm. "Do you want it or not?"

Soren reached for it, but he pulled back. "I had a taste of daylight when I wore Oliver's ring. I don't think I can handle being teased. Is this for real?"

I pinched the sun ring and slipped it on his stubborn finger. "Welcome to the daylight...you know, tomorrow."

The vampire stared at the ring like a woman who'd been proposed to, and I knew that look intimately.

"It's real," he repeated his awe.

"Get in the car," I told him. "Now you have something to celebrate too."

Soren rested a hand on my shoulder and leveled his gaze at me. "After everything I put you through, I don't deserve this from you. Yet here we are again. So, I thank you as deeply as I can. My brother is lucky to have you." He pulled me into a hug, and I squeezed him back. Never expecting Soren to be sweet, I fought back tears.

"Don't be getting all touchy-feely with my fiancée," Oliver said, partially serious but mostly joking.

Soren playfully flipped him the bird and released me. "Thank you," he said once more and folded into the back seat of Oliver's Shelby.

I claimed the shotgun seat. Despite my pleading, Oliver wore a suit tonight for the campground bonfire. I had the feeling he'd never been to one before. I wore jeans and a snug T-shirt, but I brought along a hoodie in case the air was chilly by the water. Soren chose similarly with jeans and a dark T-shirt. Nerves skittered along my skin, and I rubbed a hand along my arm.

"Cold?" Oliver asked and started up the engine. The garage door rattled during its ascent.

"No." I smiled at him in reassurance and buckled in.

Since I was little, Mom and Greg worked long hours and were hardly home. Lily was off with her friends and school clubs. I'd studied. I was that lame kid trying to earn scholarships to impress Greg and become a doctor like him someday. At that age, I didn't necessarily want his career path, but I'd wanted his approval. So, as a family, we never had any fun. Work trips were solo for Greg. Club trips were Mom and Lily. But all of that was in the past, a stain on my memories. Everyone I loved, my family and friends, were all going to be in the same place, celebrating Jamie's accomplishment. A night of laughter, drinks, s'mores—that I couldn't eat, but I harbored no regrets—and people supporting each other, something I'd wanted but never saw happening. My fingers intertwined with Oliver's on the shifter knob.

"Learning to dance by placing your feet on Daddy's doesn't work," Oliver said.

I was completely lost. "What?"

"But I like your hand on mine." Oliver winked and shifted, my hand following his.

Ah, yes, the failed attempt at lesson two. As long as I had my own car and I could borrow the automatic Mercedes, learning to drive stick wasn't that important. But something else was. "Wait. We can't go anywhere yet." I craned my neck over to the back seat. Soren sat spread-eagle, elbows out, and free of a seatbelt. "Can you please buckle up?"

Soren chuckled. "If we kiss pavement, which I doubt since Oliver is a decent driver, I'll heal just fine."

"That's not the point."

Soren rolled his eyes.

I sighed and added, "If we crash, you become a meat missile in the back seat. I don't want to be pulverized or decapitated by you because you don't want to buckle. And if we crash because of enemies, do you really want them to have the upper hand?" It was a long shot, but I figured appealing to Soren's primal side would work.

Soren grunted. "I'm only appeasing you because you gave me my sun ring." The telltale click in the back seat left me smiling.

"Then you can appease me once more. Alli set up this whole thing, bringing together witches, humans, and vampires in a *peaceful* celebration of Jamie's graduation. Promise me you won't eat anyone, Soren." I captured his gaze, demanding his compliance.

"No elves?" Oliver asked, brows raised.

"She didn't mention them," I said, grateful to avoid Pierce for once. "Maybe they'd declined the invite."

"In that case, I won't eat anyone," Soren said. "Besides, I prepared ahead of time. Oliver, you might want to restock your fridge."

Oliver frowned, pulled his cell phone out of his suit jacket, and sent a text. "Nicole will handle it. We have a baby vampire in our midst. Leaving the stash drained is irresponsible."

"Don't lecture me on baby vampires," Soren countered. "You're the one bringing one to a buffet. No offense, sweetheart."

Having also prepared ahead of time—to be responsible and careful—I frowned. Soren wasn't wrong, but I trusted Oliver to keep me in check, and I believed Soren would assist if I really needed it. "Don't worry," I said dryly. "I've had my fill."

Oliver closed the garage door behind us and brought us along Riverside Drive, across the interstate bridge, and into Menominee. The night was quiet in the small town, and we swung a right toward the shopping center without any other cars around.

The campground nestled between the strip mall and the Menominee River. With a view of the interstate bridge to the west, the mall to the north, and the dark rolling river to the south, it wasn't rustic. And across the river, the shoreline was peppered with docks, a boat launch, and a sprawling ship manufacturing company. At this time of night, the strip mall was closed, manufacturing was shut down, and all that remained were the rumbles of semis crossing the bridge. It was just like being in the middle of nowhere, while still within walking distance of fast food.

Oliver drove us along the paved roadway until I spotted the glowing firelight in the center of the campground. I pointed as if he couldn't see the line of cars or hear the music. Oliver followed the curve and pulled up behind Lily's car. We all climbed out. I carried a greeting card stuffed with cash for the new grad and a voucher for a few hundred bucks off next month's rent for all the repairs he'd done.

"Fashionably late," Soren said and stretched. "Just the way it was meant to be."

"Soren, my brother, I'm not your wingman tonight, because I'm on Daisy duty." Oliver ducked into the car and retrieved something from the glove box.

"I'm not a chore." I frowned.

Oliver showed me a freshly cut red rose. He slipped the wrist strap over my hand. "Giving you all my attention is never a chore."

He really had never been to one of these. "I'm not dressed enough for a corsage, and I don't want it to catch on fire by accident."

"The only fire you need to worry about is right here." Oliver took my hand and pressed my palm against his chest.

I grinned mischievously. "I thought more like here."

Oliver startled at my low grab, and I laughed.

"Save it for the after-party, please?" Soren said and split off into the crowd.

Oliver and I wove our way through the cars and traversed the grass. Someone I didn't know guarded the gift box. I dropped the card inside and sent a friendly smile to the unfortunate sap.

"Care for a drink?" Oliver asked.

"Free beer and you have to ask?"

"One red college cup coming right up." As Oliver fished his way to the beer table, I couldn't see him, but I could sense his movements. I could feel him, and I would never be alone. I would never feel lost. After everything I struggled through, knowing that was a huge comfort.

I scanned the crowd, hoping to find the grad to congratulate him, since I hadn't been home much to have done it already. Secretly, I hoped my sister would be chatting him up.

"There you are." Mom's voice.

I turned. Mom had cleaned up nicely. She wore a cocktail dress and espadrilles—heels that still functioned in grass. Her hair was curled along the sides of her face, and she wore shimmery lipstick. She looked beautiful, put together. "You made it."

"Of course, honey. I wouldn't miss this for anything. Where is dear Jamie?" She leaned in close, already holding a drink in her hand. "He's not dancing tonight, is he?" Her tone said she didn't want to see it, and since I agreed, I relaxed a little.

I shrugged. "Alli threw this party, so probably not."

"I'm going to find her. Excuse me." Mom squeezed between me and the strangers around me. Jamie sure had a lot of friends.

She looked like Mom, but she wasn't the same Mom I knew. Becoming a vampire changed her into someone more...selfish? Flashy? Chatty? Dressed the way she was, holding a beer in a crowd of young twenty-somethings meant she didn't care about ruining her reputation as a high-class commercial real estate agent. She didn't want her house, and at this point, I assumed she didn't want her job either. I couldn't figure her out.

But like Mom, I was out of a job. I couldn't be an EMT as a vampire. So what was I going to do now?

"What's wrong?" Pierce asked, wearing his usual cargo shorts and a band T-shirt.

My brows popped. "I didn't know you were going to be here."

"It's Jamie. Of course I'm coming. So what's with the doom-and-gloom look on your face? Oliver die?"

I grimaced. "Why would you say something like that?"

"Wishful thinking." Pierce tipped back his red cup. Apparently, I was the only one empty-handed. Pierce noticed right as I thought about it. "I'm not getting you a drink, if that's what you're thinking. Never ends well for me."

I snorted. The last time Pierce had left me alone in a crowd, Oliver swooped in and stole my heart. "That's in the past."

"And yet, history repeats itself." Pierce walked away.

I squinted in annoyance at the elf, but the corners of my lips twitched with the slightest relief. He was friendly but not possessive, pleasant but not generous, and he no longer vied for my attention or planned to whisk me away against my will. After I'd forced Oliver to bite me to save his life, my blood had been tainted for elves—no longer useful for him. Now, as a vampire, I was his enemy. I didn't want the elf to attack me out of obligation. In fact, I was thrilled to be cordial friends. That was something to celebrate, too.

Oliver returned with a pair of drinks, and he passed one to me. "This bond is great. I know exactly where you are at all times. Makes me a little less worried."

"I know what you mean. Pierce is lurking around, just so you know."

Oliver narrowed his eyes. "Great. Well, this isn't his party, so he's not going to ruin the fun."

"He's not trying anything. Actually, he seems completely ambivalent toward me."

"That's good news." Oliver swallowed from his cup.

"I thought so." I sipped the cooled hops and trembled with a chill. "Come on, let's find the new grad and congratulate him before he's too drunk."

"Lead the way."

I sensed Oliver on my heels as I wove through the crowd, but I checked over my shoulder every so often to make sure my new bond was correct, and it was. Compared to the crowd of elderly ladies watching the jazz concert in the park, my cravings weren't as strong here, so either the ratio of people to the supernatural was unusually small, or more likely, my lack of cravings had to be my preparation—fully fed and in control. I was a better vampire than a witch, and I was okay with that.

At last, I found Jamie and Allison talking on the south side of the campground, near the water. As a fun test for my new vampire hearing, I tried to pick up what they were saying, but with all the background noise, I couldn't. Just beyond the thick of the party, piles of kindling were lined up at the neighboring campsite. Near them, picnic tables were covered in boxes of graham crackers, bags of marshmallows, and stacks of chocolate bars. Roasting sticks were piled next to them. How many non-vampire, endless-keg drinkers were going to stop for a sweet treat? It was thoughtful, nonetheless.

During a break in the conversation, I approached with a bright smile. "Hi, Jamie. Congratulations."

My roommate wore a graduation cap with a dangling tassel on his buzzed head. With the blond beard and sleeve of tattoos over one arm and shoulder, he looked far less bright-eyed and bushy-tailed than most newbies launched into the real world.

Allison gave us a little space and drank from her red plastic cup.

"I'm glad you could make it." Jamie smiled at me and nodded to Oliver in acknowledgement.

"So what's next for the college grad?" I asked.

"Never mind me. The news of the day is you. How are you doing with this whole change, Daisy?"

Better than I thought. "I'm good, actually. I'm happy. We're happy." I gripped Oliver's arm. "Knowing what I know now, I'm impressed with your skills—you and Alli. I wasn't strong enough to hack being a witch, and I can't imagine the strength and work you put in to earn your stripes."

"Thank you, Daisy," Jamie said.

"You're not a failure," Allison said. "Quite the opposite. I'd say you were a survivor."

"That I can agree with," Oliver said, and patted my hand on his arm. Warmth flooded through me. Here we were. All together, all cordial, and everyone was happy. This party was everything I'd wished for.

Jamie lifted his plastic cup. "To good friends, passing grades, and gumption."

Oliver and I raised our cups along with Allison and Jamie, and we all sipped at the toast. A sharp poke, like a fang, radiated from my throat. Seriously? Now? My head swam, and a fiery burn flowed through my body. It didn't feel like the paralysis of a vampire's bite, which wouldn't affect me now. Puzzled with rapidly growing pain, I lowered my cup and turned my head to scold Oliver. The camp, the partiers, and the sky tilted like I'd had too much to drink. It all went black.

Where was Oliver?

26
History Repeats

Oliver

I couldn't recall off-hand how many decades had passed since someone last got the jump on me. A vervain syringe to the throat was unexpected, but I was so focused on Daisy—mostly keeping others safe from her—that I hadn't kept up on my surroundings.

A mistake I wouldn't make twice.

I roused with an ache in my throat and a pounding skull. My head lolled on my shoulders, and an all-over weakness wouldn't let me react, but I was upright. My arms were outstretched and bound, burning with vervain-soaked ropes. When my eyelids fluttered open, I was tied against an upright picnic table. Under my leather shoes, a brush pile with kindling flipped my stomach.

Where was Daisy? I couldn't find my voice to shout, but I craned my aching neck around. The more I moved, the more the world spun, but I had to shake off the vervain effects before it was too late. Tied to the picnic table next to me, Daisy was slumped, still under the plant's poisonous effects.

Beyond her was Stacey, likewise unconscious, and on my other side, Soren was just waking. The vervain hit the newer vampires harder than us older ones.

They were wise to attack me first.

A vampire hunt. This whole party was a ruse to destroy the town's vampires. The party-goers—namely, human—were still enjoying the festivities as if blind to the planned murder next to them. A pair of people conferred with others close enough I could listen to their conversation.

"Jamie and Allison said there's still one more lingering. We just haven't picked out the right person yet."

"Keep everyone drinking. Make sure there's plenty of beer until we can get that last fanger. We can't fail. We won't fail."

These human idiots sounded enthralled in a witch's spell, reminding me of Newt's old schemes. I tugged at my bindings, but the ropes felt like they were slicing through my wrists. Vervain didn't make the material stronger, but it reduced our strength, and it hurt like hell.

The pair set off to finish their work in hunting the last vampire. Soren groaned next to me.

"Wake up, Soren. We have to get out of here."

"Huh?" Soren blinked and opened his eyes. "Fucking vervain. That shit shouldn't exist. God, it burns."

"Can you get out of your binds?"

Soren shifted and grunted. "Negative on that."

The four of us, tied up and ready to burn, surrounded by humans under the influence of witches. This sounded familiar, and it made my blood run colder than usual. We didn't have the benefit of a drought to chase the humans away.

We didn't have the benefit of being human and hiding. The vampires burned at the stake in 1871 didn't survive—except for the one hiding in the fateful cave.

We were a long way from that cave.

Panic tore at my throat. Daisy was so young. She didn't get to experience anything yet, and her own friends were willing to sacrifice her. "Soren, if we don't get out of this—"

"Oh, stop. We've survived worse." Soren's face pinched with another attempt to escape. "Every vampire I know was here. Where's Stacey?"

"Snoozing on the other side of Daisy."

"I have a feeling the s'mores were a cover," Soren said grimly.

"You think?" I asked sharply. I struggled in my binds, gritting my teeth against the burn. It was like acid, and every move I made felt like a hot knife sliding into butter. Too much shifting, and I was afraid my hands would shear off, but that was the vervain talking.

The music from the party stopped, and at once I stilled. The crowd filtered around us to watch the macabre show.

"Well, this isn't good," Soren said, struggling in his binds and grunting at the pain. I always admired his resilience and tenacity.

Daisy groaned next to me.

My heart leaped into my throat. "Daisy? Daisy, can you hear me? How are you feeling?"

"Everything hurts." Her face pinched with pain. And she looked around, panic flashing across her face. "What... What is this? What's going on? This burns."

"Calm down. Daisy, I need you to stay calm. We'll figure this out."

Her head whipped back and forth. "Calm? We're tied to picnic tables. Mom? Mom, wake up."

Stacey groaned too. Her head lifted, and her eyelids fluttered open for a moment.

"Mom, you have to wake up."

"What happened?" Stacey asked slowly. "Ah, vervain. Damn it. Thought I'd be immune after all this time."

I hated to think of what Dr. Greg Barrett did to Stacey for her to assume that.

Our audience quieted down and focused on us, like a vampire–hunting militia. Bonfire light flickered behind them. A pair pushed through the crowd to face us. Allison and Jamie, and the fairer one carried a burning backyard torch.

Allison spoke first. "I'm sure you figured out why we invited you here tonight."

"Vampire barbecue," Soren said evenly.

Snickers zipped along the crowd.

"What?" Stacey asked, exasperated. "Alli, Jamie, you were like family to Daisy. You can't do this to her. You know her!"

"She's a vampire, Stacey," Jamie said flatly. "What relationship we had in the past doesn't matter anymore. You made sure of that."

"Me? I gave her a long life, free of elves and full of her own choices, her own decisions. She loves Oliver. As a witch, they couldn't be together, and now they can. Doesn't her happiness count for anything?"

"This wasn't how it was supposed to go," Allison admitted. "I gave Daisy a gift—stronger magic than anyone has ever known. She should've been next to me, not with you lot."

Anger curled inside me at the betrayal. I should never have trusted witches. I pulled forward, attempting to snap my ropes with blind fury. "That's why Daisy's onyx ring drained so fast. You did that to her, to us?" I exchanged a glance with Daisy, whose look was once again an apology. Allison had tried to make her kill me. I couldn't say I was surprised.

Allison smirked. "Took you long enough to figure it out."

In a pleading voice, Daisy said, "Alli, how could you? You're my best friend. You and Jamie both. I opened my home to you. I trusted you."

"Don't make it sound like charity," Jamie said. "We paid market-rate rent."

Daisy's mouth fell open. That was a low blow, even to me.

The crowd shifted once more, and Lily appeared at Allison's side. The new witch had picked her team, and I couldn't say I was surprised by that either.

"Lily!" Daisy pleaded. "Help us."

The youngest Barrett assessed the upcoming barbecue, but despite Daisy's cries for help, Lily did nothing. She was cool and calm as if under a controlling spell.

Allison wrapped her arm around the shorter woman's shoulders and smiled in victory. "Lily has a greater understanding of our society than you do. She has standards. Three witches and so many human witnesses against four vampires. You're vastly outnumbered, so don't bother fighting. The sooner we get the real party started, the sooner we can go home. Kyle's the father of Makayla's baby, and I am missing it."

"Hey, no spoilers," Soren said, offended.

"I can't believe this. Alli, it's not funny anymore. It's cruel. Let us go," Daisy said.

"The only thing cruel is allowing monsters to freely attack and kill. This area has a long history with vampires, and tonight, it ends. Consider this a mercy for you, and a rescue for them." Allison gestured with her head at the human witnesses calmly watching.

"It does have history," Daisy said, cleverly buying time while working on her binds. "And you remember how this ended last time? Witches burned. Vampires escaped. So many humans died."

With Daisy's impressive will to continue fighting, I kept working on mine, despite the blinding pain.

"And history has a way of repeating itself." The not-so-subtle threat was there, just floating around, waiting for the witches to absorb the full impact of its substance. "All I have to do is give in to the desire for blood, and I would become the unstoppable monster you all fear."

That didn't help our case any, but the witches were stunned silent.

"Soren, remember 1871?" I asked him, setting up a plan.

"I could never forget." Soren grinned mischievously.

"What's this about?" Jamie asked, frowning at us.

Soren explained, "Witches had allowed the fire to rage out of control during the drought of 1871, and our parents perished in the flames. Knowing their deaths were generations before you, we'd considered the matter buried, but since you have this itch for a repeat of history, then so do we. When we free ourselves tonight, we'll be getting vengeance for their murders."

Jamie and Allison both flinched at the dark words, and Jamie pushed a torch towards Daisy's sister. "Then time's wasting. Lily. Would you like to do the honor of lighting the bonfire? I'm getting hungry."

These witches wanted a slaughter, so they'd get one, but they actually intended to roast s'mores by our burning corpses. That was a new low, even for me. I strained at the burning binds, and my wrists sizzled.

"Lily," Daisy begged once more. "You can't do this to me and Mom. Let us go! We're your family, and we love you."

Lily stared at her sister, but I couldn't read whether her sister's pleas reached her. The witch calmly accepted the torch.

"Honey, please," Stacey pleaded. "Lily, please let us go. We can live amicably. This isn't necessary."

Lily turned to her mother, but with no indication that she actually heard. Firelight licked up her smooth features.

"Any luck?" I whispered to my hearing-sensitive brother.

He perceptibly shook his head, and I couldn't budge the damned acidic ropes either. My skin felt as if it were melting off. As a new vampire, Daisy had to be in so much pain. Anger flourished throughout my weakened limbs.

The human witnesses only watched. To control that many people at once was impressive. Allison and Jamie were far more powerful than I'd thought.

Lily stepped closer to us, staring at us like boring zoo animals, but she didn't say anything.

"Lily," I said. She and I weren't close, so maybe the witches hadn't turned her against me as strongly. The witch faced me. "We haven't known each other that long, but when I needed you most, you helped. You saved my life, Lily, and you cared. Soren and I, and your mother and sister, we don't attack people. We don't hurt others. We drink from donors who volunteer at medical facilities. Please let us go. There's no reason for this."

"No reason?" Jamie repeated with disdain. "You and your kind will always feed on humans. That blood belongs to people in need, not hungry monsters, and as witches, we forbid it. My only regret was not corralling you and your brother before Daisy and Stacey became collateral damage. But Greg assured me that Stacey's involvement was for the greater good, and we'd trusted Newt to carry out his plan. Unfortunately, things didn't work out as we intended, but this will do instead." Jamie turned and raised his voice. "As our ancestors before us, let us burn the vermin who walk among us."

The crowd cheered, and Jamie nodded to encourage Lily to finish her task.

"Lily, no, please!" Stacey begged. "Don't you remember watching movies with popcorn in hotel rooms as we traveled out of state for your meets? And when a couple was arguing, we listened and chuckled to ourselves? Remember? I do. I'm still your mother. Lily, please!"

Lily carried the torch to her mother's feet. Damn it, she was going to burn her own mother alive. I struggled harder, and Soren's grunts reached my ears.

"I was always Daddy's girl." Lily lowered the torch, and flames ate up the kindling. Lily's hair fluttered around her with the growing heat, and she moved toward Daisy next.

My heart thundered in my chest, and I purposefully smashed my shoulder against the table. I cracked the wood and dislocated the joint, but still I couldn't slide free of the ropes. The humans watched with macabre interest, but they didn't protest or cheer.

Stacey's face twisted with fear as Lily moved toward Daisy's pyre next. "Stop! Please stop. Burn me, take me, but don't hurt your sister. She's innocent." Stacey shifted her feet in a useless attempt to avoid the flames.

With dull boredom on her tongue, Lily said, "Mom, she killed a taxi driver, and the rest of you killed too many to count. This is the right thing to do."

"Daisy!" Stacey shouted, holding back sobs. "I'm so sorry for all this. I'm sorry I threatened your boyfriend and his brother, but I'm glad you're next to me instead of against me."

Daisy's face twisted with anguish, and tears rolled down her cheeks. She pleaded, "Lily, if you kill us, how are you any better?"

Stacey frantically shifted, panting and twisting, desperately trying to free herself as the flames inched closer.

Lily approached Daisy's feet. "Mom died on the day of your graduation. That is a vampire. Just like you. And it's not murder if it's not human."

I conjured all the hate and anger boiling inside me and fought through the vervain. With one last crack of my bones against the wood, I broke free and slipped out of the ropes. I rushed Lily and the fatal torch, and I shoved the witch back. Lily flew through the air, dropping the torch. I spun to rescue Stacey, but the witches knocked me off my feet, pressing me to the ground with an invisible ten-ton boulder, crushing me in place.

"Oliver!" Daisy cried.

Stacey screamed as the flames reached her feet. We all faced her. Some in horror, some with stomach-curdling smirks. And at once, the panicked woman fell out of sight.

"What's going on?" Allison asked, hands on hips and frowning at the unexpected trick.

I'd like to know too.

27

Broken Spirits

Daisy

My whole life had changed. I'd trusted my roommates and my sister, but it was my selfish, image-conscious mom I'd kept at arm's length who'd cried out to free me. I shouldn't have doubted her, and her screams of agony had torn into me like claws. There was nothing I could do. But in the blink of an eye, she'd vanished into the darkness.

Great, Mom saved herself. I supposed she was like five minutes older than me and, therefore, stronger, but why couldn't Soren and Oliver get free? Mom must've had a trick up her sleeve as usual. But as Lily was about to light the kindling at my feet, I feared Mom was too late.

Heart pounding in my chest, wrists burning as if the fire had already been cooking, I struggled. I tried to loosen the ropes or peel my flesh free of them. I tried to break the wooden boards pinning me, but my efforts were of no use. Just then, Oliver broke free and shoved Lily away from me, but he was too late. A tiny flame caught on the kindling near my feet.

Before he could free me, the witches crushed Oliver invisibly to the ground. I watched in disbelief, fighting against the binds at my wrists, waiting for Mom to pull out whatever trick she had up her sleeve, but I couldn't find her. The flame slowly lapped at the twigs, inching closer.

My friends had tricked me into coming here and bringing along my fiancé and my future brother-in-law. They'd tricked my mother into coming, too. And my sister—my own damned sister—lit the pyre at my feet on fire, intent on killing our family. When I'd begged, pleaded with, and appealed to the logical side of my friends and my sister, but still they persisted in such a brutal act, I couldn't forgive any of them for this.

But it was my sister who broke me. The golden child. Daddy's little girl. As the annoying saying went, *The apple doesn't fall far from the tree*. Greg focused on grooming the wrong kid, and his mistake cost him his life.

And it would cost Lily hers next.

Although I'd never taken a baseball bat to the back of the head, I had a feeling the injected vervain felt similar. My skull pounded like a toddler with a hammer and way too much enthusiasm. My whole body burned with heat, and sweat dripped down my back and face. And every muscle in my body ached, but nothing compared to my wrists wrapped with vervain-soaked ropes. Everywhere the vervain touched was like an open flame licking at my flesh. No matter how hard I struggled, I couldn't break free. I was too weakened by vervain, and my knees gave out. I slumped forward, facing inching closer to the flames.

My sister climbed to her feet and rejoined my roommates, and as she glared down at Oliver struggling on the ground, she smirked. Lily had called me a mosquito, buzzing in her head like an annoyance she wanted to kill, but I was a wasp, and I was about to sting hard. I inhaled deeply and pulled with all my might to break my binds, like Oliver had. Flames grew at my feet. I glared at my sister—this stranger, who didn't care about us—and I was desperate and raging for justice. And all this pain she'd inflicted made me very hungry.

The ropes snapped, and I tumbled onto and over my pyre. What the...? I did it. I actually did it. Before I could utter swears of surprise and call out to my awesome womanly prowess, I was swept up off the ground and carried away...by...Kevin? I squinted at my EMS partner, and I looked over my shoulder in fear for him. I couldn't let him become another of the witch's puppets. "Kevin? You can't be here."

Kevin Fontaine broke through the last of the stinging knots fastened around my wrists. "No witches are killing vampires on my watch."

I pulled my aching arms forward and stretched my shoulders. I rubbed the burns on my wrists and faced my partner. Needing his knife to free the others, I cocked my head at his empty hands. "I'm grateful for the help, but the others need us. I need to borrow your knife." I held out my palm expectantly.

Kevin smiled, displaying pointy fangs. *Well, shit.* All the while, Allison had been right. I hadn't been feeling the urge to kill humans in Borealis, because Kevin was never human. "Did Megan know?"

"Now's not the time to chat," Kevin said. "You get Oliver. I'll free Soren. We need to get everyone out of here, including these innocent humans."

"Where's my mom?" I scanned the dark area for her, but no one was in sight.

"Your mom's healing down by the water. She's safe for now."

"Thank you, Kev. God, I'm so glad you're here."

Kevin winked and set off in a blur. I had so many questions, like how he managed to hide being a vampire while working as a nurse in the emergency department, surrounded by staff, bosses, and cameras. Did he sneak off to the blood bank refrigerator during lunch break? Did he hide his sun ring when his hands needed to be sterile and gloved? Had he compelled anyone to get through his day? Shaking off my string of curious questions, I had people to save.

I returned to the commotion. Oliver was still pressed against the dirt. He was going to be upset about his suit when this was over. Soren struggled against his binds, eyes wide and lips parted—the first time I'd seen him nearing a panic. The humans circled the area, and now I understood what their purpose was. They weren't witnesses. They were to shield against witnesses. A human meat wall to block curious onlookers from calling authorities, and now I was even more disgusted.

I blurred to Oliver's side and dropped to my knees by his angry face.

"How did you get free?" Oliver asked, baffled.

"We have another friend here. Can you get to your feet?"

Oliver struggled. "Someone's holding me down with a spell, but I think they're losing focus in the confusion. Find who's holding me."

"What's going on?" Jamie scowled and marched toward me, but he stopped short as Soren leaped down off his pyre and stood guard between us and them.

I rose and stood by Soren's side, a shield for Oliver against my backstabbing roommate. "Let Oliver go."

Jamie's face curled into a rage, and I couldn't predict the next thing he'd try. Allison stood with the human meat wall, mumbling foreign words rhythmically. She was crushing Oliver. Allison was stronger than I ever knew possible, and I couldn't stop her no matter how much strength I threw at her.

I needed Lily's help. Somehow, I had to appeal to her overachiever-Daddy's-girl side, not this murderous witch side. I brushed my fingers along Soren's hand in a silent message, and I darted off using hyperspeed, rushing around, looking for my sister. The longer it took me to find her, the angrier I became. Allison and Jamie intended to burn us alive. Lily had been a witch for what—a few minutes?—and she'd already chosen to fight against her own family. It was truly baffling. They had to have brainwashed her. It was the only excuse I could find that made any sense.

I found Lily at a nearby picnic table, closer to where the party had been. Her burning tiki torch leaned against it, and she had a book open in front of her and a circle of candles flickering. Her eyes were closed, and she chanted. I supposed this was the second act of the night. A plan 'B' of sorts.

"Lily!" I shouted in her face, anything to disrupt whatever she was doing because it couldn't be in our favor. "Stop this right now."

Lily opened her eyes and said calmly, "Get away from me."

I was willing to pile on the guilt to get through to her and maybe break some of the brainwashing. "What happened to you? This is torture. You were going to burn your whole family alive."

Lily rose and climbed out of the picnic table. "You're a vampire. I'm a witch. It is our nature to fight. Nature decided witches destroy vampires."

"You've been a witch for like five minutes. Tell me they didn't spell you to become a mindless machine, like Newt had done to Soren."

Lily blinked and frowned. "I'm stronger than that."

Yeah, sure, whatever. I stepped closer. "Of course you are. Who else could float a syrup bottle right after gaining her magic? That's why I believe you can see through their veil. You can fight this. Lily, you see all those people out there? Alli and Jamie are willing to risk all their lives—their *human* lives. Don't you see what's wrong with that?"

Lily looked for only a second. "Jamie and Allison explained the real world to me, and I made a choice. Unfortunately, you also chose a side, but it was the wrong one. There's nothing I can do to change your mind. Dad tried, and he failed. For self-preservation, I won't copy his mistakes."

"That's it then? My own sister?" I backed up a step, shaking my head in complete disbelief. "I hoped you could see my side here, but clearly, whoever brainwashed you is stronger than me."

My sister shifted her weight, anger furrowing her brow. "I'm brainwashed? You're so dense. You *chose* to become a monster, feeding on people like a parasite, and killing them like a plague. Stop trying to appeal to my human side. My mom died on my sister's graduation day. My sister died when my fake mom crashed Dad's car on purpose."

I stepped back again, giving us reasonable space while I prepared for my next move. When I had been a witch, I'd squeezed Greg's heart until it gave up, and even if Pierce had appealed to my human side, I still wouldn't have budged. I needed a different angle—one that could turn Lily against my roommates. "Did Alli give you super strong power too?"

My super-sensitive hearing picked up a stick snapping nearby, perhaps the result of a brave-ass squirrel. Nothing that alarmed me. But that split-second distraction reminded me of how hungry I was. I had enough self-control to leave those innocent humans alone. I had a target in mind who wasn't so innocent.

"Uh, no? My magic is all my own. Everything I'm doing is because I want to. Because it needs to be done."

When I looked at her, I saw my happy little sister playing with toys and asking me to join her, but I couldn't, because Greg needed assistance, expecting the best from me, and I had to appease him more than Lily. I'd neglected her, and she turned on me because of it. It was my own fault she'd become this monster. And she was making me choose between saving her, despite how much pain she'd inflict in the process, and saving Oliver. Unfortunately for Lily, I'd lost my belief in second chances a long time ago. Without a weapon in my hands, I dove at my sister, mouth gaped and snarling.

I was hungry.

Oliver

WHILE I CONTINUED STRUGGLING against a spell meant to immobilize a vampire for an easy kill, Soren moved between me and Jamie. At any moment, I expected my brother to join me in the most unrefined, humiliating way to ruin clothing—pinned to the filthy dirt. But either the witch couldn't modify the spell quickly enough, or he wasn't the one casting it. My brother remained on his feet.

Choices came with consequences, and unfortunately for Jamie, when Soren set his sights on anything—in this case, an enemy—he moved without hesitation, which was why I'd blamed the careless bodies on him. He was impulsive and quick. He didn't harbor guilt about what he did—usually. Sometimes I envied him.

So when Soren dove for Jamie and tore out his throat in one smooth motion, I wasn't surprised by his actions, but I was surprised that a man so powerful was shredded so easily. Blood sprayed from my enemy's throat, arcing through the air. His face blanked with shock, and a hand feebly covered the wound.

Allison cried out and broke from the crowd of humans, dashing toward us. Humans looked around, lost, confused, and a couple screamed. Several started to run away. The spell pinning me severed, and I leaped to my feet at Soren's side. Jamie crumpled to the ground as Allison reached him. The light in his shocked eyes faded, his face slackened, and his hand fell from his wound. Even if I could save Jamie with my blood, I wouldn't.

Allison touched his face and mumbled teary words to him, and immediately those panicking humans calmed down, focused and armed themselves with the flaming kindling from the pyres. One by one at first, they rushed us in mindless anger. Allison had used them as a shield, and now dozens of lives were collateral damage. Witches never changed.

I had to get to Daisy, but Soren and I were rapidly surrounded by dozens and dozens of humans with flaming wooden stakes. My brother covered my back, and we fended off the feeble humans with a gentle jab, a tap at the throat, a simple trip. These people weren't fighters, and none of them were remotely a match for us, but to prevent a slaughter, we held back a lot. It was almost cathartic unleashing all this pent-up energy, but having to pull my punches, lest I snapped their necks, made the skirmish a little less enjoyable. And I was growing increasingly unhappy about the damage to my suit. Numbers were still numbers, though. Half a dozen humans jabbed at once. A few managed to cross the finish line, to the detriment of my suit. I tapped out the flames with a frown. Daisy wasn't a fighter either, and I needed to get through these mindless pawns to find her. At least I could feel her.

While distracted with my damaged fabric, a human managed to impale me with his flaming torch. And then another. I tore makeshift stakes from my flesh, blood dribbling down my skin and healing with supernatural speed. More kept coming. A broad-framed hulk of a man with a grizzly beard snarled at me, but a single punch landed him on his ass. Several dozen humans we didn't knock out returned to their feet for the next round. Despite their growing bruises and wounds, they kept returning, again and again. I had a feeling the spell forced them to continue until they were dead.

"How many for you so far?" I asked Soren over my shoulder as I confiscated a woman's stake and shoved her back. She tripped and fell over her own sneakers. I tossed the stake aside like the stick it was.

"I knocked out a dozen or so. Lost count."

If Soren hadn't come to the party, I would've been up a creek, having to choose between my life and theirs. And I wouldn't have been holding back. "I owe you a beer."

Soren swung his arm to neck-slam another attacker. "I want top-shelf shit. My help is worth that much, and you have the deep pockets to make the minor sacrifice."

"If we make it out of here alive, I'll buy you any drinks you want."

Soren cackled, as if conjuring all new ways to make my credit card cry. "Deal."

Allison pushed her way toward us, avoiding the strikes and blows of the skirmish, but she got knocked back a few times. Her mouth was twisted into a snarl, and her eyes were flaming with fury at us. Since Lily had been trained by these witches, I didn't trust the younger sister. I really needed to get to Daisy. My love would be pissed if I killed her friend, but I couldn't let the witch go free now.

"Soren, I need to get to Daisy. Mind taking this witch too?" I asked, allowing him to take Daisy's rage and buy me time.

"We still have human interference, and she looks strong. Name your price." Soren shoved another flailing human aside, who fell with a thump, and his stake clattered on the campground's paved road and hit a parked car.

"Full access to the bed-and-breakfast for three months, no restrictions."

"Will you be home?" My brother asked, ferreting out what made the deal sweet.

"Nope." I punched a human in the gut hard enough to fold him over, but not to cause any lasting internal damage—probably.

Only a handful of the strongest humans still fought. The rest squirmed on the dirt and grass, trying to obey orders but finding a lack of compliance in their bodies. Others were sleeping peacefully, knocked clean out of their consciousnesses.

Allison shook out her shoulders, preparing to strike. Time was running out.

"We are two for two on deals tonight. Go. I got this." Soren turned to Allison. "Let's dance, witch." My brother dove at her, claws and fangs at the ready.

I blew the remaining stragglers off their feet and tore after Daisy. My sensitive ears picked up Allison screaming at Soren and grunting and whaling on him with all her frustrations and pain. Magic was hard to conjure without focus, but she lost her brother tonight, and rage was effective fuel.

Daisy was talking to her sister, but not for much longer. She emanated fury and hunger. She would lose control. I slipped my whittle-sharp stake out of my pocket and gripped it appropriately for the strike. I sidled alongside a tree, snapping a branch under my foot, but Daisy took no notice. My hands trembled, and my stomach flipped. We were bloodbonded. Having to stake her was equivalent to staking myself in terms of physical pain. But the emotional anguish would be far, far worse.

I'd always promised to protect her, and now I was going to be the monster that hurt her. But asking for forgiveness was easier than permission, and in her current state of mind, there was no appealing to her logical side—a downfall of a baby vampire. Losing her friends was one thing, but losing her only sister would send her into a grief spiral she might never return from. I had to stop her, even if she hated me for it. Even if *I* hated me for it.

Daisy leaped into the air for the kill, and I dashed between the sisters, stake at the ready. Stopping a baby vampire didn't take much effort for an old vampire like me—under normal circumstances. I'd been staked more times than I could count, and I knew how gut-wrenching and painful it was, like having the wind torn from shocked lungs, unable to gasp or breathe as every nerve ending lit up in howling pain. With hands still trembling, I prepared myself for the inevitable blood bond pain. And Daisy's anguish.

My stake pierced her abdomen, a shocking blow. Daisy's hands landed on my shoulders as she gasped and choked, trying to pull air into her lungs. Her wide eyes looked up at me in surprise, in fear, and in heartbreak. Her trembling hands reached for the stake I'd rammed into her body and continued to hold firmly in place. As another soft gasp breached her soft lips, I blinked back tears—not for feeling the stake itself, but for what I knew was running through her mind.

I held steady. She needed time to dissolve the bloodlust coursing through her. Daisy gripped the stake with both hands and tried pulling it out, but the massive wound was too sensitive to touch. She cried out in pain. I had to remove it for her. But not yet.

"Daisy, I'm so sorry. I couldn't let you do this."

My love couldn't speak. Her mouth moved, but the pain was unbearable. As the hunger controlling her faded away, returning her beautiful brown eyes to their normal shade, tears rolled down her cheeks. But for what I'd done to her, tears rolled down mine too. "Promise me you won't hurt Lily, and I'll take it out."

She nodded.

"This is going to hurt. Try to relax, so your muscles aren't fighting me." I gave her a second to process what was to come, braced myself for the near-equal pain, and ripped the stake free rapidly like a bandage.

Daisy's face pinched in pain, and she exhaled. Unable to hold her weight, Daisy's knees gave out, but I caught her. She dragged in deep breaths and coughed. "It hurts." She gasped, voice hoarse. "It hurts so much."

"You'll heal in a few moments. I'm so sorry, but I had to stop you. I'm so sorry."

"I was going to tear off her head." Daisy coughed again.

"I know."

"But I wasn't out of control. I wanted to. I chose to. Getting to feed was only a bonus, not my focus. Lily was..." Daisy looked for her sister, but Lily had left. My love straightened onto her feet, already healed, which I could feel. "Where's Soren?"

Allison came charging after us, still raging and snarling like a beast.

"Good question." I'd never considered my brother would lose.

"Come back to the celebration or we'll have to do this the hard way." Allison held out her palms to conjure and strike with her magic.

I wasn't sure what her definition of 'hard way' was, but with Daisy recovered but unfed, my brother's condition unknown, Stacey unaccounted for, and Kevin missing, I couldn't risk her attacking. And I couldn't leave them behind.

"Easy, there. We're coming back." I wrapped an arm around Daisy's shoulders for support, and we walked carefully back toward the pyres, with Allison prodding us from behind.

All the humans were on the ground, knocked out or non-functional, and in the center of the mess where I'd left him, Soren stood still. Kevin was next to him. This wasn't good, but at least they were alive. Since the humans weren't keeping them busy, why had the vampires remained?

Allison guided us toward our brethren, and she stood in front of us. Jamie's body had been moved.

"Why are you still standing here?" I asked him quietly.

Soren gestured with his head at the same time I heard a nearby rustling. "She upgraded."

Several people stopped just outside of my view, shrouded in darkness, eluding even my enhanced vision. That wasn't foreboding in any way. Being able to read fellow vampires, I ruled out further betrayal. So that left more humans or something else entirely. *Upgraded…*

"What would you like to do first?" Allison asked, glaring at me. Before I could answer, Lily approached, joining Alli in standing against us.

"The humans can leave," Lily said. "They have served their purpose."

"Agreed," Allison said and waved her hands in the air. After a brief chant, the conscious humans glanced at each other in confusion, shrugged, and walked away with mumbles on their lips. They filtered into the darkness, car doors slammed, and engines started. Headlights flashed around as vehicles left. With the commotion, other humans woke up and followed suit, leaving Allison and Lily standing before us three vampires with nothing but flickering firelight now eating up the picnic tables. And still, the not-so-mysterious newcomers waited in the darkness. I frowned at what was coming, wishing I could've fed. I knew Daisy needed it.

"How many humans did we lose?" Allison asked, scanning what remained of her human shields.

"None," Lily said. "Looks like none of the vampires took advantage."

"You used them as bait?" Daisy asked. "You purposefully dangled innocent lives in front of us to prove a point? How can you believe we're the monsters? That's a serious question. Please do answer, because from where I stand, you're wrong. So very wrong."

I squeezed Daisy's shoulders, thrilled she saw things our way.

Allison stepped forward, too close for comfort, and I slipped my body in front of Daisy, partially shielding her without her getting angry about it, ready to react at a fraction of a second's notice.

The witch pointed at Soren and me condescendingly, and my eye twitched with restrained violence. "You want to talk monsters? Soren, your demon friend who'd tried to murder you several times, murdered Jamie. His brother, who you happily roll around in bed with, brought this to you. They changed you into them. You almost murdered your sister. Showing restraint once doesn't change the facts," Allison said.

"But Kevin didn't do anything to you," Daisy pleaded on his behalf. The short, young vampire remained quiet and stoic. "He's a paramedic. He was an emergency room nurse. He helps people."

Kevin puffed out his chest, and a small smile shifted his lips.

"All vampires need to die," Allison said darkly.

From the back, the newcomers emerged into the light. A whole clan of elves lined up. Pierce Evansson stood shoulder to shoulder with his grandfather, a broad-shouldered, square-jawed, and gray-haired peacekeeper. Unless they were upset, then they'd play the role of hunters. I didn't see spears or stakes, but that didn't set me at ease.

"Pierce," Daisy called, relief strong in her voice. "Help us."

Breaking away from the clan, Pierce approached at a slow lumber. He ignored Daisy while he assessed the situation, including the burning pyres and tables. Abandoned kindling stakes were scattered all over, most partially charred. The scent of blood was in the air, and where Jamie had collapsed was a puddle soaked into the dirt. Pierce's angry gaze landed on the new guy with surprise. "Kevin?"

"Hey, elf. Glad you could join the party." Kevin was way too friendly considering the imminent threat, but if someone was in high spirits, I was happy it was an ally instead of an enemy.

Pierce tilted his head in confusion. "Why are you standing with them?"

Kevin smiled, displaying his fangs. I had a silent chuckle at the elf not having figured it out before now. Dim bulb, that one. Pierce raked a hand through his blond hair, and his face fell with betrayal. "How did I not know this?"

A brush against my shoulder turned my head. Stacey returned, swiping the blood away from her lip.

"You came back," I said to her in surprise. "Your timing is terrible." Now Daisy's mother was caught in the witch's net like the rest of us.

"I'm not leaving my daughter."

"Kevin?" Pierce prompted, ignoring our side conversation for his existential crisis.

Allison clapped her hands and shouted to demand everyone's attention. "Now that we're all here, we can get started. Ms. Bennett, I thought you would've been smarter, but welcome back."

Stacey didn't reply.

"First thing, let it be known, Daisy and Oliver are engaged." No one cooed cute sounds at us, and Daisy didn't move. "Enjoy it for the short while it lasts," Allison said with a hint of satisfaction.

Pierce returned to his grandfather's side, and they exchanged inaudible words. The elf clan leader then approached the witches.

"What did I miss?" Stacey whispered in Daisy's ear.

"Sounds like war, honestly," Daisy said, a quiver in her voice.

I suspected my love was right. Soren shifted next to me, likely coming to the same conclusion. The gloves were off, and I wasn't pulling punches tonight.

28

This Means War

Daisy

Logon Larsen, the once-kind elder elf who opened his home and dinner table to me, gestured with broad arms, and the elves fanned out surrounding us. My sister and Allison welcomed their troops, and a rock formed in my hungry gut. Oliver, Soren, Mom, and Kevin stood at my side, and I didn't think the elves were going to flail around with sticks like the humans had.

I wasn't a fighter. Mom and her high-heeled espadrilles wasn't either. Both she and I were very young, and I'd just healed without sustenance, which was another negative against us. Oliver and Soren were formidable, but I didn't know anything about Kevin's age and strength. Although he was certainly stealthy. Three powerful allies against two dozen supernatural opponents didn't bode well for our odds. Vampires were faster than elves, but they had the benefit of flight.

Allison took Lily by the hand as if they were sisters, and together they climbed a nearby picnic table, as if leading whatever was to come. Standing shoulder to shoulder, Allison said, "Lily, go ahead, as we practiced."

My sister bowed her head and made rhythmic hand movements. Within a few seconds, Jamie Harris climbed onto the table beside them and joined her in synchronous movements and mumbles. Jamie was alive! The elves must've healed him. My relief was cut short as fire moved from the pyres to form a ring around the elves and their vampire prey.

The heat surrounding us whipped my hair into a frenzy. My heart thundered in my chest. There was no escape for us, and the witches could flick a wrist and crush us to the ground, like Allison had with Oliver earlier. I was genuinely afraid of what my roommate was capable of, and I feared I was going to find out.

The elf clan leader finally spoke. "The elves have been made aware of a grievance between vampires and witches. As a peaceful kind, we typically avoid conflict, but Pierce made a compelling case, so here we are to see the vampire terror ends tonight, reinstating the peace we'd enjoyed for decades."

I couldn't believe what I was hearing. I couldn't stay silent, and I wasn't above begging. "Pierce? We're best friends. You can't do this to us, can you?"

Logon Larsen nodded permission to Pierce. Breaking rank, my ex approached me, and Oliver stiffened by my side. Pierce's face remained impassive, and at that moment, I knew he wasn't on my side any longer. This was a stranger now.

"I've been trying to win you over for a long time."

"The Fully Loaded Halloween party," I added, trying to appeal to his nostalgia of when we'd first met.

Pierce smiled warmly. "I'd dressed as an elf."

I smiled in return and chuckled at the memory.

He added, "And you'd insulted my pickup line."

My smile slid away.

"You never let me in, Daisy. I stayed by your side, hoping that when danger came knocking, you'd turn to me for safety and protection. Time and again you'd let me down, but I stupidly held out hope every time I saw your name on my screen. I'd hoped our friendship could bring us down the aisle, but when danger arrived, you disappointed me. Now look at you."

But his words defied his actions. "I thought I'd lost your friendship when I'd almost killed you at Borealis, but you'd told me you were proud I kicked your ass—that I was strong."

"That was before," he said simply. "You're a vampire, and that means you're nothing to me."

I didn't believe that. "You'd always responded to my messages. Always been there whenever I'd needed you. I was never in love with you, Pierce, but that doesn't mean I don't care. I thought we were closer than that."

The dead calm in his eyes felt like I was pleading with a stranger. "You want the truth?"

I nodded.

"I can appreciate a fine vehicle, and when Oliver dies, I'm taking the Shelby." Pierce smirked, and Oliver twitched at my side. "And two, after I figured out you were a lost cause, Daisy, I hoped I could sway your sister. All I needed was your support."

He thought so little of my sister, and I frowned, but Lily didn't flinch. She continued her spell with Jamie at her side. "Turns out she has a thing for the witch." Pierce shrugged. "Her loss."

I'd taken Pierce for granted, and now whatever loyalty or friendship or....manipulation to earn favor and trust...was over. Fists of rage formed in my hands. For the very first time, I wished I had my explosive magic. My sister couldn't be compelled, but he was powerful, and his family could be charming. I wouldn't let that horrific fate be hers—I'd rather she died.

Instead, I needed to finish what I'd started at Borealis.

"Allison and Jamie share my lineage," Pierce continued. "I will always be loyal to them." Pierce reached into his cargo shorts and produced a shiny wooden stake. He spun it in his palm as if it were a fancy trick.

He might have a weapon, but I had leverage. "If you kill my mom, your vampire weapon goes up in smoke forever. She alone knows where the rest of the supply is."

Pierce startled. Clearly, that was news to him. He retreated to his clan, and they all whispered to each other. Likewise, Allison whispered to Lily, who broke off from the shared spell and listened. The ring of fire lowered. Oh, how the tables turned.

"What are you doing?" Mom asked.

"Saving your life, and changing their strategy," I whispered over my shoulder. "Go now. Get out of here."

"Are you sure you know what you're doing?" Soren asked.

"Trust her," Oliver said.

"I do," Kevin added with a friendly smile.

Appreciation bloomed in my chest.

"Then you lose your leverage. I can't leave you," Mom said.

"I'm not going to get another chance to keep you alive. Go." I truly appreciated her insistence on staying by me, but I couldn't let her waste the opportunity to escape.

"You too, Daisy," Oliver said. "Both of you can't stay here. These elves are strong fighters. Soren, Kevin, and I can focus and fight better if we aren't watching out for you at the same time." Oliver lifted my hand to his lips, and he kissed my knuckles. "Please go, my love. I'll meet you on the other side of the flames."

Tears filled my eyes, and I nodded. I didn't want to go, but I would be stupid to stay, and insisting would only increase the chance we'd all lose. "I love you."

Oliver silently mouthed the words back and released my hand. Fighting back sobs, I pulled my mom's shoulder, urging her to go ahead of me.

Mom used hyperspeed with me on her tail, and she leaped over and out of the ring of fire. Before I could follow suit, the flames returned to full height. I was trapped. I couldn't get through. That was the only plan I had. Now what? Eyes wide and panting, I spun.

"Daisy!" Mom shouted through the devastating fire. The anguish in her tone broke my heart.

"I'm okay. Just go," I called back to her, emotion clogging my throat. *Or get help. We're going to need it,* I silently pleaded.

Allison shouted in frustration, and she whispered to Lily. At once, the flames doubled in height. I stumbled back from the intense heat. Sweat broke out on my body, and my T-shirt clung to my damp skin. My tongue dried out as if it were stuffed with cotton. Regardless if anyone lifted a finger, we were going to bake to death.

Oliver rushed to my side and gripped my hand tightly, leading me away from the fatal fire. "This is going to get messy. I want you to avoid the elves as much as possible. You hear?"

I couldn't fight these flying elves, but I also couldn't accept we had to fight at all. We were adults, and mostly reasonable. I had to try something else. Gripping Oliver's hand like a lifeline, we returned to Soren and Kevin.

"Tell me something," I shouted to Pierce, capturing his attention. "Do you always carry that stake with you?"

Pierce stalked over to me, and Oliver tensed at my side. "Any elf would be stupid not to. We have to protect ourselves, because you and your fanger friends carry their weapons in their mouths." Either his inflated ego told him he was invincible with all his buddies as backup, or he was just that depraved.

"You aren't carrying stakes for defense, Mr. Vampire Hunter. We're not the monsters you paint us to be. Look in the mirror."

Pierce tapped his head with the side of his stake and smiled, amused. "I'll make sure your graves are each marked, 'Not a monster, I swear'. It's the least I can do."

My lip twitched and my body tensed, and despite knowing my odds were trash, all I wanted was to attack. I reeled back to slug him in the jaw, but a flash of movement sent Pierce soaring through the air. He knocked over several elves who tried to catch him.

War was now.

"Daisy, stay back like we discussed. I love you." Oliver's pale gray eyes sparkled, but before I could open my mouth to protest, Oliver chased after Pierce.

Soren used vampire speed to attack Logon Larsen. The vampire used fists, dodging a stake the elf had brought. Cowards—the lot of them.

Kevin was surrounded by several elves himself, but he seemed to struggle less than Soren and Oliver. The small guy was a beast, flipping and tossing elves like toys. He staked one, dropping the elf to his knees, and Kevin gave him parting words, "This would hurt less if I carried an iron blade, but since we 'monsters' didn't bring weapons to the party, I have to work with what's available."

At any moment, the elves could fly out of the ring of fire to regroup or heal each other and return, rejuvenated for more. Even with Kevin's surprising strength, it wasn't a fair fight.

Mounting frustration and anger at Pierce had me seeking a release of my own. Lily and Jamie kept up the hand movements. I homed in on my target, but a howl of pain distracted me. Soren had dropped Logon Larsen to his knees, the elf's own stake puncturing his broad chest, and his mouth dropped open with shock and surprise. The bellows caught the attention of several other elves, and the angry bees charged after their queen's attacker, swarming Soren. Kevin jumped in to assist. One lone elf attended to his leader's injuries, attempting to heal him.

Pierce and Oliver continued their fight—an elf with a stake taking unfair jabs at my love. Oliver's shirt was wrecked.

My hands covered my gaping mouth. This couldn't be happening.

"Hello, love," an unfamiliar voice said.

With a frown, I turned to find an elf I didn't recognize. He wasn't much taller than me, lanky, with wing tips rising above the back of his head. He grinned cheerfully, displaying a straight row of shiny white teeth. His eyes flashed as they roamed up and down my body.

Delay was my defense. "Have we met?"

"Nah, I'm just here because duty calls. When the vampires stray from their pen, they need to be corralled and taught a lesson, but since I have a rule about fighting girls, I'm at an impasse."

Being underestimated was my offense. Dirtbag was going to kiss my fist. "You're in luck."

Dirtbag tilted his head, amused. "Why's that?"

"I'm not a girl." My fist flew at his face, and the elf's complete surprise allowed me to connect. His head snapped back with a satisfying crunch, and he tumbled backward. To quote my sister, that was only a mosquito bite compared to the damage Soren, Oliver, and Kevin inflicted. With Dirtbag fully distracted, I moved away to give myself distance. And shake the pain out of my knuckles. I might hit like a sledgehammer, but I still felt it.

Soren yelled in pain, stealing my attention. A stab from an angry elf had caught him off guard, but he tore it right back out. Kevin took a tumble out of the snarl of limbs and jumped back into the fray. At the same time, Oliver put Pierce on the ground.

My Dirtbag, seeing the easy opportunity, snuck up on Oliver. When my love turned to give him a stronger sledgehammer hit, Pierce reared up and staked Oliver in the back.

My hands flew to my gaping mouth. The nightmares—the horror—of fists landing, bones crunching, grunts, and minor taunts just wouldn't end. I couldn't have killed Dirtbag even if I had my own stake, but because I couldn't prevent this or stop that elf, Oliver was going to die. I had to do something-anything—before everyone I loved was dead.

29

Pretty Big Pleas

Oliver

Pierce didn't intend to kill me, or he would've hit the target. Instead, he missed my heart by a few inches. No matter how many times someone staked me, it still hurt like the first time. My face pinched in pain, and I dropped to my knees, breathless. Satisfied, Piece moved on to another more critical fight, and I had the opportunity to remove the stake.

It wasn't my pain I worried about. Daisy would feel it too, and I was too vulnerable like this. With the wall of fire and the exertion of the fight, I was sweating. My hands were slick, but I couldn't concentrate on anything but relieving the pain. With one forced breath, I reached with all my might toward my back and grumbled about another destroyed suit. My fingers only brushed against it. I grunted with each stretch of my fingers, blinding white pain obstructing my vision. I just couldn't reach. Making me suffer and putting me out of the fight was his intention.

Asshole.

A hand gripped the stake for me, and I sucked in a breath of pain at the touch. Either someone was coming to help, or someone decided I didn't deserve the mercy Pierce had granted. The stake ripped from my back, and I gasped. Already low on blood, healing would take a while, so I had to be careful now. I turned and found Soren holding my bloodied stake. "You owe me again."

"We'll make another deal if we survive."

"Fair enough."

A trio of elves broke free from Kevin and rushed us. With a groan, I climbed to my feet. I'd have to heal later. "Ready?"

"I'm always ready for a fight." Soren sent me a crooked smile. "But you look like meat pulp."

"The handsome brother is allowed to have an off-day."

Soren laughed and shook his head. He took the brunt of the incoming attack, blocking them from reaching me, and I was grateful for the few extra seconds, but none of the elves attempted to attack me at all. Puzzled, I turned, seeking Daisy, but Jamie stood before me with a fury twisting his features so harshly, I almost didn't recognize him. A small amusement lifted my lips. "I didn't know zombies were real."

Jamie growled. "I'm not so easy to kill."

"I've always been a proponent of getting back on the horse. Shall we?"

A witch couldn't produce viable spells if he couldn't chant the right words, and since I had no intention of being crushed by an invisible boulder again, I didn't allow the witch the required time. I leaped at him and landed a flying right hook to his jaw. The bone splintered with a horrifying crunch, and Jamie collapsed. Did the spirits of the earth understand muffled gibberish? I was about to find out.

Jamie returned to his feet with grunts. He mumbled some words through his rapidly swelling face, but when I swung at him again, he parried with his forearm. I aimed for his face again, but a flicker of movement in my peripheral vision caught my attention.

An elf rushed me with a stake aimed high to defend his witchy friend. At the same time, Jamie gripped a knife. As the charging elf reached me, I ducked and spun him toward me as a shield. The unlucky bastard took a knife to the heart, courtesy of Jamie. The witch gaped in shock at his mistake. And as the elf slumped to the ground, he made one last leap, stabbing me right in the same damned spot in my back.

I gasped at the flash of tender pain. Using every lick of strength I had left, I lifted and threw the dying elf over the fire ring, creating a flame-free temporary gap. The quiet *thud* of his body was clear—he'd died in mid-air. Using the bond, I knew Daisy was alive and moving, and that gave me a sense of relief when I needed it most. Hopefully, she saw the gap and escaped.

Jamie moved to finish me off, but he stopped short. His eyes softened, and his face slackened. Not a sound or a breath passed his lips. From experience, that was a fatal blow. Jamie tipped over onto the grass, with a stake protruding from his back. Maybe this time he'd stay dead.

"Little help?" I asked my brother.

Soren pulled the fat stake out of my back again. "Twice now, brother? You're losing your touch."

"Go ahead. You earned that one."

Soren chuckled and pointed to the witch he'd killed for a second time. "He'll bleed out in a few seconds, so if you need to heal, have a drink."

I curled over the witch and extended my fangs, puncturing the carotid before the heart stopped. I swallowed several mouthfuls and pulled back with a hiss. The blood felt like boiling water, and the stinging acid slid down my throat, eating at my insides. I fell to my knees, coughing. "Fucking vervain. Damn it, Soren."

"I didn't know. Sorry. Hang tight. This is almost over."

"Looks like it. You're a mess," I croaked out.

Soren's T-shirt was sliced like he'd rolled through a meat processing plant. Blood stained his shirt and smeared his face. One pant leg dangled by half its threads. Almost over indeed.

Soren looked down at his extensive injuries and shrugged. "You're worse."

"Funny." I gasped, trying to breathe through the melting of my internal tissues, while Soren returned to fight the remaining elves.

I had to get to Daisy. She needed to be safe from this, but I couldn't move, and I couldn't heal.

Daisy

WITH OLIVER, SOREN, AND Kevin fighting a pile of elves who wouldn't quit until all of us were dead, I had to do something before Dirtbag returned or any of the other elves decided they could hit girls. Besides the few elves who were dealt fatal blows, the rest of the elves healed each other, and despite their clothes being in ragged shape, they didn't look injured at all.

Vampires needed human blood to heal, and caught in a towering ring of fire, we were in short supply and weakening by the moment. I glanced over my shoulder at the fight. Oliver was kneeling next to Soren. They were talking—if not joking—but the rising temperatures meant that no matter how the fight ended, their high spirits wouldn't last. I had to do something, but what could I do?

Allison remained alone on the picnic table just outside the flames, still working her magic. I stood no chance against my roommate, but I had to try reasoning once more with Lily. I uselessly searched the area for something I could repurpose to get through the flame when I noticed an elf making a bridge through the flames with his body. It was Dirtbag. He didn't scream or flail. No movement or sound came from him at all. He was dead.

Vampires were flammable to the extreme. I exhaled a deep breath. Without turning back, I climbed across the narrow, soft, uneven body. My flesh felt the agony of the fire's licks, trying to capture me, but I made it across just as the corpse's clothing caught fire. The path behind me closed, and I slowly healed.

Lily had returned to the picnic table just out of the way with the ring of candles and grimoire. She chanted a spell, oblivious to my approach. Disrupting could only help us. "Lily!"

She ignored me.

I shook her shoulder. "Lily, stop. You have to stop this."

"Quit interrupting me, or something even worse will happen," she said with her eyes closed.

She had a fail-safe, so I wouldn't kill her. I'd underestimated her. "People are dying. What's worse than death?"

Lily paused her chants and looked at me like I had two heads. "Isn't it obvious? Becoming a vampire is worse than death."

"How would you know? You aren't one. Lily, I'm still your sister. Whatever you're doing here is killing my friends and my fiancé."

"Fiancé? That's right. I already forgot. How cute. Two monsters in love."

The patronizing tone pissed me off, but I kept my cool. Lily was my best chance of ending this fight. "Pierce wants you to be his broodmate. Do you know what that is?"

"I don't care. I like Jamie."

Well then, I guess she hadn't seen the update. I said bluntly, "Jamie's dead."

"The elves healed him," she said without flinching.

"Not the second time," I said.

Lily finally flinched. She looked up at me, darkness on her features. "Who killed him?"

"Whoever he attacked. Does it matter? I'm trying to tell you more people are going to die if you don't stop this."

"Allison and I are strong. The elves are superior healers. I'm not worried."

This was like reasoning with a brick wall. "Jamie believes that elves ranked 'worse' than vampires. He told me himself. But you're okay with following along with them?"

"The elves haven't given me a reason to hate them, and the witches have been nothing but supportive and friendly." Lily stared at me pointedly.

That was my angle. This was about Greg. I'd killed her darling dad. I groaned in frustration. "There's nothing I can say that will make what I did okay. Dad believed different things than I, but I shouldn't have killed him. That decision is permanent. I can't take it back, and I have to live with the guilt and regret. If you don't stop this, how do you think it'll feel having all these lives on your hands?"

"Collateral damage is a means to an end."

The witches had her brainwashed so deeply that for a second I pitied her. "You sound just like them."

"Like who?"

"Like Allison and Jamie. A pair of bigots. We can coexist in peace just like we have been. There's no reason for any of this. I love you, Lily. You're my sister, no matter what happens. No matter what we are." I gripped her hands in mine and gritted my teeth against the magic flooding into me. "Can't you see? Soren and Oliver love each other, too. We aren't animals."

"You might not have fur, but you kill like a beast, and you eat like a monster." Lily pulled free.

Tears sprang to my eyes as the grunts, groans, and shouts breached the roar of the flames nearby. I didn't even know whether Oliver and Soren were alive. "What about Mom? She loves you. Please, Lily."

My sister said nothing, but she looked at the grass flickering with shadows from her ring of fire.

The height of the flames lowered. I was getting through to her. "We can be a family again. Remember when Mom ordered custom catering for us because she closed on that massive property downtown?"

Lily smiled. "Nachos, tacos, fried chicken, salad, and macaroni and cheese. It was a kid's dream."

"And afterward, what did we do?"

"We played catch in the backyard. All four of us. Mom's never done that since." Sadness reached Lily's eyes.

"The three of us can do that again. Put a stop to this before it's too late." I begged, and I didn't care.

"*Three* of us. Because of you." Lily's lip curled in hatred.

"Dad treated you terribly, too. He didn't have any of our best interests at heart. Otherwise, I wouldn't have been the vampire weapon, hunted by vampires, and you wouldn't have been the cure, hunted by elves, and Mom wouldn't have died, turned into a vampire, and spent months being tortured by Dad. And because of any or all of that, I wouldn't be a vampire either. All of this is *Dad's* fault."

Lily faced me with tears in her eyes. I expected to duck a pitiful blow, but she slowly rose and closed the book. "Mom was tortured?"

"In the lab."

"I...I didn't know. I wish all of this could go away. I just want to be normal again, a family. I want the mac n' cheese." Lily looked at me with sadness pulling her features into sobs.

Taking a chance, I moved in and wrapped my arms around her. I gritted my teeth against the magic and blinked back tears. I squeezed, giving my sister a proper hug—the first one in far too long. Lily hugged me back and sobbed against my shoulder. The embrace felt like forever with the war raging behind us.

Lily slowly pulled away and gave me a quick glance in the eyes, unable to speak through her own tears. Her hands moved and glowed. Screams of agony came from everyone inside her ring of fire. That couldn't be good.

"Lily, we need to stop this."

"It will be over soon."

My heart sunk. I thought I got through to her, but there was nothing more I could say. I had to get Oliver, Soren, and Kevin out of there. There had to be something I could use to free them now that I was on the outside.

I knew one big thing that could help.

30
Fast and Furious

Daisy

ARMS UP TO PROTECT my face from the heat and brightness of the fire, I found my roommate. Allison mumbled words of a spell with hands gliding in the air like a conductor, standing on top of her picnic table perch. I should just rip her throat out—a much-needed meal and the perfect end to a spell, but I figured if a witch was at risk of a vampire attack, she'd come prepared with vervain.

Beyond the crackles of the flames, weak grunts and groans reached my sensitive ears—the sounds of a fight nearing its end. I had a feeling they weren't tending wounds, shaking hands, and apologizing in there. No, it was far too quiet. Too many were dead. My throat tightened, worried Oliver was among the dead.

"Alli, enough already."

Her lips curled in a devious smile, and her arms continued to move in a dance, urging the spell to proceed. "It will be, after I finish what my ancestors started in 1871. The Great Peshtigo fire was intended to kill vampires, but the witches fell in a nasty twist of fate. This time, the vampires will go down in history, and I'll be the one to finally finish the job. No vampire gets out of that fire alive." She glanced at me, but she didn't tack on 'you included' to that threat.

"What about the elves? They're in there too."

"Collateral damage is expected."

Robots. Seriously. Where did they all learn this? Disappointment was an understatement. "You sound just like Lily."

Allison snorted. "She sounds like me, you mean. I taught her everything I know, including all my spells. She's a quick study. I'm proud of her."

"What about Jamie? Was he just collateral damage, too?"

"He can protect himself."

Present tense. She hadn't heard. "Except he didn't. Please stop this."

"I told you to enjoy your engagement for the short while it lasted, and I meant what I said. Witches started the vampirism curse. It's my duty to end it. Unfortunately, you joined the wrong team, and the losers don't get to beg the winners for mercy just because the tables turned."

"We came here to celebrate Jamie's graduation. We didn't bring weapons. This isn't us. Alli, please."

Allison sighed. "Just stop already. I'll grant you one mercy. Go ahead and find your love, but as I warned you, no one is coming out of that circle alive." My roommate waved slightly differently, and a path through the fire opened. "If you choose to enter, you will die."

"I'm already dead, remember?" I said deadpan.

Before Allison could change her mind, I bolted through the open path into the flaming ring. My skin beaded with sweat immediately. The heat was unbearable. I coughed, holding my sleeve against my mouth as a filter. Blood was everywhere, soaking into the grass, black with the night. So many were dead. Using my blood bond, I followed the mystical pull to find Oliver among the bodies piled on the ground. My heart caught in my throat. He rested on his side, displaying a fatal amount of blood on his suit, and I turned him flat onto his back. His skin was blistered from the heat.

"Oliver?" My voice was weak. Anytime Oliver was in danger, I would come to his rescue. I loved him, I was bonded to him, and I would never leave him. Oliver's face pinched in pain, but he was alive. I exhaled in relief and sucked in a fresh breath, but I was overcome with fits of cough. Although breathing was only necessary for speech, it was still natural to me.

"Daisy?" Oliver grunted as he shifted.

I brushed matted hair from his face. "You have to get up. We need to get out of here."

"I can't. Something's keeping us down."

Lily. Damn it, Lily. She crushed the vampires, but the elves...were collateral damage. "I tried to stop them both, but they're beyond reason. I'll help you push against my sister's force."

I lifted Oliver to a sitting position, and he groaned against the pressure I didn't feel. I positioned myself under his arms, helping him stay on his feet, and we moved as slow as snails across the sea of bodies, searching for Soren and Kevin on the way out.

I spotted a familiar buzzed head. "There's Kevin."

Oliver and I shuffled over, and I rustled Kevin's shoulder. "Kevin? We're getting out of here."

Kevin rolled over and looked at us, dumbstruck. His skin was blistering too, and his clothes were a mess. "There's no escape. Get down here and wait the witches out. When the flames go, we run."

"If you stay here, you'll be crispy bacon. We're going now," I said and coughed.

"How do you think we're getting through that wall of flame?" Kevin asked.

Remembering the flying elf corpse, I had an idea, but it was dark, gruesome, and...disrespectful. "I have a plan. Help me with Oliver."

Kevin climbed to his feet with little effort and took the burden of Oliver's other arm.

"How is it so easy for you?" Oliver asked him.

"I'm older and stronger than the witch's spell."

"Where's Soren?" I asked, not interested in small talk.

Kevin bent down and pushed a limp body over. It rolled, and underneath was Oliver's brother, alive. "Soren, get up. We're getting out of here somehow."

"I can't get up."

Kevin lifted Soren to his feet. Both Soren and Oliver struggled against the pressing weight of the spell. I could only assume, since I wasn't in the ring when the spell started, that was why it didn't include me.

"So, what's your grand plan?" Kevin asked, wrapping his arm around both taller brothers in support.

"Sorry," I whispered to the nearest corpse. With a foot, I pushed it across the flame. It split the wall of fire. "Go fast!"

Following my lead, we rushed through the gap like a train, and on the other side, Kevin released the younger vampires.

"Not bad, Daisy. It's been fun, but I'm out of here." Kevin disappeared without explanation, leaving me with two gravely injured vampires.

The path through the fire closed, and I shivered from the instant cold. The Shelby wasn't far. Without the strain of the spell, I could help them to the car. I loaded Soren into the back seat and Oliver into the passenger seat. I scanned the area for Mom, but I couldn't see her. After all this time, she should be long gone, anyway. I dropped into the driver's seat and held out my hands for the keys. Oliver dug them out of his shredded pocket. "Be careful."

I took the keys, and Oliver passed out before buckling in. With a groan, I leaned over and buckled him. Checking in the rearview mirror, Soren was crispy, but out cold, too, and also unbuckled. I leaned into the back seat and dragged a belt across his shoulders and clicked it in. I started the car. That was easy enough. Turning on the headlights, Allison appeared as a creepy apparition in front of us, a nasty snarl on her face. She held out her hands in preparation for a spell. I had to get us out of here now.

I mashed the pedals. Gears ground and the car lurched. Lesson two would've been very handy right about now, but

I didn't regret lesson three. I didn't have time to reminisce about Oliver's amazing hands and skilled tongue.

"Hang on. This is going to be a rough ride." I worked my feet and shifted the knob at my side, figuring it out as I went. The car lurched forward again, straight toward the furious witch. I swerved around Allison, bounced through campsites, and smacked nose first into a tree.

Swears poured from my mouth.

Clicking and hissing came from the engine. I checked on Soren and Oliver. Their buckles protected them from becoming meat missiles aimed at my head, but the car didn't fare as well. Damn it. I scanned for Allison. Behind the car, her arms reached toward us, and a brain-melting headache crushed my skull. I pressed both palms against my temples, mouth gaping in pain.

I focused on Oliver, shredded by elves, with burns not healing along his exposed skin. He needed blood, or he would die. Soren wasn't much better. They counted on me. I had to focus under intense witchcraft and drive a busted manual transmission or we all die. A few days ago, I wouldn't have thought it possible, but Oliver was always there for me, and the bond between us wouldn't be broken by a vengeful old friend. We were stronger than that. I loved him, and I could ignore Allison long enough to save us, to save our love. He was the only constant in my life that I could trust, and I would never let him go.

"Don't give up on me," I told him over the screaming in my head. "I'm getting us out of here."

Releasing my pounding head, I whimpered against the continuous needles stabbing my anterior cortex and reversed the limping car. The hood was stuck to the tree. I punched the pedals, and with more grinding gears and screaming metal, I lurched the angry car backward. The hood declined the join the escape.

Frantically trying to control the wonky tires, I worked the steering wheel until we careened back onto the road. Unnatural vibration came from the chassis. I could smell an oily gas mixture leak, and that didn't bode well. Thankfully, Oliver lived just over the bridge. We could make it.

With a last glance in the rearview mirror and seeing no one, I swept us through the strip mall's parking lot. I didn't bother to stop at a red light, since I wasn't sure I could get moving again. Traffic was nonexistent at this hour, so I slowed to turn us onto the interstate bridge. The engine roared louder than probably normal, and a high-pitched hiss made me cringe. I shifted to climb speed as we ambled up the bridge. The engine whined. The gears ground. I tried downshifting as we crested the hill, and a few more unpleasant metallic sounds had me gritting my teeth.

Sorry, sorry, sorry.

Oliver was going to forgive me for the damage, but I still felt horrible for ruining his prized car. At least he could afford repairs.

Because I couldn't.

31
Past Revealed

Daisy

I pulled us into the garage and left the door open. I didn't know what gases and leaks were oozing from the car, and I didn't think Nicole could handle the toxic vapors. Soren was completely limp in the back seat. With my new vampire strength, I hefted him over my shoulder and carried him inside the bed-and-breakfast. My sticky shoes crackled along the hardwood.

"Oliver? Is that you?" Nicole called from downstairs.

"It's me, Daisy. I have Soren, and he could use your help." At the couch in the living room, I carefully dropped Soren onto the bouncy cushion. I righted his head so he wouldn't get a crick in his neck.

"Sure, anything."

"Bring blood," I called back.

Nicole appeared with a box of sustenance. She set the heavy load down at Soren's feet, and she assessed his bloodied and torn condition with a critical eye. "Do I want to know what kind of graduation party this was?"

"A front," I told her. "For a twisted scheme to murder all the vampires in town."

"Oh, dear. Where's Oliver?"

"He's the next patient. I'll be right back."

Nicole nodded and took off Soren's shoes to make him comfortable. I returned to the Shelby and cringed. The clutch was the least concern, and there was nothing I could do about it now. My priority was Oliver. I hefted him onto my shoulder, and Oliver grunted.

A flood of endorphins rushed through my system. He was alive. I wasn't too late. "Hold on. You're safe."

He didn't say anything or fight me at all. I slammed the car door closed and carried him inside. Despite being shorter than his brother, he was heavier. My breathing strained as I hauled him up the steps and inside. Where Nicole played mother hen, I dropped Oliver down.

"How many more patients do we have?" she asked.

"This is it." I lifted a blood bag and popped the port. I fed the straw-like tube between Oliver's lips. Nicole mirrored me with Soren.

"Where's your mother?"

"I helped her escape, and she took off, but I don't blame her. Kevin is still on the loose too."

"Who's Kevin?"

"A vampire who was right under my nose all this time, a fellow nurse-turn-paramedic at Borealis."

"These two never mentioned him, and they usually keep tabs on all the local vampires."

Oliver stirred, slurping down the blood by instinct. His eyelids fluttered open, and his pale gray beautiful eyes met my gaze.

I smiled. "Hey, there. Sorry about your suit. You're going to need to call your tailor."

With life pouring back into his veins, Oliver looked at himself and chuckled. A finger poked through one of the larger holes. "The only thing worth saving is you, and I wasn't even the one to do it." His hand nestled against my face, and I leaned into it. "I'm relieved you're alive."

I covered his hand with mine. "Me too. You are my forever."

Soren stirred and groaned, the blood having jerked him back awake. His hand pressed against his temple. "That sucked. Next time you want to go to a party, I'm packing iron stakes. I'm tired of those elves and witches getting the jump on us."

"Glad to see you're in one piece, too," Nicole said.

"Thanks for the drinks, Nicole." Soren lifted another bag and popped the port.

"Ditto," Oliver said, sucking down another bag, and he sighed dramatically. I took one for myself, and the rejuvenating liquid felt like I'd had a full night's sleep and a long massage. I was a new woman.

A knock at the door put us all on alert.

"I'm not expecting anyone," Nicole said. "I shut down reservations for the B&B a while ago."

I said, "You two are still healing. I'll get it."

They didn't argue. I crossed the open space and pulled the door wide. My eyebrows lifted at the familiar face. "Kevin, come on in."

The mysterious man of the hour smiled and bumped his face against the invisible anti-vampire shield. His hand went up to rub his nose, and he patted the barrier.

"Nicole! Can you invite Kevin inside for me?"

Nicole limped over and smiled. "Come inside, Kevin."

The vampire crossed the threshold. "Thanks, Daisy." He approached Oliver and Soren with grace, putting us all at ease. The two vampires shifted to stand, but Kevin stopped them. "That's not necessary."

"Kevin, just who we wanted to see. Have a drink." Soren waved at what remained at the bottom of the box.

Kevin Fontaine gestured in the negative. "I'm good."

"Have a seat," Oliver said. "I don't think we would've gotten away if it weren't for you, and for that, we thank you. What brought you here?"

Kevin dropped into an upholstered armchair across from the couch. "I've always hopped towns, coming and going over the decades, whenever boredom or curiosity strike. Then one day, I saw you and your brother. Something about you rang familiar, so I stuck around until I could figure it out. And I have."

Oliver and Soren exchanged confused glances, clearly not recognizing him. Beyond Kevin being an emergency room nurse, Megan's boyfriend at the time, and now my partner, I didn't know what he meant either.

"I owe you both an apology." Kevin rubbed his palms together and pinched them between his knees.

"What for?" Soren leaned forward, brow furrowing.

"The year was 1871 when a nasty fire broke out, but you know the story."

"We were there," Oliver said.

"So was I," Kevin added.

Oliver rose as if recognition had just dawned on him. Soren stood too and looked at Oliver to lead. The younger vampire was still clueless, and so was I.

"What happened?" I asked Oliver.

My love loomed over the seated vampire with firm features. "I'd always told myself if I ever found you, I'd stake you without hesitation. The pain you inflicted on my family was…unconscionable."

Soren blinked and frowned. "That was you? You turned Oliver?"

Kevin stood to meet them face to face. "Like I said, I owe you both an apology. For self-preservation, I avoid turning vampires, but I wanted a few decoys around. For that, I'm gravely sorry."

Oliver closed the distance, a threatening gesture, towering over the shorter vampire. He gestured for me to join him. I sidled next to Oliver, and my love took my hand. As I faced Kevin, I smiled awkwardly, not knowing what was going to happen next.

"For decades I hated myself," Oliver said. "I hated what I'd done and who I'd become. Survival was met with all new rules, and I didn't know any of them. I hated you—even though I didn't know you. But that changed when I met Daisy. No need to apologize to me, my friend. Without you, I would've never met her, and for that, I'm eternally at your service."

Oliver looked at me, and I smiled back with salty tears. I squeezed his hand.

"I accept the apology," Soren said. "I can't speak on behalf of our sisters and mother, but for me, you kicked ass for us, so we're square."

"Thank you," Kevin said. He turned to leave, but stopped. "Daisy, I'll see you on shift Monday evening. You're still my partner, right?"

I'd planned to quit, not wanting to risk my patient's lives with my desire for blood, and since I'd almost ripped my own sister's head off, it was in everyone's best interest if I stayed far from temptation. "I'm new at this. I don't know if I can control myself well enough for the job."

"I'll keep you in line. I am six hundred years old." Kevin winked.

My mouth dropped open. Oliver and Soren cocked their heads at him as if he were some oddity.

I cleared my throat of the surprise, and a warmth flooded through me—happiness, fulfillment, and whatever mushy other labels I could slap on it. All I knew was I felt at home. I understood my place in this new chaotic world. With endless and unconditional love at my side, and Kevin keeping me from hurting anyone, I could do anything. Besides, what else was I going to do? EMS was my life. "I'd love to return to work."

"Not so fast," Oliver said. "We're going on vacation."

"For three months?" Soren added hopefully.

"And an open bar, and access to my credit card, yes. Does that cover it?" Oliver asked.

Soren celebrated quietly to himself. Apparently it was.

Oliver faced me. My heart pounded with anticipation. His fingers enveloped mine, and he kissed my knuckles. "I'm taking you on a global vacation. Wherever you want to go, we're going. No budget, no timeline, but I promised Soren he'd have the B&B to himself for the next three months. What do you say?"

"Kevin? Think you can manage without me for a while?" I asked.

My new but old partner nodded. "The ambo will always be there. Go have fun, kids."

I snorted. Kevin looked younger than me, but he'd been around since before Christopher Columbus mistakenly landed on our continent. Just picturing that was mind-blowing.

"Sounds great." But I was so tired and dirty, getting excited about a vacation would have to wait. "But I need to clean up first."

Oliver pulled me into his arms. "You and me both."

Soren's celebrations ended with a cringe. "And that's my cue to get the hell out of here."

"You and me both," Kevin copied, darting for the door.

Oliver and I chuckled.

Daisy

NICOLE HAD RESTOCKED THE fridge three times over. And Soren, Oliver, and I drained it again before finally satiating that endless thirst made worse by injuries. We'd all showered and changed and, feeling like things were moving back into a normal routine, I needed to come clean about the damage I'd done. Despite knowing Oliver wouldn't be upset, nerves still fluttered in my stomach. "I have something to show you, and it's not pretty."

Oliver frowned for a moment. "Not pretty as in a homely beast or not pretty as in something's untimely death?"

"The second one." I held out my hand for him to come with me, and he took it. My hand trembled as I brought him out to the garage. A puddle had formed underneath the bent and buckled Shelby, but the steam had stopped. The crumpled hood was still missing—not that I'd gone back to the tree to remove it.

Oliver circled the car, assessing the damage with a serious face. I couldn't figure out his thoughts, and the guilt was crushing me alive. "I'm so sorry. I didn't mean for it to get this bad."

Oliver placed a palm over his forehead. His shoulders shook.

I felt even more terrible. How hard was it to find parts for a 1967 Ford Mustang Shelby? Dread sank into my bones. "I'm so sorry."

Oliver dropped his hand and cracked up laughing. "How? Explain to me how you did this much damage in a mile of driving? Apparently, it's possible, but how?"

A wave of relief washed over me, and I smiled at his contagious laughter. "Lesson two was more important than we thought."

Oliver wrapped his arm around my shoulders and brought me back inside. "Clearly. I'll have my guys fix it. Don't worry."

Oliver brought us back inside. I knew he'd be understanding, but I didn't feel absolved. The poor Shelby was just as injured as everyone else had been, but the Shelby's wounds were my fault. "I'm sorry, really. Alli interfered, too. I don't want to imagine what she would've done to us and the Shelby had I stuck around any longer. The busted Shelby saved our lives."

At his bar, Oliver stopped and faced me. "You got us out of there alive. Don't ever apologize for it. Things can be fixed. People can't."

"Technically, people can be fixed..."

Oliver brought his lips to mine. "You know what I mean."

"I do." I smiled during his kiss.

Oliver released me before I was ready, a sparkle of excitement lighting his eyes. "We're healed and ready. It's time I made do on my promise to Soren. Pack up. We're traveling the world."

"She's not going yet." Lily's voice had me stiffening.

Oliver and I turned to face her. Standing in the front doorway, Lily held a paper folder, not a stake, and even though her posture wasn't threatening, and we'd had a cute bonding moment in the midst of the vampire barbecue, I kept my guard up. After things calmed down and time to process had passed, I didn't know if my sister's change of heart had stuck. "Lily? What are you doing here?"

At the sound of her name, Soren rushed to our side, forming a blockade. "Witch wants round two? Your timing is ill-advised. We're all powered up and ready to fight again."

Oliver shifted just slightly in front of me. With the strongest defense I was going to get, I said, "You're not welcome here."

Lily stepped inside anyway, knowing full well the capabilities standing before her, but the confidence and arrogance she'd displayed whenever she was around Jamie and Allison were nowhere to be seen. She was my little sister again, shuffling back with her tail between her legs. I couldn't garner an ounce of sympathy, but I was willing to hear her out.

Lily stopped before us and held the folder over her chest meekly. "I thought about what you said, and you were right. Look at you, all of you." She met everyone's standoffish gazes. "You care for one another, you risk your lives for one another, and you love." Lily smiled at me, a sadness permeating the tiny lift of her lips. "And I'm sorry for falling into Jamie and Allison's harsh point of view. She won't talk to me, and I haven't slept the greatest, so, like I said, I've had time to sit and think about what you said."

Lily had crossed a line that couldn't be undone, but I also didn't know how much of the witches' influence had guided her actions. Was Lily fully in control, or was she a puppet like the wall of human bait? I remembered her robotic motions, and the regurgitated viewpoints. That doubt made me angry at myself for not seeing it before, but I still couldn't just let her in again. "I don't know, Lily. You hurt me."

Lily looked at the floor and rubbed a toe on the hardwood. "I know, and I deserve all your wrath, but you believe in second chances, right?" Lily looked me square in the face, an extra plea with puppy-dog eyes.

It was because of her I'd lost that part of me. I didn't want to be that raging person again, incapable of forgiveness and remorse. I didn't want to be what she thought I was: a monster. But dishing out a second chance wasn't like popping a frozen TV dinner in the microwave and sticking a fork in it. "How can I trust you after everything you've done?"

"I brought a peace offering." Lily opened the folder she'd brought and passed me a stack of papers.

My eyes skimmed the text, but it was legalese, and I wanted the CliffsNotes version. "What's this?"

"I've made a correction in the ownership of your house. Daisy Barrett, the human, gave up ownership to Daisy Lynn Barrett, the vampire. Legally, it makes no difference, but magically, it'll allow you free access to your house, and Allison can't block you. However, any other vampire can also enter, but I didn't think you'd mind that so much." She slipped another paper free. "This one is a notice to vacate, to start Allison Kincaid's eviction proceedings."

I appreciated knowing Allison couldn't magically rescind my access, but I noticed a key name missing—my sister's misplaced crush. Not having any updates on how everyone else had fared, I added, "And Jamie's?"

Lily looked at the floor. "He won't be needing one."

"I'm sorry to hear that." Not knowing what else to say about it, I looked at the papers in my hand. Having Lily fix my human-to-vampire technical issue was...thoughtful, but my sister wasn't a real estate guru by a long shot. "Where did this come from?"

"Mom gave me some pointers."

Mom and Lily made amends? "Where's Mom?"

"She's healing and regrouping. Mom and I are finishing the house cleanout before she moves on."

Lily gave me a lot to process, but I had one more question. I didn't want to ask, but curiosity had the words leaving my lips before I caught them. "What about the elves?"

Oliver twitched next to me, but he and Soren silently waited for her answer.

"The elves are mourning their dead. Pierce was hit the hardest by the loss of his grandfather. Turmoil will follow as they reorganize and choose a new leader." Lily paused awkwardly. "You asked about everyone but me. Where do we stand?"

It took guts to reconcile with our mother and craft all these documents for me. She didn't have to do any of it. But if Lily didn't hate me for killing Greg, and she came here unarmed, risking her life, and begging for forgiveness, then I could prove to her once again I wasn't the monster she thought I was.

"Lily, you're my sister. I can hate your mistakes as much as you can hate mine, but I'm always going to love you. Come here."

Lily teared up as she embraced me, and I hugged my sister back and bit down against the magic. I wanted my family together, and if Mom was leaving, then my trip with Oliver had to wait. I released my sister with a sad smile. "Oliver?"

"What is it?" Oliver's concern always made my heart flutter. He was my protector forever.

"I want to get married before we go, and I want Mom to be there, and I want Lily to be my maid of honor, if she'll have me."

Lily's eyes turned red with suppressed sobs, and we both looked for Oliver's approval. He was an important participant, after all.

My love smiled sweetly. "Anything you want, it's yours." He raised his voice and called into the next room, "Nicole, can you whip up a wedding in two weeks?"

Nicole popped her head into the room, a beaming smile spreading across her face. "With your credit card, I can do anything."

Soren snorted. "I hope you have a high limit, because between a wedding, and my three months of celebrations, and an open bar, you're going to need it."

Oliver slyly smiled. "I have no limits on any of my cards."

Soren's brows lifted.

Oliver began delegating. "Nicole, that's perfect. Get started at once. Daisy, you and your sister can have whatever you want. Tell Nicole, and she'll take care of the arrangements."

"I don't want to be a burden..." I started, feeling uncomfortable at the blank check before me.

"Daisy," Oliver interrupted. "When we're together, never concern yourself with the price of anything," he repeated his reassurance.

I would need time for that concept to truly sink in. "Because money is not an issue," I finished for him. "I got it, but if Lily, Nicole, and I are handling all the wedding details, what about you? What are you doing?"

"Two weeks isn't a lot of time. I'm putting together the guest list." Oliver leaned forward and kissed my forehead. He vamp-sped by me.

"Wait, right now?" I asked, surprised.

He really wanted to marry me right away. I couldn't wait either.

Oliver

ALL THINGS CONSIDERED, I had one guy on my guest list that would take some effort—something more than a delicately handwritten invitation. I hated him, truthfully, but he chose to stake me painfully instead of fatally, and I needed answers for that, because Daisy would want him at the wedding. I knocked on the door of Pierce's humble home with a bottle of wine as a peace offering.

Pierce Evansson opened his door, gazed upon my handsome face, and slammed it shut.

I couldn't say I hadn't expected that. I knocked again.

"I don't want to see you," Pierce said through the door. "Doesn't slamming this hunk of wood in your face make that point clear?"

"I just want a few words."

Pierce opened the door a few inches, and I passed him the wine. Pierce took it. His angry face was beet red with tears, but whatever his grief was telling him, it wasn't aimed at me. Pierce was ashamed of being seen crying.

Apologizing for being a victim of a witch hunt was like grating sandpaper in my ass crack, but the things I'd do for Daisy knew no bounds. "I'm sorry for how things happened. That wasn't what I wanted."

My surprising words lifted his brows, and Pierce stared hard for a beat. "The witches said it would be an amicable party, but just in case, they wanted us there as bodyguards for them and the humans. When the ring of fire went up, a thirst for the hunt took over, and no one wanted to leave until you were dead. Once things got too messy, we tried to leave, but a spell stopped us—just like you. I didn't know the humans were a test for you, and I didn't know the whole party was a setup at first. I'm glad you didn't lose anyone, but I lost family and friends. So pardon me for not wanting company right now."

If the elf was offering apologies—which color me shocked—I'd wring every last one out before deciding if he was worth Daisy's time on her wedding day. "And that barbaric speech you gave?"

"Caught up in the moment of my grandfather's values from past generations. I was hurt and angry, and I needed to save face."

In the heat of the moment in years past, I'd said plenty of stupid things, too. I was convinced this levelheaded Pierce was telling the truth. He passed my test. "The witches are good at stirring us against each other, but since we're still standing, we're stronger than them. For Daisy's sake, you and I have been mostly cordial, and it's because of Daisy I'm here today."

"What happened?" Pierce asked, quiet defeat in his tone, as if he couldn't handle one more piece of bad news.

Whether my news would cheer him up depended entirely on his point of view. Better to rip off the bandage. "We're getting married, and I want you there."

Pierce jerked back in surprise and rubbed his eyes clear.

I continued, "You and I fought, but time and again, you chose to spare me rather than deal a fatal blow. I can't say I understand why, but I appreciate it."

Pierce looked at my shiny leather shoes. "For some stupid reason, Daisy adores you. As much as I want you dead, I didn't want to cause her more pain."

"Thank you," I said.

"Thank her."

"Can I count on you to be at our wedding?"

Pierce thought for a moment. "I'll be there."

"Great," I said cheerfully. "Open bar. Bring your drinking hat."

Pierce frowned.

"Or whatever you elves do to celebrate." I bowed my leave and turned away. Daisy would be thrilled to see her old friend supporting us, and even more thrilled to see we had buried our hatchet—for good this time. Before Daisy, I never would've believed it, but we could coexist in peace.

Free booze helped.

32

The Bells Chime

Daisy

A FLURRY OF ACTIVITY had me floating through the preparations in a whirlwind of pampering. Samples were draped and stacked all over the bed-and-breakfast in little stations arranged by type and in order of deadline. Temporary tables were erected to help organize the chaos. While I sat on the couch, sipping tequila, Nicole showed me choices, and I pointed. The elder woman had a smile on her face, but the constant stream of phone calls and bringing me samples with a limp had me feeling guilty.

"Are you sure this is no trouble?" I asked her.

"Honey, I've waited my whole life to marry off one of these two. Don't let the bum hip deter you. I'm having a roaring good time. Now if only I could find someone for Soren, then I could die easy in my old age."

With how sweet the woman was, for my sake, I hoped Soren stayed a single bachelor.

"The tailor will be here this afternoon to take your measurements, and he promises the dress will be ready in a few days." Nicole slid a finger along the screen of her tablet. "Next up is cake." Nicole stared at me wistfully. "The design is fully up to you, but I can choose the flavor if you prefer."

Vampires didn't eat, but frankly, my hips didn't miss it...yet. "That would be great, thank you."

Even though I trusted Oliver and Soren's niece to handle the preparations like a seasoned wedding planner, I checked off all the major items on my mental list, but one item was glaringly missing. "Nicole, I've made selections in almost every aspect of the wedding, except one. Where's the venue?"

"That's a surprise." Nicole winked.

Huh. "Okay."

Lily walked through the front door, empty-handed this time. "I'm here to help. Where do you want me?"

Nicole pointed to a table where wedding favors were piled, ready for assembly. I got up and followed my sister. I couldn't do absolutely nothing for my own wedding, and apparently Nicole didn't need me for the moment because she didn't protest.

Lily and I sat across from each other at the table. "Nicole's got a handle on everything. What's left for the maid of honor?" Lily asked with a sly grin.

"I don't think there's anything besides these favors, really." She and I assembled the little party favors of candies and a card inside tulle baggies.

"Oh, come on. You're missing the pinnacle of a wedding." I waited, not sure what Nicole had overlooked.

"Bachelorette party," Lily said, beaming.

A wave of sadness washed over me. Jamie Harris should've been the featured entertainment, but he could never accept me and Oliver as we were, and he died for those misplaced values. "I think I'd rather skip it."

"Nooo!" Lily said with a dragged-out sound. "We have to celebrate the loss of your singlehood properly."

"I don't know. It's just not right without Jamie."

Lily held a moment of silence for the loss of her crush and friend. "There are other dancers. Besides, isn't it weird to have your roommate shaking his mostly naked ass in front of you?"

I did think of him as a brother. "I'd already seen him dance too many times, but I'd want him to be there, you know? And I'd tell him to keep most of his clothes on." Those were moot points. Jamie was gone, and nothing could bring him back now.

"I'm still getting you one of those sparkly tiaras with 'bride' written on the front. I always wanted one."

"Maybe someday you'll get your own," I said with an encouraging smile.

Lily's excitement waned just a little. "It's hard to find a man who can accept the hidden world...and a powerful woman."

"No kidding."

For Oliver, the situation had been reversed. He had to find a woman willing to accept the hidden world and his...powerful...side. I'd needed a long time myself. But a lot of men still wouldn't accept a woman as strong as a witch. Something about their masculine sensitivities. I hoped my sister could find happiness too.

"I hear a wedding is in order." Mom's voice.

Lily and I both lifted our heads from our tedious task. Our mom had dressed in her usual business attire, not a scratch on her. If we hadn't survived her 'accident', funeral, my second car 'accident', and all the chaos with the bonfire, I wouldn't never known it had happened. She looked exactly how I'd remembered, but now she was different. More like...a mom.

Who would've thought dying and torture made a person reflect on their life and try things a little bit differently? Perhaps I too was guilty. As I smiled at my mom, who'd chosen to be here instead of disappear, the second chance that I'd valued above all had returned. I could definitely hate what she'd done, but I couldn't hate her. I loved my mom.

"We're so glad you're here," Lily said.

"We're all here—one big, semi-dysfunctional family, but I'm proud of you girls. Who would've guessed what was necessary to bring you together?" I declined to answer that. "But I can't be a spectator at my own daughter's wedding. Let me help. Where do you want me?"

"You can assemble favors with us," I said. I might not be able to have children of my own, but all I really wanted was a family, and mine was finally getting bigger.

"I'd be delighted." Mom sat next to Lily, and together we swapped stories and laughed over shots of tequila. I was sure some of the favors were missing candies, but it wasn't my fault. I could hold my liquor these days.

Daisy

IN THE BACK OF the limo, I wore a wedding dress custom-made for me—a beaded and fluffy princess-shaped dress, but guilt over the extravagance lingered in the back of my mind. Lily and Mom rode with me. Mom's mother-of-the-bride dress was navy blue, sleek, and slimming, just as she was. Lily wore the maid of honor dress, an off-the-shoulder sweetheart, floor-length gown in mint green—my favorite color. She was stunning.

Oliver and the best man were in a separate limo. I assumed it was Soren. Oliver hadn't told me. Butterflies reenacted World War II in my stomach. I shouldn't have been nervous, but this was so fast, so fancy, and so many aspects were a surprise, which also made me nervous.

Including the guest list.

The limo driver brought us toward the mysterious venue, which Oliver didn't want me to know ahead of time, and as the darkened streets became familiar, those butterflies quieted in surprise. I squinted through the tinted windows into the dusk. I knew where we were heading. The home where Marc, Lisa, and Abby had lived, where Abby's beautiful wedding in the garden crafted warm memories, where I'd first met Oliver. I smiled to myself, wishing Pierce had never erased that memory—twice.

"He chose Uncle Marc's house, didn't he?" I asked carefully, trying not to let the full impact of that thought in. My makeup wasn't getting touched up anymore.

"It seems we're headed that way," Mom said.

But *how*? "The house was sold shortly after the accident. Did Oliver rent the property?" With his funds, he could make anything happen. I fanned my face to prevent my makeup from running.

"I broker commercial real estate, but Oliver and I have an agreement for other properties of interest. When you said it had been sold, I went digging. Too bad I'd been a new vampire locked in a lab. I missed out on a nice commission."

I tried to piece together the details while ignoring old Mom's sudden reappearance.

"Oliver didn't rent it, honey. He bought it."

Oliver and I had met at Abby's wedding, but my memories had been erased. So when he'd made this leap, I didn't even remember him. "He knew back then?"

"He's quite the charmer, isn't he?"

The limo pulled into Uncle Marc's driveway, and the driver shut off the engine and exited the stretched car. With a white-gloved hand, he assisted my mom and Lily out of the vehicle, and when he helped me, Mom lifted my fluffy dress hem so I wouldn't drag it on the ground. I bunched the fabric to keep it clean and braced myself for a wave of memories. I inhaled deeply and slowly let it out.

With the porch light guiding our steps, together we entered the house. My stomach was in knots. All personal effects were gone, as if it had been staged for sale. Beautiful, airy, and clean. The dozens of flower bouquets left a floral scent in the air. Uncle Ed shuffled through, oblivious to me and Mom, and I smiled at him. I remembered younger cousins running around, playing hide-and-seek with ribbons fluttering behind them. I remembered uncles and aunts on both sides of the family talking and laughing in the kitchen, telling stories, and drinking punch. The house was full of the happiest memories I had, and because of Oliver, I got to add more to the list.

Curious to see Nicole's fortitude at throwing together a quick but extravagant wedding, I stepped onto the back deck and gasped. People mingled, awaiting the ceremony, and all around them was a stunning display of beauty. Clear lights were hung around the backyard, near the garden. White chairs, with mint strips of satin wrapped around them, lined up in an orderly fashion on the grass. More bouquets filled the space, and the floral scent was intoxicating. Near the arch positioned at the head of the ceremony, a band tested their equipment. Gentle strums of a guitar brought a smile to my face. Oliver really wanted this to be unforgettable.

It certainly was.

"Wait," I turned to my sister and mom. "Who's going to walk me down the aisle?"

"If it's not too much trouble, I'd like to volunteer." The masculine voice stopped my heart. My throat closed. I didn't know what to say as Pierce appeared from around the corner, wearing a very nice suit. He carried a bouquet—not daisies—and a sad smile lifted his lips.

I guess the elf really could figure something out.

He approached me cautiously, and my family backed away to give us space, making an excuse about checking with the caterer. I had nothing to say, so I waited for Pierce to explain.

"You look good, Daisy. Better than good. You're beautiful."

His compliment was kind, perfunctory, basic, as usual. "Thanks."

"I don't deserve you. Never have. But I thought about what you said, and I'd rather have you as a friend than not have you at all. I would be honored to walk you down the aisle."

I didn't understand how he made the leap from hating me and wanting me dead to being honored to stand by my side. "You said some terrible things to me."

"Oliver and I exchanged words. He understood my position and invited me here today. I'm sorry for what my grandfather said, and I'm sorry for agreeing with him. In the heat of the moment, I had to show the clan I was on their side, but there's no excuse. You know I don't live with them. There's a reason for that."

Words were easy. Actions were harder. But it was true he lived alone, and I wanted to believe him. "You tried to kidnap me to make a new serum."

"I tried to keep you safe...from yourself, and I was desperate to have you see our side. At the lab, your father and I would've watched over you. Helped you. But now you're formidable, Daisy, the strongest woman I know. I mean, you kicked *my ass*. That says a lot."

I couldn't help but chuckle.

"I want you to know I'll always be there for you as a friend...if you want." Pierce smiled and dashed away tears.

I blinked back tears of my own so my makeup wouldn't spoil, and I nodded, swallowing back the emotion. "I would love for you to walk me down the aisle."

Nicole rushed my bouquet to me, and I took it from her. She was in her element—radiant, happy, youthful. My heart sang for her. In her hurried words, she reminded me of the steps from the rehearsal—which had been held at a local hotel's banquet hall to keep Uncle Marc's house a secret. When I assured her I remembered what to do, Nicole explained to Pierce his duties, since he hadn't been there.

"The maid of honor and best man are going to line up first," Nicole reminded us. "And it's still bad luck for the groom to see the bride, so I need the two of you out of sight." She opened the door to the guest bathroom, and Pierce and I stepped inside and listened for our cue behind the door.

"Uncle Ed, this way," Nicole said, and I chuckled.

"You know forever is a long time for a vampire, right?" I heard Soren ask through the door. I wasn't surprised Oliver's brother was the best man. Okay, actually, I was. Only a few months ago, this was never in the realm of possibility. Now the brothers were back together, and I was once again trying not to cry.

"With Daisy, it's never long enough," Oliver said.

My lip quivered as I fought back tears. I fanned my face and blinked rapidly. I still couldn't believe I was so lucky, and that we had literally forever.

"Someday, maybe I'll find a woman who makes me turn to mush like you, but I doubt it."

"I'm not mushy."

Soren chuckled. "You are soggy bread. You are a wet paper towel. You are as mushy as three-day-old noodles—"

"Enough." Oliver laughed. "If being in love with the most wonderful woman in the world makes me noodles, then stick a fork in me and call me ramen."

"I'm surprised you know what ramen noodles are," Soren said, and I covered my mouth to muffle my laugh.

"I might have expensive taste, but I'm still cultured."

"Let's get on with it, shall we?" Soren asked. "Then I can use your culture to mingle with the ladies and the open bar."

"Promise me you won't eat anyone tonight."

"I promise. Lily, are you ready?"

My sister didn't respond, but footsteps left the kitchen area and creaked on the deck. The band's tune shifted to something slower, and footsteps left the house.

"That's our cue," I said to Pierce. The elf looked at me with a shimmer in his eyes. I asked, "What?"

"Let's get you married," Pierce said, opening the door and guiding me out. Tears fell over his eyelids, but he didn't brush them away.

I couldn't wait.

Oliver

Despite my grievances with the elf, I easily ignored him on Daisy's arm. Paper lanterns lit her path with the bond casting a warmth toward me. Her hair was curled around her shoulders, topped off with a ring of diamonds nestled on her head. Her dress, exactly what she wanted, was hand-beaded by the finest tailor in the state, and he assured me every detail was precise. With each step, her dress shifted, and my love glinted in the lights like she was a precious jewel herself. The diamonds were genuine, of course. I didn't think Daisy realized, but that detail and quality was what I paid him for, and he was worth every penny.

The radiant smile on her face swelled my heart, and I struggled to keep my tears at bay. Daisy was perfect—donning her favorite jeans and a T-shirt or sparkling with thousands of diamonds. She was it for me. She was everything. When I'd been dying of the serum in her father's backyard and I'd given up on living, I'd been certain I would never see her again. Instead, here I was. Daisy's beautiful eyes—more beautiful than the fairest sunrise on a calm bay—were for me only, and my brother stood proudly at my side. For the first time in my life, I was truly happy. The tears fell.

Pierce shook hands with me to give her away, and of course, he took the opportunity to squeeze my hand painfully. I squeezed back harder, and the elf's lips subtly lifted. Pierce sat down in the front row, and I faced my bride. The officiant read off the pre-planned, human-safe words and paused for me to give my vows. Daisy's eyes sparkled with tears, and I rubbed her knuckles gently in reassurance.

"Daisy Lynn Barrett, when we'd first met at a wedding quite like this, I was certain of one thing: you felt like you were alone, unheard, misunderstood. I was determined to fix that, and in the process, you saw the best in me. No matter what happened, you never gave up. Since then, you've grown to become my best friend. I promise to love you, to protect you, and to treat you right every day until my dying breath. And I promise you'll never be alone. You are my forever, and forever is a long time." I sent her a sly grin, and Daisy beamed. "I wouldn't have it any other way."

Daisy's beautiful lips lifted and quivered as she fought tears. I rubbed her knuckles with my thumbs, and she cleared her throat. "Oliver Herman Rockwell," Daisy let out a wet snort. "You saved my life one pre-dawn morning, and I remember every detail. You told me I needed to find someone who lit a fire in my heart, who made me sing when no one's looking, and who would always be there for me. That was someone I deserved, but you were describing yourself, even if neither of us knew it at the time. Everything you've done was to protect me and keep me safe, and for that and everything else...I love you. I will always love you. Oliver, you are my forever, and I promise to love you until my dying breath, a long, long time from now."

The officiant gestured, and Soren handed a ring to me, who winked encouragingly, and Lily handed one to Daisy.

My fingers deftly slipped the diamond-encircled wedding band up her finger. "With this ring, I thee wed, the love of my life."

Daisy smiled, and her hand trembled as she slipped the ring onto my finger and repeated the words. "With this ring, I thee wed, the love of my life."

The officiant announced we could seal our promises with a kiss. I leaned in and wrapped my arms around my love's waist. Daisy's hands slid up my chest to the back of my neck. Her fingers nestled in my hair, and she pressed me closer. Oh, the things I wanted to do to her right now.

"Did you laugh at my middle name?" I whispered.

"I couldn't help it," she said. "I still love you."

"Kiss me." Daisy lifted up on her toes, and I captured her mouth with mine. My heart pounded in my chest. She was it; she was the one.

The band played a bright tune, and the audience rose, clapping and cheering. I pulled away from my love's lips to spare my niece's sensitivities, and we marched down the aisle. My niece's blowers created a soft breeze of flower petals floating over all of us. The photographer shifted all over the place, shutter snapping. The videographer glided along, capturing our moments with a steady hand. Sniffles reached my sensitive ears. I gripped Daisy's hand. There was only me and her.

Forever.

33

A Dance With the Snake

Daisy

I'D NEVER BELIEVED IN fairy tales, but with Oliver, anything was possible, even witches, vampires, elves, and humans behaving themselves with an open bar. Nothing had gone wrong, no one got hurt, and the police hadn't been called. The only fire was candlelight. I still couldn't believe it. Oliver had been perfect. The night had been perfect.

I'm sure most of the credit belonged to Nicole.

My house was empty. At first it was eerie, but I was glad Allison was away, probably looking for a new place to live. A clean cut was best for both of us. She and I had performed spells right here in my room. Allison had also cast a spell on me, amplifying my magic, making me out of control. The living room had been destroyed, sliced, and patched. Pierce had put his elf hands on me to heal me after I had been attacked and nearly killed. Every memory in here was...negative.

I cuffed socks and stuffed them into my suitcase. My love sat on my bed next to it, helpfully keeping me company as if he had nothing more important to do. "I don't think I can live here anymore. There's too many bad memories."

The only good one was the night I'd taken Oliver home from the bar...

"I happen to know a great real estate agent," Oliver said. "And I happen to have a bed-and-breakfast with plenty of bedrooms."

"I like that idea." I'd spent more time at his house than my own lately. It only felt...right. I tucked a bag of toiletries into my suitcase. "What kind of clothes do I need for Europe this time of year?"

With vampire speed, Oliver moved behind me. His hands slid around my hips and pressed my stomach closer to him. He whispered into my ear, breath sending a flutter of heat through me, "None." Oliver brushed the hair off my neck and kissed my throat, teasing me. "Are you sure you want to jump on the plane right now? It's a long flight."

"There's a mile-high club for a reason, right?"

Oliver groaned in my ear. "You're killing me, woman. I love it."

I turned to face him. "I would never kill you during sex, but you might wish you were dead when I'm done with you."

Oliver's eyes glowed red with desire, and in the blink of an eye, he freed my shirt and flung it aside. "Challenge accepted."

I unbuttoned his shirt while his mouth explored my shoulders. As soon as I opened his expensive shirt, revealing his smooth curves, I pushed him against the wall with my vampire strength. Picture frames rattled, and the drywall buckled around him.

Oliver smiled, amused. "Oh, Nicole's going to have work to do while we're gone."

The poor old woman had done enough for us. "I'm not asking Nicole to fix my house, and you're not either."

"She'd be proud to do it. Also, I pay her well."

Still, I hesitated. "Are you sure?"

"She'll upgrade half the house and get you twice the sales price. I'm sure."

I slid a finger along his smooth-shaved jaw, no longer concerned about the survival of my house. "Let's demo the bedroom for her, shall we?"

"That sounds incredibly thoughtful of you."

I laughed. Oliver kissed along my throat while his hands freed my jeans. I unbuckled his belt and eagerly unzipped his tented pants. Before I could expose the glorious snake in my new husband's pants, he flipped me up and tossed me on the bed. The frame cracked.

He approached my ankles and freed the tight denim. Before he could claim me, I shoved him backward into the dresser. The wood crunched, and drywall dust fell. A lamp tumbled to the floor with a crash.

"I like to make people happy," I said, closing the distance. I pulled his hair back to expose his throat, and I bit down. Oliver groaned as I drank from him, his erection firmly begging for attention.

"Is that how it's going to be?" he asked.

Through mouthfuls, I mumbled an affirmation, and Oliver freed my hand from his hair and bit my wrist. We exchanged blood until we were both messy, and Oliver lifted me and threw me onto the mattress again.

The bed frame cracked for a second time. Oliver launched himself over me, and he cradled my face, eyes blazing red with a surge of the blood bond between us. He took my lips as he nudged my eager legs apart. I wrapped my thighs around his hips, and my husband stretched me firmly with his lustful length. I cried out and arched my back in pleasure, and Oliver grunted.

Slowly at first, he slid in and out while his satisfying mouth tickled every inch of my throat and lips. Faster and faster he pumped, gaining momentum like a locomotive, and further cracking the frame.

"Don't stop," I begged.

Always a pleaser, Oliver listened. Sweat broke out on his back, and his breath puffed against my throat. He nipped, teasing, and I groaned under his touch. Too much of a good thing existed. We'd ignored the warning cracks until a loud bang startled us, and we fell to the floor, cocked at an angle.

We laughed together.

Oliver brushed the hair out of my eyes. With a gravelly voice filled with lust, Oliver said, "I can't be upset with that. Now where were we?"

"I think we upgraded to the fast portion of the morning's entertainment." I checked the clock on the end table. "We don't want to miss our flight."

"Your wish is my command." Oliver's thrusts banged against me, sending my breasts bouncing. My fingers toyed with his hard nipples, and he reached a hand down to my clit. The acrobatics alone were award-worthy.

Sated with blood and raging with need for my new husband, the surge of heat and tensing of muscles in anticipation of soaring to new heights spread rapidly. "I'm coming, Oliver. Come with me."

Oliver panted and wiped the sweat from his brow. "As my sexy bride commands, so shall it be." His words jerked out of his mouth with his frantic thrusting. "I'm almost there. Almost...almost...right now."

I came with him, and we both cried out, locked in place in orgasm. Slick with sweat and panting with exertion, Oliver rested himself upon my chest. "Do we have time to shower before catching the plane?"

"I don't want the passengers next to us to smell sex on our skin."

"Passengers?" Oliver cocked his head.

"Other people on the plane," I added, the sex having knocked our plans firmly out of his head.

"It's a private plane. Still, the pilot gets upset if the itinerary isn't followed exactly."

I chuckled and shook my head in disbelief. Of course, it was a private plane. How was this my life?

"What's amusing?" Oliver asked and nibbled my ear.

"You are. Everything about you is just...perfect. We need to shower fast because I don't want to miss our honeymoon."

His kisses trailed down to a breast—the one that jiggled first when I moved, and I arched against his mouth. He licked around my nipple and blew cool air on it until it hardened.

Tingles of need grew down low, and I squirmed for his touch again. As his mouth reached for the other nipple, I groaned. "We're going to be late."

Oliver reeled back, suddenly snapping out of his lust. "And now it's time to catch our flight."

"Wait, what? You can't do that and quit on me."

Oliver's sly smile frustrated and amused me at once. "The mile-high club beckons." He held out a hand to assist me up, and I took it. Oliver effortlessly lifted me to my feet.

Between the tourist traps and shopping, I was going to spend all our honeymoon wrapped in his arms, and after that cute stunt, he was getting punished. That reminded me I needed to pack my leather whip.

"And when we land," Oliver added, "I'm renting us a manual transmission, because you sorely need lesson two."

I smiled. My life was finally complete. I had my family back in one piece, and I'd added to it. Now that I was a vampire, we had unlimited time before us to enjoy each other, and I wasn't going to waste a minute of it before I had to get back to work.

Dear Reader,

BEGIN THE NEXT TRILOGY in the series with **Elf Bound (Immortal Protector Book 3.5)**, the dramatic war-torn backstory of Indiara Niskatar, long before she meets Soren Rockwell.

Or dive right into **Vampire's Demand (Immortal Protector Book 4)**.

As an indie author, I'm thrilled you shared your time with me, exploring the crazy worlds residing in my head and keeping me up at night. Your reviews are very important to me, so if you enjoyed this book, please consider leaving some stars for the last installment of Oliver Rockwell and Daisy Barrett's story, **Vampire's Promise (Immortal Protector Book 3)**.

If you found any typos or errors, I blame my cat. Rat her out at: support@stephanieflynn.com.

Thank you for your support!

Also By Stephanie Flynn

Find my catalog at StephanieFlynn.com

Immortal Protector series

0.5 Vampire's Distraction

1 Vampire's Deception

2 Vampire's Secret

3 Vampire's Promise

3.5 Elf Bound

4 Vampire's Demand

Immortal Protector Side Tales

Deer Holiday

Love Claws

Depths of the Heart

Matchmaker in Time series

0.5 Minutes to Live
1 Seconds to Act
2 Hours to Arrive
3 Days to Hide
4 Years to Savor

Pirates in Time series
1 Pirate's Prize
2 Pirate's Treasure
3 Pirate's Plunder

Time Travel Romance Shorts
Fateful Time
One Crazy Time

If you like your urban fantasy without the romance, too, check out Stephanie Flynn's other name, Marie Flynn!

About Stephanie Flynn

Stephanie Flynn writes action-packed paranormal romance filled with adventure, suspense, and danger. She lives in Michigan, USA, with her husband and kids, and she spends her writing time surrounded by a herd of normal cats who bat everything off her desk, including her coffee. Check out her website for more books: StephanieFlynn.com

9 781952 372605